PRAISE FOR MICHELLE MARCOS AND

SECRETS TO SEDUCING A SCOT

"TOP PICK! 4½ stars! Marcos brings her latest Highland Knaves book to life in a way that sends shivers of anticipation through readers. The depth of emotions, realistic characters, history, and sensuality make her novels keepers."
—*Romantic Times BOOKreviews*

"Michelle Marcos expertly weaves history and romance in this exhilarating tale. The action begins at the first page and flows effortlessly throughout the novel. Marcos weaves a Regency-era romantic tale with witty banter, romance, action, and drama into one tightly bound package. For fans of the author, this book is not to be missed. For new fans such as myself, you will enjoy it. I recommend giving Michelle Marcos and *Secrets to Seducing a Scot* a try!"
—*Romance Reviews Today*

"4½ stars! *Secrets to Seducing a Scot* has rocked my world! A wonderful breath of fresh air in the highly saturated world of sexy Highlander historical romance. Michelle Marcos most definitely knows her craft, her talent ultimately shining through her characters' inner mettle, charisma, and heartfelt journeys. A winning read from start to finish!"
—*Romance Junkies*

"Michelle Marcos is famous for her interesting and intriguing heroes and heroines and she definitely does not disappoint in this new release! The interplay between Malcolm and Serena is rapier-sharp and fascinating. The story line is strong, filled with interesting secondary characters, and unanticipated happenings. This is a treat Scottish romance lovers will not want to miss!"

—*Fresh Fiction*

"Plenty of snappy banter, steamy sex, and a wealth of historical detail . . . make this a nice bridge between Regency and Highland historicals." —*Publishers Weekly*

"*Secrets to Seducing a Scot* is an enthralling and adventurous Scottish romance. The characters are entertaining and the dialogue between Serena and Malcolm is razor-sharp . . . the series promises to be a treat for fans of romantic tales filled with Highlanders and lots of action."

—*Night Owl Romance*

"Seduced me from the very first page! Marcos is a masterful storyteller who brings the Regency period to vibrant life. Passionate and pleasurable!"

—Teresa Medeiros, bestselling author of
The Devil Wears Plaid

WICKEDLY EVER AFTER

"A scrumptiously sensual and delightfully witty historical romance . . . I absolutely loved this story. Brimming with mystery, humor, witty repartee, an interesting plot, charismatic characters, and intrigue, this book is a winner! I look forward to reading Ms. Marcos's future works as well as those she already has out. I highly recommend *Wickedly Ever After* to anyone looking for a terrific read."

—*Romance Junkies*

"4½ stars! For this installment of Marcos's Pleasure Emporium series, the once infamous brothel becomes a school where young ladies learn the art of seduction. Playing on several erotic romance themes and adding her own delicious brand of sensuality, Marcos delivers a fast-paced, sexy tale." —*Romantic Times BOOKreviews*

"The strong lead characters for which Michelle Marcos is becoming known are also present in this newest of the Pleasure Emporium novels. *Wickedly Ever After* is a sensual treat for historical romance readers everywhere."
—*A Romance Review*

"Richly drawn characters, the spice of desire, and a bit of mystery combine with undeniable emotion to make this a treat you'll want to savor over and over again."
—*Romance Reviews Today*

GENTLEMEN BEHAVING BADLY

"4½ stars! Marcos gives readers another taste of desire and danger, along with an enticing adventure/mystery in the second Pleasure Emporium novel. Strong and likable characters, as well as a unique setting, should have readers longing for her next book."
—*Romantic Times BOOKreviews*

"Michelle Marcos infuses plenty of humor and suspense into this historical tale which readers won't want to put down." —*Romance Junkies*

"A talented storyteller, Marcos gives a very human face to all her characters and the moral dilemmas and situations they face. A solid gold read!" —*Fresh Fiction*

WHEN A LADY MISBEHAVES

"Marcos delivers a refreshing, creative take on the typical Regency, carried by the spirited heroine and buoyed throughout by lively plot twists."   —*Publishers Weekly*

"Her heroine is a spunky delight, and her dark, hostile hero is an ideal foil . . . Marcos displays talents that are sure to grow with each new title."

—*Romantic Times BOOKreviews*

"*When a Lady Misbehaves* is the first in a bold and original new series by a bold and creative new voice in the romance world. Michelle Marcos is impressive in her debut. The characters in *When a Lady Misbehaves* are complex and immensely fascinating, the story is imaginative, and the plotting is excellent. Ms. Marcos makes some clever twists on the traditional romance. I highly recommend *When a Lady Misbehaves* . . . newcomer Michelle Marcos is an author to take note of."

—*Romance Reviews Today*

"This rags-to-riches story by debut author [Marcos] absolutely sizzles. *When a Lady Misbehaves* is beautifully done and I highly recommend it."

—*Fresh Fiction*

"*When a Lady Misbehaves* is loaded with smolder and charm . . . It was a joy to read this inventive, sexy, and ultimately moving story. When I want a great historical romance, I'll reach for anything by Michelle Marcos!"

—Lisa Kleypas, bestselling author of
Love in the Afternoon

Lessons
in Loving a Laird

Michelle Marcos

St. Martin's Paperbacks

For Jesus

This is a work of fiction. All of the characters, organizations, and events portrayed in this novel are either products of the author's imagination or are used fictitiously.

LESSONS IN LOVING A LAIRD

Copyright © 2012 by Michelle Marcos.

All rights reserved.

For information address St. Martin's Press, 175 Fifth Avenue, New York, NY 10010.

ISBN: 978-0-312-38179-0

Printed in the United States of America

St. Martin's Paperbacks edition / March 2012

St. Martin's Paperbacks are published by St. Martin's Press, 175 Fifth Avenue, New York, NY 10010.

10 9 8 7 6 5 4 3 2 1

ACKNOWLEDGMENTS

No book goes from concept to shelf without some help along the way, and this novel was no exception. So I'd like to take a moment to thank some great people who helped put this book into your hands.

First, I want to thank my sisters, Mabel and Marlene Marcos, and Marlene's husband, Juan Cabral, for their help during our plotting session. It really helps to bounce ideas off of some really smart people who aren't afraid to tell you when something is utter crap. Thanks also to my friend, Vanneta, a voracious reader of romance, who helped me fine-tune my ideas into something resembling an outline—even if it was scribbled onto five dinner napkins.

I want to thank my editor, Rose Hilliard. She has an amazing instinct for great storytelling, and I've benefitted enormously from her guidance and creativity. Thanks also to the rest of the team at St. Martin's Press, whose mission it is to give this story an appealing physical shape. You all are fantastic at what you do.

Finally, I'd like to thank Jesus Christ. He is the reason I am able to live my dreams every single day.

PROLOGUE

RAVENS CRAIG HOUSE
ROSS-SHIRE, SCOTLAND
TWELVE YEARS BEFORE

"Mumma?" asked Shona, her pink lips pouting.

Fiona straightened, her unlaced ghillie still clutched in her hand. "Aye?"

"If God made spiders, why did ye try to squoosh that one just now?"

Fiona shook her head as she searched for the beastie beneath the table. It took her a moment to compose an answer for her eight-year-old daughter. "Well, he doesna belong in my kitchen. If the good Lord made a creature with so many legs, He must've meant for it to be oot-side where there's plenty of room to run around."

Shona's mouth formed an *O* as the sense of it dawned on her. Excitedly, she jumped down from the chair. "I'll take him ootside for ye, Mumma." Her black hair sprayed around her shoulders as she crouched on the wooden floor.

The black spider was no bigger than the tip of her finger, and she watched it slowly climb the leg of the kitchen table. Mumma was cutting tatties and neeps for supper, and it was dangerous for the wee spider to be here. Her

younger brother, Camran, was playing on the floor, surrounded by toy king's men their father had carved.
Shona took the empty wooden box and placed it on the
floor underneath the spider.

She leaned closer, her large green eyes rounding over
the tiny creature. He seemed so alone, so far from home.
Everyone should be home with his family. *I'll take ye
home,* she thought at it, feeling sure he understood her.
She puckered her lips and blew.

The startled spider let go of the wooden surface, and
supported by a single thread, it landed squarely in the
wooden box.

"I got him, Mumma!" she shouted excitedly. She lifted
the box so her mother could see.

"Well done, Shona," Fiona cheered flatly, barely able
to suppress a shudder. "Mind ye put him ootside where
he belongs."

Her older brother Malcolm always kept the wood-
pile outside well stocked. Shona had seen spiders among
the chopped wood, especially around the base of the pile
where the logs were oldest. This must be where Wee
Spider's family lived.

Shona upended the box onto the pile, and Wee Spider
scampered out and disappeared between the dried logs.

"Ye've got too many legs to be in the house," she said,
bouncing an admonishing finger in the air. "Mind ye
don't stray inside again."

In the distance, beyond the footbridge, she saw three
figures approaching. Her father and older brothers
were returning from the hunt. From a pole shouldered
by Thomas and Hamish swung a large dead boar.

"Mumma!" cried Shona. "Da's come back!" As she
ran through the house shouting the news, she passed

her thirteen-year-old brother, Malcolm, who'd been sullenly dragging about the house, moping because he wasn't allowed to go hunting with them. Her twin sister, Willow, squealed in delight. She dropped the bannock she was shaping and ran out of the house.

Shona wanted to be the first to greet her father, but Willow raced ahead of her down the footpath. John lifted Willow in his meaty arms, swinging her round and round until she laughed convulsively. Even in the waning light of the setting sun, Shona could see the radiant smile upon her father's face as he embraced her pretty blond sister.

He carried Willow in the crook of his elbow, her corkscrew tendrils dripping around his cheeks. "Have ye been a good lass, then, Willow?"

"Aye, Da. I made the bannocks for tonight."

"Happy I am to hear it," he said as he strode toward their front door. "I'm as hungry as a bear in the springtime. I want them all for m'own!" Willow giggled as he tickled her.

Shona hugged her father around his waist.

"And ye, Shona? Did ye mind your mother while we were away?"

"I saved a spider."

"Is that for my dessert?"

Shona laughed gleefully. "He's not for ye to eat, Da!"

"Oh!" He tousled the black fringe of hair over her forehead.

As they walked across the threshold, Fiona came to greet them, wiping her hands upon her pinafore.

"Glad I am ye're home," her mother said as she kissed her father on the mouth, something which always struck Shona as repulsive even though they always smiled when they did it. "I'm over the moon for ye, John MacAslan."

"I'll meet ye there, Fiona MacAslan."

Her older brothers flopped the boar upon the butchering table, and pulled the pole out from between his tied legs. Malcolm trudged over to see the kill he hadn't been permitted to make. His face hung low. Malcolm was the only member of the family who wasn't celebrating.

John squeezed Malcolm's shoulder. "I know ye wish it had been ye to bring in the hunt, son. But boar hunting is too dangerous for a man who's yet to grow."

"I'm big enough, Da," the thirteen-year-old protested.

"Aye, ye are," John replied. "But tall is not the same as grown. Have no fear . . . we'll get some weight on yer arms over the winter. Next season, I'll take ye with us. And *ye* can be the one to wrestle the boar to the ground."

The corners of Malcolm's mouth lifted. "Promise?"

John smiled. "Aye. That I do."

Blam! A sudden forceful pounding on the front door startled a scream from her mother. A group of men battered through the door, and began to stream into the house. Their clothes were soaked red, and blood caked around their wounds.

Fiona grabbed Shona's arm, and shoved her behind her along with Willow and Camran. John pulled out his hunting knife and shielded them all from the intruders.

"Who the devil are ye?" demanded his father.

An angry bearded man spoke. "Aye, the de'il indeed. Did you no' expect a visit from yer own clan? Or did ye think yer cowardice would go unnoticed?"

"Get out!" her father ordered.

The bearded man laughed hollowly. "Ye see that, lads? Now he's found his balls! Where were they when the clan was musterin' for battle yesterday, eh? Where were *ye*?" The bearded man held his sword to her father's chest.

Fiona turned around and knelt in front of Shona, Willow, and Camran. Her hand was trembling upon Shona's arm. Shona had never seen her mother so frightened. "Hide yerselves. Go!"

Breathlessly, Shona nodded. She took hold of Camran and shoved him inside the larder cupboard. Willow refused to let go of her mother, her tiny fists balling Fiona's skirts. Shona yanked at Willow's hands, and folded her into the cupboard next to their brother. But now there was no more room, so Shona crouched beneath the scullery table.

"I made my case before the chief personally," John explained. "I have no quarrel with the McBrays—my son Hamish is to be married to a McBray lass. I could not fight them."

"Ye mean ye *would* not fight them. Ye and yer tenants would have increased our showing on the battlefield. It may not have come to a head if they had seen us strong in number. But without ye we were outnumbered, and the McBrays saw it. They tore us to strips. The battle was lost in only two hours."

From beneath the scullery table, Shona could only see the dirty, muddy legs of all the men. *Too many legs to be in the house*.

"I'm sorry," she heard her father say.

"Sorry?" A man advanced upon him. "I saw both my sons slain on that battlefield. I found my William with a claymore in his chest. My boy Robert had his neck broken. It took an hour for him to die." His voice warbled with anguish. "Ye don't know the depths of sorry yet!"

"I know ye're grieving," said her father. "But the blame for yer boys does not rest on me."

"Aye, it does," said the bearded man. "His sons' death, as well as every man oot there who lost life or limb, is on *yer* head. You and every man jack of yers who hid with yer womenfolk inside the safety of yer homes. Lads, let it not be said that there is no justice among our clan. An eye for an eye. If Angus here lost two sons, then John must not be allowed to keep his!"

"No!" Fiona screamed as she dove in front of her older sons.

Shona heard a crack, and then her mother crashed to the floor, clutching her cheek. Then she saw her brother Thomas take a run at the man, just as two more men joined the fray. With his dagger high in the air, her father swung into the mob.

And then everyone was fighting. Her heart pounding in her chest, Shona began to cry.

Fists and daggers flew inside the kitchen for what seemed like forever. She could no longer see her father among all the angry men. Her mother grabbed her kitchen knife and dove on top of a man who was beating Hamish. But one of the angry men grabbed her from behind and called her a bad name. Then he raked his knife across her throat.

Her mother fell to her knees, blood oozing from between the fingers clasped at her throat. Her face was twisted in horror, and she made an odd, gulping sound. Mumma's pretty yellow frock ran red with blood. Shona watched in terror as her mother's eyes flew around the room like those of a frightened horse. Finally, Fiona's gaze landed upon the tear-streaked face of Shona, huddled under the scullery table, and a strange serenity came over her face.

"Mumma," Shona whispered, the saliva in her mouth stringing between her lips.

But her mother didn't answer as she fell forward into a pool of her own blood.

Horrified, Shona watched as the lifeblood poured from her mother in an ever-widening pool. The image of her mother's face blurred as tears crested over Shona's green eyes. She cringed against the wall as the awful red syrup inched closer and closer.

The yelling and the noises suddenly stopped. The angry men were no longer fighting, only breathlessly talking with each other. Shona's gaze lifted from her mother to a spot beyond the kitchen table. Her father lay upon the floor, a *sgian achlais* sticking out from his chest.

Get up, Da, she thought to him, but knew he would not understand. His body only convulsed slower and slower as blood poured from the wound.

Suddenly, a shod foot stepped right in the puddle of her mother's blood, and a hand gripped her wrist. She screamed.

A man lifted her into his arms. "Is this the wee mouse ye're after then? Ye're a pretty thing, aren't ye?" he said.

Her despair turned to rage as she beat her fists against the man's hairy face. The vinegary smell of sweat and hate assaulted her nose. Though Shona was only eight, she was strong, and his head jerked backward with each of her punches. Aggravated, the man dropped her, and she fell hard on the floor. He seized her by the hair, and dragged her over to the fireplace where another man held an iron in the fire.

"Here's yer first *slaighteur,* Seldomridge. Burn her."

Shona tried to pull away, but her hair was wound tightly in the bearded man's fist, and he wouldn't let go. The shorter man grabbed her wrist and held it aloft while he aimed the glowing iron at the back of her hand.

Shona struggled against them, but their strength was too mighty. She watched as the iron drew closer to her hand, her fingers splayed impotently. Then she heard a sizzling sound, and pain exploded inside her. She screamed shrilly as the darkening iron seared her skin. She had never known such pain. Or such malice to inflict it.

They let her go, and she ran into the corner. All her insides ached, and no amount of crying was enough to quench the pain. She looked at the back of her hand. Blistering on her skin was a squiggly figure. They had burned a snake onto her hand.

But she soon realized that she wasn't the only one blubbering, and she could easily hear her twin sister from within the cupboard, her sobs disclosing her hiding place. Instinctively, Shona ran in front of the cupboard, shielding it. But they had already heard—already expected—the presence of her siblings. The bearded man grabbed her by the shoulder of her frock and threw her forward. She landed upon her dead mother.

He threw open the doors of the cupboard and pulled Camran out. He too fought, but his child's body was no match for the man's strength.

Just then, Malcolm's eyes fluttered open and he groaned.

"Malcolm!" Shona cried, grateful he was alive. If he

helped, they might be able to escape. But he never moved. Blood seeped from his ears.

She heard Camran screaming, his small boy's voice filling the air as they branded him, too. Shona had to do something. She reached into the cupboard and yanked on Willow, whose eyes were clenched tight. Pain flooded her as she curled her fingers around Willow's arm. But Willow wouldn't budge.

"Come with me!" Shona cried, and Willow's eyes fluttered open. Fixing her gaze upon her twin sister, Willow climbed out of the cupboard. Hand in hand, they ran over the bodies of her family on the kitchen floor.

But a mob of kilted men were looting in the hall, blocking their escape.

"Where do ye think ye're going?" said a voice that Shona would never forget. The bearded man seized both their arms in his meaty fists, and yanked them backward toward the kitchen fireplace.

"Leave my sister be!" Shona cried as the bearded man hauled Willow into his arms. Shona's other half, the one that her father delighted in, was about to be painfully disfigured.

And as the iron drew closer to Willow's little hand, her legs scissoring helplessly in the air, Shona cried over that vision of suffering and thought just one thing.

Why?

ONE

MILES' END FARM
DUMFRIESSHIRE, SCOTLAND
1811

"I'll kill her!"

The front door slammed, thrusting an exclamation point on the threat.

Iona rolled her eyes as she wiped her sticky hands on her apron. "What did Shona do this time?"

Her husband lumbered into the kitchen, and wedged his hatchet into the wooden table.

"It's no' what she did. It's what she has no' done. I ordered her to bring in the flock from the field before midday. Farragut's will be here any minute to take the lambs to be butchered. She's disappeared and taken the damned sheep with her!"

Iona's loose bun wobbled as she turned back to the task of stuffing the chicken with the oniony skirlie. "Well, what did ye expect? Ye know how she gets. As soon as ye mentioned the word 'slaughter,' she was bound to rescue the lambs. I told you to send her off to market today. Getting those lambs away from Shona will be like tryin' to pry the cubs from a she-bear."

Hume jerked the worn tam off his head, revealing a shiny white scalp. Though his face was bristling with thick ginger hair, there was not a single strand above his bushy eyebrows. "Every blessed year we go through this."

Iona hoisted the pan heavy with two stuffed chickens and hung it from the hook inside the fireplace. Her back screamed as she righted her rounded frame. "After near ten year workin' for ye, ye should know the lass well enough by now."

"If I had only put my foot down in the first place. I knew she'd be trouble from the moment I laid eyes on her. I told ye so, didn't I? I told ye we should ha' only taken in the fair one. Every time I listen to you, I end up having to eat ma own liver." He stuffed a hunk of bread into his mouth.

"Och, Hume. Ye know perfectly well we couldna take one sister and no' take the other."

"Aye, we could ha'!" Crumbs of bread flew out of his mouth. "T'were required we take only one parish apprentice, no' two. And *slaighteurs,* no less! Two mouths to feed, two backs to clothe—"

"And two pairs of hands to do all the work that ye're too old to do, so shut yer pie-hole."

Hume grumbled. "Why can't Shona be more like her sister? I don't understand it. They eat the same food, sleep in the same bed, wear the same clothes. We grew them alike. Why is the one so obedient and docile, and the other so full of her own mind?"

Iona's thoughts turned to the gentle Willow. The twin sisters could not be more dissimilar. Not just in looks, but in disposition. The murder of their parents must have affected them in entirely different ways. The fair-haired Willow was a beauty, but terrified of her own shadow. She was not docile; she was dominated.

Shona, on the other hand, had grown fangs and claws. Since the night she had witnessed the brutal slaying of her parents and older brothers, Shona had grown into an untamable wildcat, and it was not to Hume's liking. Oh, they got along well enough, whenever they shared funny stories in the evening, or when they were of one mind on an issue. But if Shona Slayter had to stand up to him, stand up she did, and woe betide him if he tried to put her in her place. Yet there was a chink in her armor, and Hume knew what it was. She had a weakness for all things defenseless, especially her twin sister. And, of course, lambs destined for slaughter.

"If she doesna bring back those sheep before Farragut's arrives, I'll . . . I'll—"

Iona ignored him and began to slice the carrots. Hume never could finish that sentence.

The sound of carriage wheels crushing the gravel outside made Hume groan. "Och! Farragut's has arrived! Damn that lass! So help me, Iona, I'll make that girl obey me if it's the last thing I do!" He wedged the cap back on his head and stormed off as fast as his bowed legs would carry him.

There would be the devil to pay for this. And Shona Slayter knew she was about to become the chosen currency.

She slumped upon a felled tree trunk about a mile from the farmstead. Two dozen sheep fanned about her, dotting the emerald hillside, blissfully munching away at the moist grass. So joyfully ignorant of the fate that awaited them.

The brisk Lowland wind leaned against the grass,

and it lifted the black tendrils from her face. The breeze was thick with moisture, heralding a heavy rain. She sighed in irritation. Her work had to be done whether it be fine weather or no, and she dreaded having to spend the day in a sopping wet dress.

A three-month-old lamb ambled up to her, his white eyelashes sliding over his glossy black, questioning eyes. Her heart melted. How perfect his trust in her. The little creature followed her everywhere, came whenever she called. Hume had ordered her not to give the animals names, lest she get too attached, but she didn't care. This lamb was born with a gauzy nap of snowy white fleece, and she had named him Pillow.

She untied the pouch that hung next to her dagger on a cord around her waist. Inside a folded cloth was her untouched breakfast, plus a treacle-sweetened oat biscuit she had snatched from the kitchen window where Iona had been cooling them. She tore the chewy biscuit in pieces and held them out in her hand to Pillow. His nostrils puffed air onto her palms as he smelled the crumbles and then nuzzled them from her hand.

Shona smiled, resting her chin on her fist as Pillow finished off the biscuit. Eagerly, he sucked on her sticky fingers, massaging them between his flat upper gums and his short, dull bottom teeth. It was a pleasant sensation, and she chuckled when he weakly tried to bite off her fingers.

"Away with ye, now. Those are my fingers, not blades of grass!"

He bleated, and it sounded like a child's laughter.

Pillow sought her other hand, searching for more sweet things. But she had nothing more to give him. Her smile began to dissolve. The thought of Pillow being turned over to Farragut's chilled her more than did the distant thunder. When it came to slaughtering animals, Farragut's was careless and inhumane. She shuddered as she thought how Pillow's joyful bleating would turn to screaming as he was torn from his mother's side, hoisted onto a wagon, and hauled thirty terrifying miles over rocky roads to Dumfries. Then some brute of a man at Farragut's would cram Pillow into the slaughterhouse pen. He'd swing a hammer onto Pillow's tiny skull, knocking him senseless. Then he'd hang Pillow upside down from the lamb's delicate rear legs before slicing open his neck, leaving him to bleed out until dead. She wanted to—*had* to—save Pillow and the other lambs from that experience. She might not be able to stave off the slaughter forever. But today, at least, Farragut's would leave empty-handed.

The rumble of the thunder seemed to get closer, until Shona realized it was the muffled sound of a horse galloping toward her. She stood up from the tree trunk and looked behind her. Willow was quickly approaching atop General, the plow horse.

The sheep scattered as General came to a halt in front of Shona. Willow slid down the horse's bare back.

Shona crossed her arms. "Willow Slayter, if ye came to wag yer finger, I'll tell ye instead where to shove it."

Willow shook her head, her blond corkscrew tendrils bouncing against her face. "No, I didn't. I wanted to find ye to tell ye that a man came to see Hume just now. A town man! He had a big book with him . . . and papers. I couldna hear what they said, but whatever he came aboot, it made Hume very cross."

Shona's eyes widened. "Was it someone from the parish authorities?"

Willow shrugged. "I couldna tell."

Shona's breathing quickened as her excitement grew. "Maybe it was. Maybe Hume has to sign papers to release us from our apprenticeship. After all, we're nearly twenty-one." It was a day that Shona longed for, when she and Willow would no longer be wards of the parish. As much as she liked living with Iona and Hume, as a parish apprentice, Shona chafed at her lack of freedom. But one day they would reach maturity, and they'd be free—free to live and work wherever they wished, and no longer subject to a master's dominion. That glorious day was still three months, eleven days, and fourteen hours away.

Her freedom was so close she could almost taste it. She knew precisely what they would do. Upon their birthday, they would pack their belongings and head back to the Highlands to find their little brother Camran. If he was still alive.

They hadn't seen Camran since the Day. He'd been taken by the bearded man, and Shona and Willow were taken away by the man who'd branded them. Mr. Seldomridge was his name, and she'd never known a crueler human being. He used to punish them by making them kneel on brambles or locking them in a dark closet with rats. Thrice they'd run away, thrice they were caught, and each time they were badly beaten. After nearly a year, the two of them finally succeeded in escaping Mr. Seldomridge. They ran as far from the Highlands as they could, and made it as far south as Thornhill. There, they sought refuge in a church, and the vicar gave them food and a place to sleep. Eventually, though, the vicar had to surrender them to the care and protection of the parish authorities, which then arranged to apprentice them to learn trades befitting their station in life. Hume and Iona Findlay agreed to take in both sisters, and train them in farming and animal husbandry.

Shona had no idea what had become of Camran, but he was the only family they had left. She simply *had* to locate him. She glanced at the back of her hand. Like her, Camran had an *S* seared on the back of his hand. It identified them as *slaighteur*—knaves. Finding work or even friendship would be difficult for anyone with that damning brand, but there was one good thing about it—it might make Camran easier to find.

Willow tucked a lock of hair behind her ear. "I dinna know who that man was, but he must have a lot of power. When Farragut's wagon came, the town man sent it away."

Shona's eyebrows drew together. "The *town man* sent the wagon away?"

Willow nodded. "I saw him, clear as daylight. That's when Hume began to plead with him, but the town man just shook his head. Then I saw the town man get back in his carriage and leave."

Bafflement twisted her features. She picked up her pouch, and tied it around her waist again. "Come on, help me get the flock back to the sheep paddock. I want to find out who this town man was."

Willow shook her head. "Hume isna too pleased with you right now. If I were you, Shona, I'd stay clear of him. Hiding the sheep might've just earned you a lifetime of trouble."

Shona glanced at the horizon. Trouble, aye. A lifetime, no. Just three months, eleven days, and fourteen more hours of it.

* * *

To Shona's surprise, Hume didn't reprimand her for hiding the sheep from the butcher. In fact, he didn't even look for her. He spent the entire day inside the house, away from the farm. Even the chatty Iona was uncharacteristically tight-lipped about the strange visitor who had come that morning.

It rained throughout the night and into the next morning. Willow had developed a sniffle, sneezing and moaning throughout the night. When they awoke the next morning at half past four, Willow's eyes were puffed into near slits, and her nose was the color of Solway salmon. But at least she'd not had any of her nightmares.

Shona leaned over and touched her cheek to her sister's forehead. "Ye do no' have a fever. That's a blessing. Ye'd do well to stay abed today."

"No. I'll be all right. No doubt I look dismal."

"No worse than usual," Shona ribbed. "Still, I wouldna want ye to get a cough. Sleep the morning. I'll bring ye some tea after I do the milking."

Willow threw off her covers. "I canna let you do both our work. Besides, it's my turn to do the milking. I'll be fine once I shake the dew off me."

Shona felt a stab of remorse, but couldn't help feeling relief at sharing the task of milking. It was backbreaking, repetitive, exhausting work, and it had to be done twice each day, dawn and midafternoon. It took about twenty minutes to milk each cow, and there were three of them. Then there were the nanny goats, and there were seventeen of them. It was hard enough between the two of them, but for Shona alone, it would take all day.

Willow had washed and dressed before Shona had much time to object. Willow didn't seem to mind the quiet, patient work of milking as much as Shona did. Shona would rather pull a plow over a rocky field than have to do the milking. Cows could be peculiar, inscrutable creatures. It was easier to milk them from the rear, but that was not their most attractive side. Plus, it was the most dangerous. When she wasn't dodging a kick, she was dodging something else.

Shona stepped behind Willow to tie her pinafore. "All right, ye can help milk . . . but ye must stay inside the byre. The rain's coming down in buckets, and I dinna want you getting wet. I'll bring in the cows and nannies from the field to ye. Agreed?"

Willow snuffled, and nodded.

The morning lasted twice as long as any other for Shona. Her dress was glued to her wet body as she brought in the goats one by one from the paddock to the dairy. While Willow milked them, Shona tended to their other work. She mucked out the horse stalls; filled them with fresh, dry hay; collected the chicken eggs; and hauled water from the brook. By noon, even though it had finally stopped raining, she was nearly done in.

As Shona was hitching up General to the wagon, she saw a carriage approach the farm. Her eyebrows drew together as she edged toward the stable door. Hume and Iona had such few visitors that Shona immediately suspected it was either very good news . . . or very bad.

Willow ran into the stable from the kitchen courtyard, where she had been washing and candling the eggs. "Shona! That's the carriage that came yesterday! The town man . . . he's back!" She pointed at the carriage from behind Shona's back.

It was a fancy carriage, very unlike the kind seen in this part of Dumfriesshire. An older gentleman alighted from within the black lacquered coach. He had a compact, thin frame, and his body moved with great purpose and ease, even though his hair had become snowy white. He was dressed in a tartan jacket, vest, and trews. Under his arm was a large, flat book.

Shona took a step toward the driveway, but Willow gripped her arm. "Where are ye going?"

"I mean to find out exactly who this man is."

"What if he's from Mr. Seldomridge?" Willow's large green eyes had curved fearfully.

A streak of vengeance stiffened her spine. After all, she was no longer a frightened eight-year-old girl. In fact, she would very much like to cross paths with that monster once more. "Only one way to find out," she said as she wiped her hands on her sopping wet pinafore.

She walked out of the stable, her hands clasped behind her back, and stood in front of the team of horses. "Good day to ye."

The man turned his face to her. He touched his hat. "Good day, lass. Can ye fetch Mr. Hume Findlay, please?"

"Aye. Can I tell him who ye are?"

"Horace Hartopp. Factor to the new laird of Ballencrieff."

Shona let her guard down an inch. She turned in the direction of the house to call Hume over, but he was already coming toward the carriage to greet the visitor.

"Mr. Hartopp! Just having me tea. You're a wee bit earlier than I expected, sir."

The elderly gentleman held out his hand. "My apologies, but Ballencrieff has matters of a pressing nature this afternoon, and he hopes to settle business affairs with his tenants as soon as possible."

"Well, I'm afraid I've no' been able to scrape together the amount due the laird. Would he consider extending the time I have to repay?"

The elderly gentleman waved his hand. "We already discussed this yesterday, Mr. Findlay. Ye're nearly eighteen months in arrears, and I sent ye notice of collection six months ago. Ballencrieff has now arrived to take the reins of the estate, and he will not permit his tenants to live *gratis* upon his lands."

" 'Twere not our fault the estate has been ungoverned this past eighteen-month after the old laird passed away. No one came to collect the rents."

"All the more reason I would expect ye to have the monies from the sale of last year's crops."

"No, sir. We put all that money back into the management of the farm. Bought a new plow, got a stronger horse. We rotated our crops, and that required additional tilling and fertilizing."

Mr. Hartopp pasted an artificial smile on his face. "I appreciate the improvements to the land, Mr. Findlay. But the fact remains that the rent must be paid."

"We need more time to make up the debt, Mr. Hartopp. Can the laird just give me until the harvest?"

"Ye may wait until harvest to make up the rent past due for this year. But as I informed you yesterday, Ballencrieff must have the last twelvemonth rent."

"I tried to sell all my lambs yesterday . . . did ye at least tell the laird that ye yerself stopped me from doing so?"

Mr. Hartopp shook his head. "Selling off your livestock was a step ye should have taken a long time ago. As the new laird's factor, I could not risk that ye would abscond with any new profits. It is now simply too late. The laird has the right to confiscate this land for nonpayment of rent."

Hume turned pale. "The wife and I are advanced in years, Mr. Hartopp. Ye can't throw us off the homestead we've had for nigh on three decades."

"That decision is for the laird to make. But in the meantime, these crops are now forfeit to Ballencrieff."

Hume's voice shot up. "But I worked these crops, sir. They're mine."

"Not in the eyes of the law, Mr. Findlay. This land belongs to the estate of Ballencrieff. Under yer agreement with the landowner, ye were permitted to live upon and cultivate these forty acres for a rent of thirty-five pounds sterling per annum. As ye have provided the estate with neither monies as rent, nor provender to the stables, nor produce to the house, it now falls to the laird to determine how the estate can recover its losses. It will be my recommendation to rent the arable part of the land to a new tenant, thereby making good on most of your arrears."

"That's not fair! The fields are already planted and cultivated. A few more months and they'll produce a full harvest. This year, I've got wheat, peas, barley, and oats. They'll bring in enough money at market, I promise. If I could just have more time. Maybe if I speak to Mr. Carnock, the former factor?"

A note of pique sharpened his tone. "Mr. Carnock is no longer working for the estate. I'm the new laird's factor, and ye'll have to deal with me. And I do not look the other way when I see a scrounger living off my employer's generosity. In fact, if the laird is agreeable, I will suggest that he scrape you off his land this very day."

Hume had been a strict master, but a fair one. In all the time Shona had worked for him, she'd never seen him swindle anyone. Everyone in these parts could attest that Hume never asked for a farthing more for something than it was worth, nor did he pay less than its fair value. Indignation leaped within her. No one insulted Hume that way and got away with it.

"Ye will, will ye?" Shona retorted, taking a step toward the white-haired man. "Then ye're as wicked as ye are ugly. Hume is no scrounger, and he's never cheated a soul. The man's as good as his word. If he told ye ye'd have yer money at the harvest, then ye'd be smart to believe him. But ye seem more interested in showing off yer fancy suit and crowing like a cockerel on a pile of pigswill. Ye're nothing but bully and bluster, and I'll wager ye don't have the goolies to do it. Away with ye, and tell yer master he's got a whey-haired old goat for a servant."

Mr. Hartopp's face flushed to red, and even the whites of his eyes had colored to pink. He looked as if he'd been winded by a fist to his gut.

The carriage door opened. A glassy black Hessian boot emerged and landed on the muddy path. A second followed, and the door closed. Standing beside the carriage was a man almost as tall as General, the Clydesdale she had just been harnessing. His mouth had thinned to a razor-blade line across his face, and his eyes were blue flames burning beneath a scowl. He was dressed unlike any Scotsman she knew, with a tailcoat of navy blue and breeches made of fawn. A white cravat was tied underneath his square chin, and a gold brocade waistcoat outlined a trim torso. If she didn't know better, she'd think the new laird of Ballencrieff was an—

"You can tell me yourself, young woman, for I'm right here."

Shona's open mouth closed slowly. The man towered over her, filling her range of vision with his forbidding presence. A quake of fear erupted in her belly.

She swallowed hard, trying not to betray her trepidation. The man was an unfamiliar threat, but he clearly had both the status and the physical strength to enforce his own will. He was not in the least singed by her words. And that was the only weapon she had at her disposal.

"What game is this?" she demanded, forcing the steadiness back in her voice. "Do ye really expect us to believe that the laird of Ballencrieff is an . . . an—"

"Englishman?" The handsome man cocked an eyebrow. "I'm afraid so."

Now it was Shona's turn to be winded. His clothes, his accent, even his arrogance all screamed English. Despite the dominating stance, he was incredibly, incredibly handsome.

"Bah!" Hume punched his forefinger in the man's direction. "Ballencrieff was a patriot. A head-to-toe Scotsman. He would ha' nothing to do with Sassenachs."

The man's jaw tensed, and his eyes grew flinty.

"I appreciate neither my uncle's politics nor your disparaging remark, sir. Do not now pretend you two were allies. As for your daughter here, you'd do well to teach her to respect her betters. Or at least to keep a civil tongue in her head."

Hume's mouth sealed to a tight-lipped snarl.

The Englishman continued. "As for Mr. Hartopp's generous offer, it is hereby nullified. You will repay your debt—in its entirety—to my estate. If you don't like that arrangement, perhaps a spate in debtor's prison is in order, there to remain until every last penny is settled. Now, what's it to be?"

Shona could kick herself. Her outburst served only to worsen Hume's position. And put a smug smile on Mr. Hartopp's face.

Hume grumbled into his chest. "I've got five pound in the house."

The Englishman gave a curt nod. "And?"

Hume's nostrils flared. "I'm owed four pound thruppence from some in town. I can have it to you on the morrow."

"And?"

Hume shrugged. "Crops will come in by fall."

The Englishman shook his head. "I won't wait that long. You can make up the difference with the livestock. Hartopp, what was your accounting of his animals?"

Perfunctorily, Mr. Hartopp opened his book to a marked page and scrolled down with his finger. "Three milk cows, seventeen dairy goats, two bucks, one plow horse, twenty-four sheep and lambs, fourteen laying hens, and one rooster."

"Take them. Have them conveyed to the estate until I decide what to do with them. You can reduce Mr. Hume's debt by the fair market value of his animals." The Englishman turned on his heel, followed closely by Mr. Hartopp.

"But you can't take my animals, my lord," Hume pleaded. "You'll leave us with no milk or cheese or meat. We need them for sustenance."

The Englishman didn't even turn around as he spoke. "I'm certain you'll think of something."

Hume removed his cap and held it to his chest in humility. "My lord, please. My family will starve without them."

The Englishman stopped in his tracks. He heaved a ragged sigh and turned around. The Englishman's eyes landed upon Shona. His expression softened.

"Very well. In light of your years, I'll allow you to keep the plow horse to help you bring in the harvest. You may also keep one cow, and half of the poultry. That should keep you and your daughter from immediate want."

"I'm no' his daughter," erupted Shona.

"Pardon?"

It felt so good to toss his mistake into his face. "I said, I'm no' his daughter."

"I see," he said, his irritation palpable. "You're incredibly opinionated, but I find you a bit scruffy to be his solicitor. Who are you then?"

Hume took a step toward her. "She's a parish orphan, my lord. The wife and I took her and her sister in. We've been taking care of them for almost ten year now. I taught Shona the business of farming. Growing crops and raising livestock."

The Englishman crossed his arms at his chest. Slowly, his eyes took their fill of her, and she grew uncomfortable under his perusal. She could just imagine how she looked to him. Horse manure caked her shoes and lined the hem of her dress. Her wet, shiny hair hung down her head like long black snakes. Her once-white pinafore was now mottled with smears from handling the rain-soaked animals.

A thread of embarrassment coiled inside her. The image she presented to him was little more than mud, moisture, and manure. At least her branded hand was behind her, out of his sight.

"How much were you given for her?"

Hume wrung the tam in his hands. "Er . . . two pound, my lord."

The Englishman scratched his jaw. "I've not hired any outside servants yet—other than the gamekeeper, that is. I'll need someone to look after the livestock that Hartopp is conveying to the estate. As you'll have little enough need of Shona yourself, you can article her to me. And for that, I'll reduce your debt by a further four pounds."

Hume silently considered the proposition.

But not Shona.

"Ye've a bloody cheek!" she told the Englishman, her hands pinned to her hips. "How dare ye trade me aboot like an animal! Who do ye think ye are? I won't be bought and sold like a heifer."

Mr. Hartopp rolled his eyes. "My dear young woman, there is little enough difference between a parish apprentice and a farmyard animal. In fact, if it were left to smell alone, I doubt the laird would be able to distinguish between a heifer and yerself."

The Englishman suppressed a chuckle. Shona, however, was not similarly amused.

"Why, you ill-begotten, half-bairned son of a cur!" She lunged at Mr. Hartopp, determined to scratch the smug look off his face. Before her nails made contact, a long arm snaked around her middle.

"Whoa!" shouted the Englishman. "It was only a jest."

" 'Twas no jest," she said, struggling against the Englishman's superior strength. " 'Twas an insult, clear and deliberate!"

He laughed. "You thrust first in that swordfight. It was not so long ago you called him a whey-haired old goat. Now sheathe your claws."

Shona stopped wriggling. When she did, she became vividly aware of the feel of the man holding her tightly. Behind her was a wall of strength—a wide chest dense with muscle, narrowing to a firm waist. His long legs prevented any retreat, but she wasn't making any. She grasped the arm wrapped around her middle. The fabric of his sleeve was soft, but the muscles beneath were marble-hard. Her waning fury was quickly replaced by a surprisingly agreeable sensation.

He released her, and she backed away from him. Her body was still tingling wherever it had made contact with his.

He jerked on his waistcoat, straightening his clothes. "Now, the fact remains that my estate is not yet fully staffed, and your services will be required. Apprentices don't usually get paid, but I am prepared to offer you a small wage, in addition to bed and board. *If* you're industrious and well behaved, that is. And I'll give Mr. Findlay here until the end of the year to make up the balance owed. Now, are we in agreement?"

For the first time, hope winked inside her. Not only would Hume have more time to pay his debts, but she would finally be able to earn a wage. Her mind reeled with the possibilities of how her and Willow's lives would change if they went to work for the Englishman. Surely with some money jingling in their pockets, they would be in a better position to seek their own lives—and Camran—once they turned twenty-one. Also, she'd be able to tend to Pillow and all the other animals she'd come to love.

On the other hand, the Englishman might prove to be an evil taskmaster. She'd heard stories of Sassenach lords and the advantages they took of servant girls. For all his boorishness and bluster, Hume was no lecher. She wasn't so sure about the Englishman. Better the devil you know than the devil you don't.

The Englishman's eyes gazed at her in bemused curiosity. He was handsomer than she had at first surmised. His eyes were blue, like the sky on a summer day, encircled by a darker cobalt, like the color of a loch in winter. Beneath his long eyebrows, his eyes were edged by a thick fringe of dark brown lash. The wind picked up a sandy brown whorl from above his forehead. His jaw was clean-shaven, but tomorrow's beard lay submerged underneath.

Maybe this would not be such a bad move after all. "Sounds fair enough. Aye. Willow and I can be there on the morrow."

The crease between his eyebrows deepened. "Willow? Is that the cow's name?"

Shona laughed. "No. Willow is my sister."

His dark lips thinned. "Willow is not part of the bargain between myself and Mr. Findlay. She can stay here on the farm."

The smile drained from her face. "Nay. Willow must come with me."

The Englishman sighed. "I'm sorry. Findlay, please sort this out. Hartopp will draw up the articles of indenture. I want the girl on my estate before nightfall." The Englishman stepped onto the carriage.

"I'll not leave without Willow," she protested.

Hume put a hand on her arm. "Leave it be, Shona. I want Willow to stay here with me."

She jerked her arm free and ran to the carriage door, holding it open. "Ye *must* take us both. Keep the wages if ye wish, but I'll not leave Willow behind."

"Shona, hush yerself!" Hume admonished. "Take no notice of her, my lord. 'Tis sisterly affection between them. But they are of age now, and must learn to live apart."

"No," she insisted. "It is both or none."

"Young woman," began the Englishman, "I am not in the habit of being issued ultimatums, least of all by those in my employ. Now I strongly suggest that you—"

His voice trailed off and his eyes lifted to a place just behind her. She turned to look. Willow was standing behind her.

"Please, my lord," Willow said. "Don't separate us. I'll be no trouble, I promise."

He blinked. "You're Shona's sister?"

"Aye, my lord." Willow cast her face toward the ground, her blond hair falling forward along her cheeks.

He gave Willow a leisurely appraisal. His expression was one that many men had when they set eyes upon Willow. "Very well, Shona. I'll take you both. I think I might be able to find something for her to do. Gather your belongings. The carriage leaves in ten minutes."

Within five minutes, the girls had tossed their wardrobe—the frocks that they shared between them—and their few belongings into a worn leather valise they had brought with them from the orphanage. Iona stood in the doorway of their room and wept, swearing all sorts of curses upon Hume's bald head.

"Don't cry, Iona," said Shona as she changed out of

her wet dress and into a dry one. "The estate is only five miles away. I promise Willow and I will be back every chance we get."

Iona's nose looked like a wet cherry. "Five miles? It may as well be fifty. Ye'll never make it out to the farm from that distance. And even if ye could, there's no telling what that Sassenach laird will be like. He might refuse to let ye leave the estate. He might be just as bad a tyrant as his uncle, may that man rot in his grave. Oh, God. What if he's a scoundrel? What if he takes advantage of ye?" Iona dissolved into tears again.

Willow embraced Iona from behind as Shona grasped the older woman's hands. "We're not going to let that happen," Shona assured her. "Don't ye worry. We can take care of ourselves."

"Ye, perhaps. But Willow, sweeting, ye must promise to be strong." She turned toward Willow, whose own tears had begun to fall swiftly. "Men are animals, the lot of 'em. They want only one thing, especially from a pretty girl like ye. Ye mustn't let anyone bully ye into giving them favors. Not yer master, not the other servants. Ye're a sweet girl, and ye don't understand the effect ye have on a man."

Shona looked away, stung once again by the realization that she was not the prettier of the two. Willow's effortless loveliness drew men to her like flies to honey. She could see why. That creamy, unblemished skin, which invited caresses; the childlike shape of her face, which lent her an ageless beauty; those full, shell-pink lips that formed a perpetual pout; her long, shiny lashes, which made her appear as if she had just been weeping. Yet there was an unawareness of her own beauty, making Willow much more susceptible to men's flattery, leaving her as helpless as a tethered goat outside a den of wolves. Iona's advice was a truth that Willow needed to hear.

"And ye," continued Iona, placing both her hands on Shona's cheeks, "take care of yer sister. Ye're a sensible soul, and ye've sound instincts. If anyone makes unreasonable demands of either of ye, or hurts ye in any way, promise me that ye'll run away straight home. D'ye understand? Hie yerselves here."

"I promise," she said.

A crest of tears spilled over the rims of Iona's blue eyes. "Dear Lord, what am I going to do without m'girls?"

They went downstairs to the kitchen, where Iona placed some treacle biscuits and the kidney pie she had made for Hume's dinner into a basket. She stumbled over her own sobs, trying to pour overdue motherly advice into their heads. All she managed to do was stammer unintelligibly.

The driver placed their bundles in the rumble of the carriage. He then held the door open for them and helped them onto the coach.

The interior of the coach was even grander than the exterior. Burgundy-colored leather seats faced each other, and the matching walls were accented with gold trim. The clear glass windows were elegantly etched at each corner.

Shona glanced at the other occupant. Not only did the carriage seem to belong to another world, but so did the Englishman. He had a manner that bespoke generations of breeding, completely at ease with his own power and wealth. His tall frame filled the cabin, and his long legs extended out almost to the opposite seat. He was immensely attractive . . . for a Sassenach. Shona edged past his lap and sat opposite him, while Willow took her place beside her sister, their gloved hands clasped nervously in their laps.

The Englishman smiled at Willow. "So you're the one that Mr. Findlay wouldn't part with. I can certainly see why."

Willow smiled sheepishly, a blush whispering across her cheeks. Shona's protective instincts immediately became alert. To Shona, Willow looked a mess—her hair was uncombed, she was at the pinnacle of her cold, and her clean pinafore was already smudged. But to a man, she probably looked as beautifully rumpled as if she had just risen from a lover's bed.

"Your name is Willow?"

"Aye, my lord. Willow Slayter, at yer service."

"What do *you* do for Mr. Findlay?"

Willow glanced up from her downcast head, and shrugged. "Whatever's required, my lord. Milk the cows, see to the chickens, mend the clothes, do the washing—"

"Do you have children?"

Color flooded her face. "No, my lord. I'm a maiden."

"I see," he said, a smile touching his eyes.

"But I love children. When the women of t'other farms would give birth, Iona would ask me to look after the wee ones while the mums got their strength back. I love seeing to bairns."

"Do you?" he replied, his interest even keener. "In that case, I have a special position I think you might be able to assume."

The words "dirty sod" flashed through Shona's mind. "And just what *position* would ye be talking aboot?"

The Englishman flashed a puzzled glance at Shona. "I have an infant son—a two-year-old—and his nursemaid fell ill midway on the journey from London. She simply couldn't continue, so I had to put her on a coach back home. Consequently, I must engage a nursemaid to look after the boy. Perhaps you, Willow, might be able to fill that station."

Willow's face brightened. "I'd love to, my lord!"

The Englishman asked Willow a barrage of questions as to her health, cleanliness, morality, temperance, habits, and specific experience with children. She answered each question with self-effacing candor and meek respect.

The Englishman turned to his factor. "I think Miss Slayter here can serve as Eric's nursemaid—on a trial basis, of course. Hartopp, ask the housekeeper to get adequate clothes for Miss Slayter. She'll also need to be given accommodations in the nursery. You'll ask Mrs. Docherty to see to that as well, won't you?"

Mr. Hartopp scribbled into his ledger. "Of course, sir."

Shona became immediately suspicious. "And where is this nursery?"

His brows drew together. "On the uppermost floor. Why do you ask?"

"Will yer bedchamber be adjoining hers?"

"Shona!" Willow admonished.

The Englishman's lips pursed. "Are you implying that I'm arranging a sordid dalliance with your sister?"

She straightened. "I've a right to know what yer intentions are toward her."

Mr. Hartopp came to his employer's defense. "Young woman, ye're speaking to a gentleman and the laird of the estate. If he—"

The Englishman raised his hand and Mr. Hartopp stopped speaking. He leaned forward and brought his face to within inches of hers. "In the first place, I do not care for being upbraided by a servant, however well intentioned it may be. In the second place, if you are accusing me of desiring to take liberties with innocent maids, you have much still to learn about me. And finally, if I *were* to take liberties with anyone in my household, there is nothing you could do to stop me. So I will thank you to remember your place, for if you cannot control your impudent tongue, I will send you—and only you—back to that farm."

He retracted his imposing frame back to his chair, and Shona could finally breathe again. His threat had winded her, robbing her of speech. During their brief acquaintance, he had accurately discerned what her greatest fear was—to be separated from her twin sister— and he knew precisely how to use that weakness to his own advantage. She now understood that although the Englishman was well groomed and genteel, he was infinitely more dangerous than she had initially thought him. Ownership of the sisters had passed hands from Hume to the Englishman, but she was no longer certain that it was a good thing. A lamb never fared better at the *second* place it went to.

No one spoke during the remainder of the trip. Shona gazed out the window, hands in her lap, her left hand instinctively covering the right. The familiar woods near Hume's property faded behind them, and the carriage rumbled into unfamiliar terrain as it neared Ballencrieff House. Shona had seen the house only once or twice—and only from afar—because Iona had warned them both to stay clear of the "wicked laird of Ballencrieff." Even after that man's death, unmourned by everyone she knew, she still kept her distance. As she was fond of saying, she had lost nothing on the estate, and even if she had, it was not worth going back for.

Now the carriage turned onto the very property she had avoided. The wheels crunched on the gravel in front of a large mansion that seemed about three hundred years old. The one-time fortress seemed to make an effort to be welcoming and warm, but failed utterly. The beige stone walls rose high into the sky, dwarfing the leafy woods that receded from it. The walls were studded with narrow windows, more brick than glass. The façade was crowned by a crenellated wall and several small, sharp turrets, looking for all the world like a row of fangs in the mouth of a large beast.

The Englishman jumped off, extending himself to his full height.

"Hartopp, see to Miss Slayter's clothing. Then have her report to me in the study for inspection. Also, tell Mrs. Docherty I got her her very first dairymaid. She can tell Cook to expect fresh milk, cream, and butter soon. And tell her to prepare a room in the servants' quarters for the other Miss Slayter."

The other Miss Slayter. A flicker of jealousy had already been burning inside Shona, but it flared at his dismissive attitude. Despite his authority, she would make the Englishman respect her. As she always said, start as you mean to go.

"In the first place, I am not 'the other Miss Slayter.' You can call me Miss Slayter, or by my given name, which is Shona. And in the second place, my sister's place is with me. We live together, we work together, we stay together."

It was the last thing in the world she expected him to do. The Englishman tilted back his head and laughed.

"Clearly, you've been accustomed to a great deal more latitude than I am prepared to give you. So let me paint you a picture of what your life is about to become. I am the master, and you are the apprentice. You belong to me now. On this estate, I am the supreme and final authority. If from my lips you hear that I want you to work in the dairy, then that is precisely what you can expect to do. And if your sister is wanted in the nursery, then that is where she will serve. I demand swift and absolute obedience, and anything less is blatant disobedience. The sooner you learn that fact, the more inclined I will be to hearing your *requested* privileges." He dipped his head curtly. "Shona."

Despite his admonishment, she enjoyed hearing her name on his lips. Perhaps it was his English accent, which softened her name into something that sounded elegant and romantic. Or maybe it was that she had won some measure of his respect, as he had done precisely as she had asked him to do. But she greatly suspected it was the way his mouth curled into a slight smile as he looked her in the face.

"What shall I call you?" she asked softly.

An invisible smile touched his eyes. "You may call me Master."

A dog bounded out from the open front door of the house, a white English pointer with blue-black spots and pendant ears that flapped in the air as he ran toward the Englishman.

The man's face transformed into something she had not yet recognized. He smiled widely, revealing straight white teeth, and his eyes became playful crescents. The dog's tail whipped side to side as he reared up and pushed his forepaws into the Englishman's abdomen.

The Englishman grunted, laughing at the dog's squeal-ing salutation.

"Good to see you, too, Dexter!" The Englishman ruffled the dog's ears with both hands. The dog jumped higher, trying to lick the man's face, but not quite reach-ing it.

Shona took in the joy that man and dog felt in each other's presence. Aye, she liked seeing the Englishman contented. Aye, she relished seeing the happiness he brought to the dog. But if the Englishman thought she was going to call him Master and lick his hands like his dog, he was in for an unpleasant shock.

TWO

Shona was pleased to discover that the estate's new housekeeper was Esther Docherty, wife of the town's printer. They were a lovely couple. Mrs. Docherty had been out of work for some time—since the day that her former mistress moved the entire family to India—and they had been struggling. Whenever Shona would travel into Stonekirk, Mr. Docherty secretly supplied Shona with his mistakes—books and bills that had come off the presses smeared or typographically incorrect—and Shona would cut him off a hunk of cheese or some scented soap that she had brought to town to sell.

Now Mrs. Docherty's bony frame was zipping about the linen room like an overexcited bee.

"Just look at the state these table linens are in. Old Ballencrieff was a miserly codger. I'll just have to get some new ones brought in. The new laird's lived all his life in London . . . no doubt he's accustomed to grander things. We can't ask the family to wipe their mouths on this. It looks more like a cheesecloth than a napkin."

Shona took the apron Mrs. Docherty had given her, and tied it about her waist. "Family? What family?"

Mrs. Docherty hardly looked at Shona. The cap she wore revealed the dull copper color her hair had turned once the gray had set in. Her angular profile reminded

Shona of an engraving she had seen of the Greek Furies. "Well, now o'course it's only the master and his son. But the master's brother will be arriving soon. Och! If these English folk get a look at these napkins, they'll think we Scots live like animals."

Shona turned over one of the folded white cloths in her hand. The napkin looked perfectly suitable to her, even if they were a little frayed at the edge. "Would you like me to go into town and buy some?"

Mrs. Docherty sighed. "No, thank ye, Shona. The master informed me that ye're to work in the dairy, and I should see to it that ye have what ye need to start. First thing ye'll need to do is clean it out. Come along with ye, then."

The older woman grabbed a few sheets and towels from the far end of the linen closet and proceeded down the stairs. Shona followed closely behind, their combined footfalls making hollow noises in the servants' hall.

"So what do you know of the new master of Ballencrieff? Seems a right arrogant bugger to me. He won't even tell me his name."

"His name is Conall MacEwan."

"Conall?" She wrinkled her nose. "That's a Scotsman's name. I thought he was a Sassenach."

"No! He was born in this very house. Must have been, oh, about thirty-five years ago, after war began with the Colonies. I remember his father, Niall. He was a kind man, a scholarly man. Devoted to his studies. Which was probably just as well, as Niall was the second son and would never inherit the estate. So when the old laird died, Niall's older brother Macrath became laird of Ballencrieff. 'Twas a dark day for Stonekirk when Macrath inherited the estate. That man squandered all the income, and joined in devil's bargains with the tenants. It wasn't long before Niall stood up to Macrath and his unjust ways. But Macrath never could abide insults to his authority, and ordered Niall to leave the estate for good. So Niall took his young family and hied to England, where Conall grew into a man. I'm given to understand that Conall became a doctor, just like his father, Niall."

"So this is his first time back to Scotland?"

"Aye. 'Twill be good to have the bloodline of Niall MacEwan in charge of the estate."

It didn't make one bit of difference to Shona. Be it Conall MacEwan, Hume, or someone else, she was indentured to serve at the pleasure of a man. Her freedom was little more than a twinkle of starlight in the distance. But at least it was in sight. All she had to do was bide her time a wee while longer.

"The apple doesna rot far from the tree," muttered Shona. "Is his wife any kinder?"

"The laird is a widower. I was not told how his wife died. But she left behind a wee baby. Might have died giving birth to him, poor thing."

"Oh," she replied, her head jerking back in surprise. It was a pity he had lost his woman. She stiffened once more. "Mayhap that explains his crabbit ways. Do ye know what he had the cheek to tell me?"

Mrs. Docherty turned around. "Shona, I've known ye since ye were a short lass in long pigtails. Let me give ye a wee bit of advice. Bow yer stiff neck. If ye do as ye're told and mind yer tongue, there'll be food aplenty for ye and yer sister. Don't challenge this man. He'll not have it. Do ye ken me?"

Shona pouted. "I'll no' take his spleen."

"Ye won't get any unless ye defy him. Or call him a Sassenach."

Mrs. Docherty led Shona to a cellar below the house. The air in here was cold and thick, like the inside of a cave. "This is the cold room. Ye can bring the milk and cream in here to keep. Just keep out of Cook's hair. She's one of them English. She is *not* happy about moving up north. I've already had a few run-ins with her. The only way she'll have us Scots is if we're baked in a pie."

Shona picked up two milk pails and the stack of old linens Mrs. Docherty gave her. "Well, if any of these Sassenachs think they're going to get on their high horse with me, I'm going to make them dismount!"

He was not cut out for this.

Conall glanced down at the untidy stacks of paper on the desk, which had belonged to each Ballencrieff laird for the past two centuries. The last time he'd been in this room, he was five years old. He'd torn yellowed strips from the historical charter and papered the floor with them, while he dripped water on the ancient ink and watched fascinated as it swirled and disappeared. His uncle Macrath was so furious that his face had purpled, and he spit out every foul word he could think of in both Gaelic and English.

Now the papers on his desk were screaming for *his* attention, and he wanted nothing more than to run from them back to his familiar life in England.

He fell into a chair, his long legs splayed wide. How was he ever going to run a large estate like this? His father had certainly not taught him, as there'd been no need. Their house had been a modest residence in the cosmopolitan center of London. There had been no tenants to manage, no local commissions to oversee, no need to understand harvest seasons or livestock prices. In London, meat was purchased at the butcher, vegetables at the market, and government handled the workings of government.

What cruel joke of fate was it that had dropped him in the remote hinterland of the Scottish Lowlands, trying to rescue a crumbling estate from longtime mismanagement and neglect?

He rubbed his tired face. He'd been willing to make bet that it would be a frosty day in hell if he were to inherit Ballencrieff. Back when his grandfather was laird, there'd been two sons born to him. Niall, Conall's own father, was only the second son, and so would never inherit the estate. The estate logically went to the eldest son, Macrath. Growing up in England, Conall never had to give Scotland or his uncle Macrath more than a passing thought. But when Conall's father Niall passed away four years ago, and then his uncle Macrath died without issue, Conall found himself dubiously honored as the laird of Ballencrieff.

Clearly, the devil was playing with snowballs.

And so he went from being Dr. MacEwan to laird of Ballencrieff. Conall looked around the study, its mahogany-paneled walls groaning under the weight of stag heads, taxidermied trout, and hunting weapons— all symbols of an indolent sporting life. Conall was not a man of idle gentility, content to while away the hours fishing or shooting game. He was hard-pressed to find any meaning at all in collecting rents and living off the sweat of another man's brow. That lifestyle, he thought with a shake of his head, was better suited to his reprobate brother, Stewart.

Conall, on the other hand, was a man of science. He loved the elegant marvel that was the human body. Its ability to move, change, procreate—and heal itself— always left him in thrall. So he became a doctor, like his father before him. As a physician, Conall was well-known in the loftier social circles, and he was frequently called upon by those among the *ton*. Indeed, it was from them he was able to make his living. But he always made himself available for those who were unable to afford a doctor's pricey fees. Consideration for the poor had something to do with it. But if he were honest with himself, he'd admit that it had more to do with his eager fascination with the workings of the human body, which provided no end of wonder.

Or horror, he thought as he picked up an antique pistol that was used as a paperweight. Conall detested weapons. He'd seen what damage they could do on the human body. Earlier in his career, patriotic fervor got the better of him, and against his father's advice, he'd gone to sea on one of Lord Nelson's ships as a surgeon. The battle he witnessed at Copenhagen in 1801 would scar him for the rest of his life. The broken bones, the torn limbs, the charred skin. And everywhere blood. Each young seaman looked at him with mortal dread and desperation, and asked the same question—one that he was unable to answer. *Will I live?*

He threw the pistol into the bottom drawer. Conall had sworn he would never use a weapon on another human being. When steel met flesh, it was rarely the latter that emerged victorious. And with the dead and dying all around, even a battle won offered too little over which to celebrate.

Battle. It seemed that once again he was engaged in a battle—only this time with a woman.

His mind quickly turned to the two girls he'd just brought on as maids. The one called Willow Slayter was soft-spoken and bashful, and as pretty a girl as he'd ever seen. He took to her immediately. She was respectful and industrious, and he liked the tender way she cooed over his son. All told, it was a promising start to her position as nursemaid.

But then there was that other Miss Slay— *Shona,* he corrected himself with a smile. God, she was impertinent. She was clearly the more stubborn of the two sisters, and the one with the greater cleverness and instinct for survival. But her impudent manner got right up his nose. That one would definitely need to be taught some manners.

She was a handful, and in more ways than one. He remembered the way she felt in his arms, bucking like a wildcat when she tried to tear Hartopp's face off. And she was a tall, strong woman, too. He doubted Hartopp would have emerged unscathed if Conall had not been there to hold her back. But as he'd held her, he'd become keenly aware of how her body gentled under his, and the hitch in her breathing when he spoke into her ear.

She was pretty, too, albeit in a rustic, Gypsy sort of way. Despite the stringy wet hair and the holes all over her dress, he liked the way she fit into his embrace. He allowed his mind to darken as he imagined what sort of a lover Shona would make.

A knock on the door jarred him out of his thoughts. It was the new housekeeper, Mrs. Docherty. A sharp-looking woman, with bony cheeks and a pointed nose, yet quite probably the most efficient servant he'd ever had. She was almost single-handedly making the house not only livable, but comfortable.

"The guest ye were expecting has arrived, sir. He's in the hall."

"That'll be my brother. I presume you've already seen to his rooms?"

"Of course, sir. All is prepared. Tonight promises to be chilly, so I'll just see to it that the fireplaces are lit in both your bedchambers."

Conall grinned, grateful for his prize find. "You are a treasure, Mrs. Docherty."

When the housekeeper left, Conall cast a baleful glance at the desk full of bills, letters, boundary disputes, rent tallies, and produce reports. Though unwieldy and irritating, comparatively speaking, these were the easy problems. In the hall awaited the challenging one.

In the servants' quarters, Shona fell backward onto her bed fully clothed. Her hands and knees were red and raw, and her nose burned from the lye in the soap. But she had succeeded in scrubbing clean the dairy to a shine.

From the look of it, there hadn't been a cow in it for some time, and no one had bothered to clean up after its last occupants. The dust had been gray and thick, coating everything in sight. Ancient cobwebs, streaming from the rafters, got tangled in her hair. A mound of hay below an open window had turned green from rot, and was no doubt a tiny cottage for whatever was squeaking inside it. But by the time she had finished, there wasn't a speck of dust on the wood beams, the walls had become a few shades lighter, and the air had been infused with the perfume of fresh hay.

Thankfully, she didn't have to do a thing to prepare her bedchamber. Someone else had done her the kindness of making it cozy for her. Against one wall there was a small cupboard for her clothes, and in the corner was a washstand. A brass candle stand, a dented relic probably discarded by the family, sat on a table next to her bed. There was a window that looked out onto the rear garden, and it was draped by a soft green curtain with pretty pink flowers. Although the room was small and sparsely furnished, it was clean and warm, and was considerate of its inhabitant. The only thing missing was her twin sister.

But there was another heartbeat in the room. Curled up in the basin of her washstand was a black cat, the same one that had watched her labor in the dairy all afternoon. Its jade-colored eyes were regarding her with languorous interest, as the fluffy tail with a kink in it swayed gently over the lip of the basin.

Shona tried to rise, but the dagger of pain in her back sank her back down again. "Dinna get too comfortable, Little One," she groaned aloud to the cat. "Ye'll be moving just as soon as I find the strength to wash myself."

"Mayhap I can help?" came a familiar voice from the doorway.

"Willow!" Shona bolted upright, the jarring pain making her wince. "Where've ye been?"

The blond sister smiled and sat beside her on the bed. "In the nursery. Oh, Shona, the bairn is a wee bit of heaven! Smiles all the time, he does. He's as sweet as can be. And he looks just like the master. Wee soft curls on his head, and the longest lashes you've ever seen. He's named Eric."

"What aboot the Englishman? Is he treating ye right?"

" 'Course he is! His lordship is a real gentleman. We even had tea together, and Shona, ye should see the pretty cups and saucers! They brought up the most lovely warm scones, and they served it with raspberry jam and butter."

Shona's stomach would have growled, but she suspected it was too tired to do so. Willow reached into the pocket of her pinafore and pulled out a napkin that Shona recognized immediately from Mrs. Docherty's linen closet. "I didn't know if ye'd had yer tea," Willow said, "so I saved ye one."

Shona smiled, and unfolded the napkin to reveal a lovely browned scone sliced through the middle and filled with creamy butter and a thick line of black jam. "Thanks, Will."

Shona took a huge bite, and instantly, all her senses came alive. As the salty-sweet taste filled her mouth, her body began to awaken from its death of exhaustion. "Mmm . . . at least the Sassenachs can cook. Tastes better than Iona's."

"I would think twice before telling Iona that," she chuckled.

Shona took another bite, her upper lip ringed with raspberry jam. As she did, she began to inspect her sister. Willow was uniformed in a beautiful sky-blue frock with a matching cap. A pristine white pinafore was tied around her waist. Not a single wrinkle could be found anywhere on her garments.

"Where did ye get those clothes?"

Willow cast a glance down at her dress. "They were meant to be the nursemaid's. Poor thing."

With her clean hand, Shona lifted the hem of Willow's dress. "Those shoes. Are they . . . are they silk?"

"Aye," Willow responded, lifting her foot into the air. "I think these were in a trunk somewhere. I don't know whose they were, but he asked Mrs. Docherty to give them to me."

"Why would he do that?"

"Well, he didn't care for the look of my ghillies. He wants to order me some proper shoes, such as English servants wear, and he gave me these in the meantime."

Shona wiped her mouth with the napkin that, according to Mrs. Docherty, was only fit for animals. "Wait a minute. Why is it that ye get to work with the master's child and have tea and get a nice new dress and real silk slippers and sleep in the main part of the house, while I get to scrub old cow pats out of the dairy in my own clothes and sleep in the servants' quarters?"

Willow shrugged. "I'm sorry, Shona. It isna fair, is it?"

"I should bloody well say no'." Shona's lips formed into a pout.

Willow put a hand on Shona's shoulder. "Why don't I have a word with the master? Maybe he'll let ye sleep in the nursery with me. There's enough room in there for the three of us."

That was neither a wise idea nor a useful one, but Shona was having too much of a sulk to say so.

Willow looked around the room. "Ye know, Shona, this room really isn't so bad. It's actually quite cheerful. Much better than our room at Miles' End Farm."

Shona had thought so, too, but in light of where her

sister was staying, it now seemed like a hovel. She crossed her arms in front of her.

The crease deepened in Willow's forehead. "I must go. I have to get back to the bairn. I'll come visit again tomorrow. All right?"

Shona turned away as Willow walked out of her room. As her sister's footsteps faded down the hall, regret crept in. She didn't begrudge Willow those comforts. If it had to be one or the other, she was glad that it was Willow who'd been favored. It just irritated her that the Englishman had lavished so much attention on her. She was certain he was up to something, and her sister was sure to be too naïve to see it. She sighed heavily. Only three months and eleven days more until they had their freedom, and she let that thought infuse her with hope.

A chilling fear snaked through her, and that hope began to evaporate at the edges. What if Willow got attached to the child? What if she didn't want to give up the relative comfort of her life here at the manor? What if, in the end, Willow wouldn't want to leave? Would that force Shona to set out on her own? The thought of being all alone in the world terrified her.

She trudged to the washstand. The cat lifted its head, and jerked its kinked tail. Shona picked up the animal to set it on the floor. But for some reason, she couldn't let the cat go. She sat upon the bed, and sank her face into the creature's soft fur, consoling herself in the rumbling purr amid the dreadful silence in the room.

THREE

After a sumptuous dinner of salmon in white sauce, venison steaks, potatoes in gravy, asparagus in butter, and gooseberry pie, Conall sank contentedly into a leather chair in the library. It was good to see and talk to his younger brother again. But Conall wished that, for once, Stewart could be a little less . . . *Stewart*.

Conall passed the candelabra to Stewart and watched him light his cigar. The puffs of smoke billowed about his golden head, dissipating above his tailored black coat and neckful of ornately tied linen. Clean-shaven with a stylish amount of sideburn, and ever self-confident, Stewart always looked as if he'd just posed for a portrait. Secretly, Conall appreciated Stewart's princely good looks and sense of fashion. That is, of course, until Stewart opened his mouth.

"Had any good Scottish totty yet?"

Conall sighed into his whisky. "No, Stewart. I've had a great deal of work to do. Besides, I didn't come four hundred miles just to have some 'Scottish totty.'"

Stewart waved his cigar. "You've been gone three weeks already! Don't tell me you've been here all this time and haven't had the odd itch. I'd have spread good English cheer all over Stonekirk by now."

Conall chuckled in spite of himself. "I'd be careful

if I were you. Remember, this is Scotland. Chasing skirts indiscriminately may deliver up the occasional surprise."

"What a ghastly thought." A single blond eyebrow shot up. "Well, I hope your celibacy isn't due to a dearth of crumpet in these parts. A man has needs."

"And few more than you."

"I shan't dispute that. I know! Why don't you and I take a ride into the next village tomorrow? We can dress as tradesmen, have a drink at the pub, find a couple of lusty lovelies—" A brilliant gleam sparkled in his eye.

"No, thank you."

"Come along, old boy. It's been far too long for you. Surely you remember the kind of thing."

"Of course I remember the kind of thing."

"Well then, let's get you back into the hunt. I've heard it said that if a man doesn't have sex for too long a stretch of time, he completely loses the ability to . . . stiffen his resolve."

Conall rolled his eyes. "That statement has absolutely no basis in medical fact."

"I don't care. And if you insist on being drearily sensible, I intend to leap right back onto the carriage I came in on and head straight back to London."

That brought the subject of Conall's troubled thoughts to the fore. He hadn't wanted to broach the subject on Stewart's first night in Scotland, but he may as well have it out now.

"I think you should consider very carefully making Stonekirk your home. I've been giving this a lot of thought, Stewart. I'm going to have to sell the house in London."

Stewart's blue eyes widened. "Sell the house? You must be mad! No one *sells* a house in London."

"We must. If we don't, there won't be enough capital to keep this estate afloat."

"But you can't, old boy! London is the only place in the world where beautiful women are just as inclined to have intercourse *under* the dinner table as over it. Sometimes at the same time," he added with a sidewise grin.

"Stewart, you're insatiable. I swear, if that bust of Socrates were wearing a dress, it would be in physical peril of you."

"Don't stray from the subject. You've got to let me keep our house in London."

"I'm afraid that's impossible. There are a lot of expenses on this estate. My God, Uncle Macrath nearly ran it into the ground. It baffles me. I remember Father telling us how profitable the estate used to be when he lived here. What on earth has Uncle Macrath done with all the money?"

"Damned if I know. Why don't you sell this house instead? Let some other fool take over the estate. Then we could keep the house in London, and live like kings."

"I can't do that. Ballencrieff is our family's ancestral home. It's belonged to the MacEwans since the days of Henry the Eighth. I don't want to become the one MacEwan remembered for losing the estate. Besides," he said, downing the last of the whisky, "assuming we even *could* find a buyer, with all the estate's financial entanglements, I doubt there'll be any profit in the sale."

Stewart crossed his legs. "Let's not think of selling the house yet. What if we were to sell yourself instead?

This giant white elephant," he said, waving his hand about the room, "has made you a catch in some women's eyes. What if you were to marry some rich old girl or other? Her dowry might turn things around."

Conall narrowed his eyes. "Thank you for your considerate suggestion. Only please do me the favor of allowing me the consolation of having a bride of my own choosing."

Stewart straightened. "You can't afford to be so selective. You'll need to marry into some money very soon."

"Why don't *you* make the sacrifice and marry for money?"

"No woman will have me. At least not the ones that know me. No, I shall just have to content myself with remaining an impoverished wretch."

Conall shook his head, engulfed by the woodsy aroma from Stewart's cigar. From amid the fog, something glinted on Stewart's hand. "If you're so hard-pressed for money, then why did you acquire that? You can't afford to wear a gold ring."

"Not exactly," he replied. "I can't afford to *buy* a gold ring. This was a gift from a lady friend for, shall we say, services rendered."

"You and your appreciative ladies. And when that comfortable stream of income diminishes to a trickle? What then?"

He exhaled a worried breath. "I'm afraid it's already dried up."

"Hmm. I told you it would eventually. You've spent—or misspent, I should say—far too much money seeking your own pleasures with wave after wave of good drink and bad women."

"Conall, if this conversation is going to degenerate into another one of your lectures, then I'm going to bed. And no thanks to you, an empty one."

"All right. I apologize. I'll save the lecture for another time."

Stewart's eyes drifted above Conall's head and fixed themselves on the far wall. "What have we here?"

Conall turned around. The nursemaid stood in the doorway. "Ah, Willow. Do come in."

Willow took a few hesitant steps into the library. "Beg yer pardon, sir. Master Eric is cryin' for ye. Being as this is my first night with the bairn, mayhap ye could put his tiny wee mind at ease just this once?"

Stewart glided past Conall's chair and affixed his hand to Willow's. "Of course he shall, my dear. And while he puts young Eric to bed, won't you please join me for a drink, Miss—"

"Willow, sir. Willow Slayter."

"Willow," Stewart repeated, the smile inching across his face. "What a delightful name."

Conall put an admonishing hand on his brother's shoulder. "Stewart. This is Eric's nursemaid. A *servant*," he emphasized, in a tone that was full of meaning.

Stewart cast a momentary backward glance that acknowledged Conall's implication. But he shrugged it off and returned his gaze to Willow.

Conall looked down at the girl. "Willow, this is my brother, Stewart MacEwan."

She gave a brief curtsy. "My lord."

"What a charming accent," Stewart continued. "How fortunate that my nephew will be privy to such a lovely voice. And how fortunate my brother is that he found such gentle hands to pamper his one and only child. Miss Willow, on behalf of the men in my family, I offer you our sincerest gratitude."

Stewart bowed over Willow's hand to place a kiss upon it.

And froze.

"Good Lord," he exclaimed.

Willow retracted her hand and hid it behind her back.

"What is it?" asked Conall, suddenly concerned.

"Her hand," said Stewart. "It's . . . it's—"

"Forgive me," said Willow, a heady flush coloring her face.

"May I see it?' asked Conall gently.

Her cheeks coloring furiously, Willow haltingly brought her hand out for his inspection.

Conall studied the back of Willow's hand. "Good Lord," he repeated.

Gnarled scars welted up from the soft skin on the back of her hand, the result of a gruesome burn. He raised the candelabra and brought it closer. The light illuminated a deliberate form that had been etched upon her hand. It wasn't just a burn, he realized. It was a brand. The pale skin behind her knuckles was shaped into an *S*.

"What happened to your hand?"

Willow drew her hand back. "'Tis nothing, my lord. Please . . . pay no heed. Master Eric awaits yer pleasure."

"Willow, won't you at least tell me—"

But she cast away her reddened face and darted out of the room.

Some time after breakfast, Kieran, a hauflin who lived near Miles' End Farm, arrived on the estate with Hume's cows. Despite Shona's happiness at seeing Daisy and

Precious again—she'd known them since their birth—their arrival reminded her of a depressing reality. Nothing in her life had really changed. She had been a farmhand at Hume's, and she was a farmhand still. Three months, ten days, and fifteen hours to go . . .

While Kieran put the cows into their stalls, Shona got everything prepared. She doubted Hume had been able to milk the cows since Willow and Shona had left Miles' End Farm, so she suspected the cows were in real discomfort from their fullness. Precious was the biggest, so Shona began with her.

She walked the cow into the milking pen, and locked her neck into the stanchion. Shona shoveled some sweetened grain into the feed bucket to entertain Precious while she was milked. After some cooing words and a few reassuring pats, Shona gently cleansed Precious's teats with a soft cloth to wipe away any dirt and hair. Precious's poor udders were stiff and full, and they had begun to leak. Using her thumb and forefinger, Shona encircled Precious's teat high up, and then squeezed each finger around it until a stream of milk came out. Precious's flesh felt familiar and warm, and the soft teats filled up with milk just as soon as they were emptied. Shona's practiced hands soon rendered a full pail of thick warm milk. She lifted the heavy pail, and poured it out into a five-gallon milk bucket.

Behind her, a shadow filled the doorway. The sunlight inside the dairy dimmed.

"Good morning, Shona."

The Englishman. His deep voice resonated through her, and she was startled by the unexpected flutter it caused inside her. His accent made her name sound different—somehow more refined—and for just an instant, it took her out of a dairy in the Scottish Lowlands and put her in a salon in a London palace. She turned in his direction, suddenly uncomfortable with her appearance. Her clean apron was now dotted with drying milk drops, and her faded russet-colored dress was also her most frayed. A tendril of hair escaped her cap, and she pushed it back from her face.

"Mornin'," she replied.

He walked over to her with slow, easy steps. What was it about this man that made her feel so ill at ease? Perhaps it was his clothes, which bespoke a level of wealth that no one in her circle of acquaintances had ever aspired to, let alone achieved. Perhaps it was his Scottish birth but foreign ways, which made him such a puzzle to her. Or perhaps it was his handsome face and heavily muscled body, which called up sexual desires that she had no intention of *admitting* to him, let alone *expressing*.

"I see the cattle have arrived." The Englishman placed a leather-clad hand on Precious's head. His thick dark eyelashes dropped as he regarded the animal. The sleeves of his royal blue tailcoat stretched over his thick arms, and her gaze drifted to the cream-and-gold waistcoat that gleamed across his chest. His face was freshly shaved and washed, evident from the still-damp hair at his temples. Spikes of dark hair fell forward over his forehead, stealing years from his age.

"Aye. 'Twas a long journey from the farm, but they are none the worse for it."

"Glad to hear it. I've sent the young man back for the goats. They'll be here this afternoon. I trust you'll see to them, as well."

She nodded, waiting for him to say how beautiful the dairy looked. She had really outdone herself trying to make it spotless. In some measure, her efforts were for the benefit of the cows. But, in truth, she really wanted her new master to notice.

He took a deep breath and a crease deepened in his forehead. "I came to talk to you about your sister, Willow."

Her heart squeezed tight, but she swallowed the crushing disappointment. "That doesna surprise me," she muttered, anger fomenting within her. It had to be a blind man that did not notice—and desire—Willow's beauty. But *this* man . . . it bothered her that he took such an interest in her pretty twin.

"Yesterday evening, I noticed that Willow had a mark on the back of her hand." He gestured with his own hands. "It was a scar . . . a sort of brand. Where did that come from?"

A thread of panic coiled within her. She moved to the other side of Precious, instinctively hiding her own hand from his sight. "Did ye no' ask her?"

"I did, but she wouldn't discuss it. When I pressed her to tell me who had done such a thing to her, she became quite flustered and flew out of the library. I saw her again this morning, and she'd taken to wearing gloves. I can't imagine what she'd done to deserve such a horrible disfigurement. She seems very ashamed of it. I thought you might be a little more forthcoming. How did she come by the brand?"

Shona stroked the cow's neck, her eyes feathering over her own burled scar. She never forgot about the mark. Never. How foolish of Willow to drop her guard and leave her hands uncovered. "I canna say."

He narrowed his eyes. "You cannot? Or will not?"

"Either way, it is the same. 'Tis a private matter."

He expelled a tortured breath. "Are you always this obstinate?"

Her back stiffened. "Are ye always this meddlesome?"

He took a step toward her, his large frame looming high above her. "What do you think I am . . . a gossiping fishwife? I am master of this estate. It is my responsibility to know the kind of persons I have in my service. Was Willow in trouble with the law?"

She shook her head as she grabbed hold of Precious's halter. "I canna tarry. I must see to milking Daisy now." She spun the cow around to put her back in the stall.

The Englishman stepped in front of them both, his anger barely leashed. A fire ignited in his blue eyes, and the tone in his voice was just a breath away from dangerous.

"I can appreciate your loyalty to your sister," he said through clenched teeth. "But I am your master, and your first loyalty should be to me. When I ask you a question, I expect you to answer it."

"Ye may be my master, but ye dinna own me. I belong to no man."

"That's where you're mistaken. While you are apprenticed to me, you are my charge. It is my responsibility to feed you and clothe you and teach you a trade. It is your responsibility to work diligently and to do as you're told."

"I have done so!" she said, pinning a fist to her hip. "See you the dairy? It is clean, as ye commanded. See you the cow? She is milked, as ye commanded."

"And now I command you to answer my question. What does the mark signify?"

"Ye want an answer? Very well. She tried to brand a horse, and the iron slipped."

His lips pursed. "You must take me for a complete idiot."

"Oh, so ye can read minds, as well?"

The look of shock on his face gave her a perverse thrill. It was just a taste of revenge, but it was sweet on her tongue.

He crossed his arms at his chest, barricading her between the cow and his imposing body. "If you think your disobedience will go unpunished, you are gravely mistaken. Defy me and I shall bring you before the magistrate and hand you over as a willful and indolent apprentice, for which the punishment is imprisonment in a house of correction until such time as you are agreeable to serve. And for every one day you spend in prison, the law adds two days onto the end of your indentures."

The sweet taste quickly turned to bile. The hope of her imminent freedom was the only thing that kept her going, and his threat to delay it silenced her. Three months, ten days, and—

"Was the brand inflicted for robbery?"

"No."

"Brawling?"

"No."

"Murder?"

"No!"

His expression chilled to suspicion. His eyes narrowed to slits as he regarded her with renewed awareness. Suddenly, his hand shot out and clamped around her wrist. She tried to wrench it away, but gained nothing—the man's body was stone.

He brought her hand up to his gaze. There for him to

see was the hideous scar that disfigured her hand. A gruesome *S* burned into her flesh so many years before, marking her as well as her sister. Inside, she was quaking.

"Must have been quite a horse to make the brand slip onto both your hands."

Her body was flattened against his, her wrist trapped in his strong grip. "Let me go."

"Now I understand why you were so reticent to speak. Honor among thieves. Answering for your sister would mean betraying yourself, as well."

He loosened his grip, and she tore her hand away. "We've done nothing wrong."

"Two women branded for all to see. Now it's clear to me what the *S* upon your flesh stands for. You're a couple of slatterns!"

A violent anger sprang up within her at that accusation. Instinctively, she swung her open hand and slapped his arrogant face. Hard.

His face stilled in the direction of her smack. But when his face swung back at her, she immediately regretted her impetuous outburst. The blue eyes that she had found so seductive the day before were now glaring hotly at her.

"I shall enjoy spending the next three years making you regret your disrespect."

His threat made her heart pound an uncomfortable beat, but two words alone stood uppermost in her mind.

"Three years? What do you mean? I reach maturity in three months, ten days, and fourteen hours. Upon that day, I will claim my freedom from my apprenticeship."

"No, my sweet," he said, a cheerless smirk touching

his reddened cheek. "The sand in the glass has just started falling on your newest indentures. To me."

The tasty dish of freedom she had so long hungered for was now dashed to the floor. Three more years locked in her indentures was appalling enough. But trapped in submission to the arrogant Englishman would feel like three centuries.

"No . . . no!" Shona ran from the estate as fast as her legs could carry her.

FOUR

Iona rubbed Shona's back as the girl sobbed into her clenched fists. The sound of her sadness filled the kitchen at Miles' End Farm.

"There now. Hush, child. No use crying over what can't be helped."

"But why, Iona?" Her face was slick with tears. "Why did Hume agree to this? Willow and I were meant to be free in three months."

Iona shook her head. "'Twas that villain, Mr. Hartopp. He said the laird would no' assume the care of another's apprentice for a period too short to teach a trade and then profit from it."

"Trade?" she yelled. "What trade? The Englishman has me milking cows! The man just wants to shunt me away to the dairy and forget aboot me." She blew her nose into the cloth Iona had given her. "I canna endure three more years of this torment."

Iona wrung her hands. "Have some more tea."

"I don't want any tea!" she exclaimed. "Oh, Iona, I must find a way to be free. Do ye know how it can be done?"

"Well," she said, serving herself another cupful. "Apprenticeship is not enslavement. There are rules. If ye have a grievance, ye could file a complaint with the overseers of the parish. But to be heard, ye'd have to wait for the assizes to convene, and ye know how long that can take."

Shona squeezed the cloth in her hand. "I canna wait, Iona. I won't. I have to get oot. What if we were to run away? Just run back to the Highlands, or doon to England—"

Iona pounded her fist on the wooden table, and the sound stole the words from Shona's mouth. "Don't ye even think it! An apprentice can't run from her master! 'Tis again' the law. Ye'll be thrown in prison. Both of ye! Now, ye get that thought right out of yer head!"

Her eyes twisted in despair. "But I dinna want to stay a farmhand the rest of my life. Each day is an eternity. I canna carry on."

"Runnin' away is no' the answer. I can't bear the thought of ye in prison. Bad enough, that. But Willow? She'd never survive."

The despair Shona had been feeling chilled. "There's no need to fear for Willow. She *likes* it there at Ballencrieff. Of course, she lives in the main part of the house and has high tea with the master and is given new clothes every four minutes. Why should she want to leave?"

"Now, Shona . . . I'm ashamed for ye. I never thought ye'd begrudge yer sister a gift."

Shona shook her head. "I don't . . . it's just that . . . I miss her." The thought brought out fresh tears.

Iona patted her cheek. "It's only been a day, Shona. Ye two have never slept apart. It's only natural. Chin up, now. Ye don't know what changes tomorrow will bring."

Shona shook her head, black strands adhering to her wet cheeks. "I won't endure another day knowing I've got three more years under the thumb of that man.

I've got to find my brother. I need to find a way oot!"
The chair screeched across the floor as Shona bolted
from it, taking Iona by surprise.

Iona nodded slowly. Shona was an excitable girl, and
she might take the wrong course of action out of sheer
desperation. If Iona wanted to avert catastrophe, she
had to offer wisdom, not solace.

"Very well," she said, her hands stretched out on the
table. "There are ways to break an apprenticeship."

Shona fixed her soggy eyes on Iona.

"There's the death of the master . . ."

She blinked expectantly.

". . . his insolvency . . ."

Shona sat back down at the kitchen table.

". . . physical violence, or if he fails to provide for yer
needs . . . or if ye get married . . . or if ye become inca-
pacitated by, I don't know, losing yer arms or something."

Shona was quiet a long time as she considered these
options. "Marry . . . what if I *were* to marry? If I can
find a man to marry me, the Englishman would have
to let me go, wouldn't he?"

"Aye. Ye'd need his permission, o'course, but I've
never heard of a master refusin' a young woman gettin'
married. If he were to give ye permission, yer marriage
would break the indenture."

She bit her thumbnail. "Aye . . . I think that'll do.
That will buy me my freedom." Her expression light-
ened. "If I could find some lad or other—"

"Hold on, now. Think what ye're saying. What do ye
think marriage is, anyway? To the wrong man, marriage is just another form of indenture. Why would ye
want to step out of the griddle and into the fire? And

there's no escapin' that indenture, I can tell ye. Till death do ye part."

"I'll take that chance."

"Will ye, now?"

"Aye, I will," she crowed. But the smile dissolved from Shona's face. "Wait. What would happen to Willow?"

Iona shook her head. "Nothing. She'd have to remain."

Shona's eyebrows sank. "I can't leave her behind."

"Now ye're asking too much, Shona. There's a price for everything, and ye just don't have the currency."

"Perhaps both of us could marry somehow—" She leaned back against the chair, and covered her face with her hands. "But I know Willow. She will no' marry a man if she does no' love him."

"Nor should ye."

Shona heaved a profound sigh, her eyes closed in exhaustion. "As ye said, there's a price for everything."

Iona rose from the table and put the dirty cups in the basin. "Well, I canna see it happening. Short of marrying the laird himself, there's no way ye can both be free at the same time."

Shona's eyes slowly opened. "What did ye just say?" she whispered.

"There's no way you can both be free at—"

"No. Aboot marrying the laird." The pieces of the puzzle in her mind began to snap together. "If I were to marry my own master, I'll no longer be his apprentice but his wife. And my sister will be his sister-in-law, and therefore also free from her indentures." A wild, hopeful look danced across her face. "Iona, ye're brilliant!"

Iona's eyes widened in appalled amazement as she stabbed a finger in Shona's direction. "Don't ye be crediting that madness to me. Are ye listenin' to yourself? Do ye honestly think the laird of the manor is going to marry a poor milkmaid?"

Shona didn't want to consider whether or not something was *probable*. She only wanted to know that it was *possible*. "Why no'? It's happened before."

Iona crossed her arms over her generous bosom. "Ye've gone daft, ye have. A girl like you isn't going to be a suitable wife for someone like him. If he isn't already married, he'll be after a lady of breeding and wealth. He'll be wantin' a lady that comes in the front door, not one who has to use the servants' entrance."

Shona only partially heard Iona's objections. Her gaze darted back and forth across the table, as if a plan were somehow written on the wooden surface. "It won't be easy to make him fall in love with me. He can barely stand the sight of me. But I think I can do it. I'll have to seduce him."

A hollow laugh erupted from Iona. "In the first place, I doubt ye know how. In the second place, ye're the one that stands to be the loser in all this. Just because ye seduce him doesna mean he's going to marry ye. Many a servant girl has found herself in the family way—and no self-respectin' laird like him is going to acknowledge the bastard. He'll just chuck ye oot into the street. And with a bairn to raise, there'll no' be another man to have ye."

Shona bit her lip. The very fate she was afraid of befalling her sister, she was now willingly risking for herself. Iona was right. It was a dangerous plan that stood little chance of succeeding.

But little chance was better than none.

* * *

It was a long, depressing walk back to Shona's home. Her *new* home.

The buttery Scottish sun hung low in the sky, and the warmth had been leached from the air by the encroaching evening. As had her hope.

Marriage to the Englishman. It was a foolish idea. A desperate plan cobbled together in a moment of desperation.

The Englishman would never deign to marry someone like her. The expression on his face that morning spoke his contempt loud and clear. And it was well deserved. Shona had given him the sharp end of her tongue. She had accused him of every vile intention. And she had struck him! No master would ever tolerate such reprehensible behavior. How could she expect anything but scorn when that was all she had shown him?

Suddenly, a terrible sound split the stillness of the dying day. It was a yelp, high and shrill . . . an animal in pain. A heartbreaking ache sliced through her as the animal cried. Pity, compassion—and some unnamed natural instinct—combined to propel her in the direction of the wounded creature.

The forest was much darker than the field outside, but her legs carried her true. The leaves riffled as she whizzed past, the dog's high-pitched screaming growing louder. A bolt of fear heightened her survival instincts. She knew feral dogs roamed the forests, and where one was found, more were sure to follow.

Breathless from running, she stopped and listened. Only one yelp filled the air. Thank heaven for small blessings—the beast was not joined by its pack. The dog squealed piteously, wringing her heart. Whether it was wild or no, Shona simply could not abide the suffering of another creature.

In a clearing, she found the source of the sound. Behind a rotten tree lying on the ground was a shallow gully, and inside was a lean white dog with large dark splotches around its drooped ears. It was struggling to get out from the steep crevice.

She knelt down on the edge of the crevice to get a better look. It looked like the Englishman's pointer, but she couldn't be sure. The dog was panting and weak, unable to jump out. His front leg hung at an unnatural angle.

Two men with rifles stopped short behind her. Immediately, her hackles were raised.

"Did the dog fall in there?" one of them asked.

"Aye," she replied. "I think he's broken his leg."

"Damn and blast," said the other. "I knew that fool dog would be more trouble than it was worth. It frightened away all the rabbits we were hunting. George here almost shot it accidentally."

"Would have been a happily met accident," joked the man called George.

Shona gritted her teeth. "Help me get him out of the hole."

"Dinna bother, miss," said George. "If it's broken its leg, the best thing for it is to be put out of its misery."

Shona looked aghast. "Ye mean to kill him?"

"There's no way to care for a broken leg, miss," he insisted. "Dog, horse, cow—if it's bashed a leg, best thing for it is to die quickly."

"No," she said, wincing at the horror. "We should try to mend it."

"The laird would want his dog to die without more

suffering. Now stand aside." George lifted his rifle and came toward the hole.

Shona jumped in front of him, a look of ferocious anger burning upon her face. "Take one more step toward him and I'll turn that rifle again' you."

The man held an open palm in the air. "Settle down, miss. I'm only trying to help the dumb animal. I'm a good shot. He'll die painlessly, I promise."

She gave it a moment's thought. The dog was helpless, hobbled, hopeless. Just what she'd been feeling. But if there was even the merest chance of salvation . . .

"No. Get away. Now!"

George took a step backward.

Shona turned around and looked inside the gully. It was difficult to see into the darkened hole in the diminishing light. Slowly, she climbed over the dead tree and negotiated the rock face until she came to the floor of the gully. The dog was sitting on its haunches, the wounded forepaw trembling as he tried to keep it off the ground.

From the lip of the ravine, George grumbled something about the foolishness of women. "Don't try to touch him, miss. A hurt dog don't know you're trying to help it. You'll only get yourself bit."

Shona was already aware of this. Cooing and murmuring, she held out her hand below the dog's snout—precisely where he could do the most damage if he chose. The dog turned its head away, unwilling to make friends, but equally unwilling to run away. Shona held her ground, and finally, curiosity got the better of him. He touched his nose to her hand, sniffing her scent. His warm, moist nose stamped wet patches on her hand, and finally, he let her touch the top of his head.

"Right, ye. Ye're coming with me. Don't ye be thinking of biting me, or I may drop ye, and sure I am ye won't like that."

She went around to the dog's side. She wrapped one hand below his chest and another under his haunches. He was heavy, well over three stone. And though she could manage the weight, with a large dog in her arms, she found it difficult to see the way to climb back up out of the rocky gully.

Carefully, she let her foot feel around for a secure foothold. Slowly, she began to make her way up the side of the ditch, groaning with the weight of the dog. One of the hunters came down halfway, took hold of the dog, and walked up the rest of the way with it while George helped her climb out.

"Ye're a headstrong lass, ye are. But all ye've done is get him out of the ditch. He's still lame."

"Ye just go aboot yer business and leave him to me."

The hunter handed the dog back to her. Gently, she took him into her arms. The dog's whole body was trembling. But at least he was no longer yelping.

She could see the manor peeking through the trees. And even though it was still a long walk back, her heart was lifting already. She had snatched the dog from the valley of the shadow of death—literally—and the hope that had eluded her once again threaded its way back into her heart.

The long-case clock in the hall chimed eleven as Conall handed his hat to Bannerman, his valet.

"I'm relieved to see you well arrived, sir," said Bannerman, his bushy gray eyebrows knitting together.

Along with Cook, Bannerman was one of those indispensible servants whom Conall had insisted on bringing with him from London. "We were exceedingly worried when night came upon us and you hadn't yet returned from your rounds."

Conall growled. "This country is going to be the death of me, Bannerman. It's bad enough having to deal with the tenants, the local commissions, the creditors, and the tax collectors. Now, I discover that some ruddy poachers have dammed up the stream on the northern border of the property."

"I'm sorry to hear that, sir," said Bannerman, the long grooves deepening on either side of his flaccid cheeks. "No doubt the long absence of a laird on this estate has encouraged some people to take liberties."

Conall removed his coat. "A few liberties I wouldn't mind, but not the whole ruddy stream of fish!"

"I've instructed Cook to keep supper warm for you, sir. Would you like to dine in your rooms?"

Conall sighed. "No, thank you, Bannerman. I can't really claim any hunger right now. I think I'll just go to bed."

"Sir, before you do . . . I regret to tell you that there's been a small accident."

Conall's mind immediately flew to the hot-tempered milkmaid who'd run off earlier that morning. "Shona . . . it's not her, is it?"

"It does concern her, yes, sir."

"Is she all right?"

"*She* is fine. Your dog, sir—the pointer—it seems he's broken his leg."

"Oh, no," he breathed, his head dipping.

"I'm afraid so, sir. I understand the dog sustained the injury when he tumbled into a ditch while in pursuit of a hare. The gamekeepers he'd gone out with told me that they wanted to put the animal out of his misery, but the girl refused to permit them. They reported her actions to me, and I took it up with Mrs. Docherty, who oversees her. The girl was ordered to let the dog be put down, but she flagrantly refused, insisting she could heal him. I understand that she used the most intemperate language, sir, while shielding the animal from the muzzle of the rifle. She was so adamant that we were obliged to let her do as she wished."

"I see."

"I shall of course see to it that in the morning she be disciplined for her insubordination. But I thought that tonight, as both laird and the dog's owner, you might be in a better position to demand your rights concerning the animal."

Conall bit his cheek. "Where's the girl now?"

"In the stable, sir, with the dog."

Conall nodded. "Very well. Get me a lamp."

Bannerman went to the kitchens, and Conall put his coat back on. Bannerman returned with a lit candle lamp, ensuring that the glass door on the lamp was tightly shut before handing it to his master.

The courtyard was heavy with quiet. Unlike the residents of London, just about everyone in the country retired with the loss of light. Most of the staff, except perhaps those who had been waiting for his arrival, had long since gone to sleep.

Conall walked into the stable, his lamp held aloft. The air was thick with the smell of horses and leather.

His boots made no noise upon the hay scattered underfoot, and he advanced without disturbing the silent horses in their darkened stalls. But at the far end of the stable, where the birthing stall was located, a sphere of light glowed.

Conall approached slowly. A lit lamp hung from a hook on the wall, chasing away the darkness. The stall was empty. Conall looked in each corner of the wide stall, but saw no one. Then, a shadow shifted in the window, drawing his eye upward.

In the center of the thick stone wall, cracked from the weight of the centuries, was a spacious window opening. And upon the wide windowsill lay a woman.

Conall blinked. Shona was reclined upon the sill, asleep, her legs climbing the side of the window. Atop her abdomen lay his dog. Shona's shift had slipped down, revealing a pair of long, shapely calves and a generous view of thigh.

The vision sucked the breath right out of him.

He neared the spectacle. The dog lifted his head and pricked his floppy ears in Conall's direction. But he made no movement toward his master. And Conall could see why. One of the dog's forepaws stuck straight out from his body, encased in a thick sausage of padding, two wood shafts, and bandages—russet-colored bandages. The same shade, he noted, as the dress she'd been wearing that morning.

He looked beneath the window, and spotted what was left of Shona's dress after long strips had been torn from it. Other debris—bits of leather, wood chips, and what looked like a horsewhip cut into pieces—were lying about. It seemed she'd been trying to splint the dog's leg using whatever she found in the stable. The girl never left the dog alone, even for a moment, for fear that they'd shoot him at the first opportunity.

His heart sighed gratefully. His dog was alive. Thanks to Shona.

For the first time, Conall studied her. She was fast asleep, poor thing, exhaustion heavy upon her features. Her hair was free of its cap, and the long, black tresses poured down the side of the stone wall. Thick lashes curled over her cheeks, which were dappled with tan freckles. Thin, black eyebrows feathered out toward her temples. Her mouth was soft and slightly parted, as if she were about to give someone a kiss.

She was . . . lovely.

Conall's eyes crinkled as he smiled. Funny how he'd never noticed it before now.

He glanced at his dog, Dexter. He was so happy to see him. He'd had Dexter since the dog was nothing more than a wriggling pup, a fat little cur with a piglet's tail and more ear than face. For the past eleven years, Dexter had been more than just a pet—he'd been a comforting companion, especially through the excruciating tragedies that Conall had most recently experienced. The thought of Dexter's body lying in a forest ditch somewhere, a bullet lodged in his head, pained him beyond words. He reached out a hand to pat the dog's head.

And felt the tip of a dagger dimple itself in his belly.

"Stand down." Shona had pulled an unseen knife from beneath her, and pointed it unflinchingly at his waist.

"Shona, please calm yourself. It is I, Conall Mac-Ewan."

She drove the point in further, pushing him backward. "I don't care who ye are. Don't ye even *think* aboot harmin' this dog."

He raised his arms defensively. "I wouldn't dream of it."

"A nightmare, more like, if ye put per hands on him once more." Her eyes flashed danger.

"You mistake me. I love my dog."

Her green eyes narrowed suspiciously. "Ye're not trying' to put him doon?"

He shook his head slowly. "You saved Dexter's life. I assure you I'm not angry. I'm grateful." He pointed at the animal. "May I see him?"

Hesitantly, she lowered her weapon, letting Conall advance. He patted the dog's head as he examined the injured leg. "Was the skin broken?"

"No."

"That's a relief. Did he suffer any other injuries?"

"There's a scratch under his chin. Probably fell upon it when his leg gave oot. But I think that's all. No reason to have him shot, is it?"

The dog wagged his tail as Conall looked him over. "Certainly not."

Shona's defensive posture seemed to unclench. Her attachment to his dog was fiercesome. She cared so very deeply for the animal, it was indistinguishable from her behavior whether the dog was his or hers.

"May I put him on the floor?" he asked.

"Very well. Gently, now."

Tenderly, he lifted the dog from Shona's abdomen. The splinted leg fell downward uselessly, and the dog whined in protest. Conall murmured soothing words to his dog as he set him on the ground. Meanwhile, Shona straightened from her uncomfortable position, and Conall found his eyes wandering to her.

She sat up on the windowsill, her chemise floating back down her legs. As she stretched her back, he noticed that the web-thin garment did little to conceal the contours of her naked form underneath. The weak yellow light from the lamp on the wall whispered over her face and figure, revealing a valley between her breasts that caused a stir in his loins.

Despite his injury, Dexter appeared strong. The dog sat on his haunches, panting calmly under Conall's hand.

Shona hopped from the windowsill, and her chemise slipped lower over one shoulder. Now he could see the curve of one freckled shoulder, the resilient sinews of one arm, and the gentle slope of one breast. For a single instance, he indulged in the thought of a forbidden entanglement with this servant girl, pressing her half-nude form against his body. The pleasurable fantasy began to cloud his head.

But the gentleman in him ordered him to act upon his manners. "You must be chilly. Please put this on," he said, shrugging out of his royal blue coat.

"Thank ye," she replied, tossing it around her own shoulders. As she did so, a line of light appeared through her parted legs, and Conall felt an immediate tightening underneath his fawn breeches. He almost regretted his own gallantry.

"We should be going now."

Shona stiffened. "Where are ye takin' him?" she demanded in a tone that spooked the horses.

"To my bedchamber. I promise you no harm will

come to him. I'll bring him food and water, and give him someplace comfortable and warm to rest while his leg heals."

Her eyes bored into his, and he could feel her assessing whether or not he was telling the truth. Finally, relief washed over her expression, and she seemed to breathe a little easier.

"All right," she responded hesitantly. "But if he should take a turn for the worse, ye'll send for me first?"

He grinned appreciatively. "Of course I shall, doctor. Er, why don't you . . . that is, won't you—" He didn't quite know how to say it.

"Aye?"

He took a deep breath. "Won't you come upstairs with me?"

Her beautiful black eyebrows drew together. "Why?"

He was happy for the diminished light, for he felt his face betraying the thoughts that were running riot in his brain. "So that I may thank you properly."

The girl spoke nothing for a few seconds. He could almost read her thoughts as she seemed to sift through the double meaning of his words.

"Very well," she responded quietly. She seemed to extend him some trust.

Conall lifted the dog into his arms. He led the way back to the front door of the house, and the valet opened the door for them.

"Bannerman, is that dinner still warm?"

"Yes, sir."

"Good. Send it up to my rooms, won't you?"

"Of course." Bannerman looked querulously at Shona. "Shall I handle the issue of Miss Shona tonight?"

"No, thank you, Bannerman. I'll handle her." Conall

was having a difficult time keeping his secret urges to himself. "That is, I'll resolve the matter myself."

"As you wish."

Conall led the way up the grand staircase to a corridor. Lit wall sconces framed either side of an ornate wooden door. Shona opened the door, and let Conall and the dog through.

Whereas Conall's home in London merely whispered of wealth, his uncle's Scottish estate screamed it—and the laird's bedchamber was no exception. A massive mahogany four-poster inhabited the center of the room, looking as if it were carved from a single enormous piece of lumber, and its Gothic wooden canopy scalloped downward over the edge of the bed. Miles of windows lined one wall. A massive fireplace, draped by a mantel of polished Italian marble, warmed the room. The room gleamed of brass and crystal, all of it too ostentatious for someone like him.

Shona walked away from him, circling the room. Wide-eyed and openmouthed, she mutely drank in the room's grandeur. But when she began to walk back toward him, it was his turn to gape. In the well-lit room, Shona's transparent chemise practically vanished, revealing a thick triangle of black hair where her thighs met.

Unwilling to stare, he cast his eyes away. But the image would be burned in his memory forever. Shona, dressed only in his coat and practically nothing else, utterly oblivious to her own naked beauty. And the effect that it was having upon him.

Conall tried to tame the thoughts in his head, but their intensity proved too powerful for him. It had now become easy to picture the two of them together, up against the papered wall, her long legs wrapped tightly around his hips as he lowered that triangle onto his hardened member. Or better yet, upon the settee, her raven's wing hair sliding over the tufted arm as his hands mounded her full breasts into his hungry mouth. Or better still—

"On the bed."

"Eh?" Shona peered at him quizzically.

Conall licked his dry lips. "I thought Dexter would be more comfortable on my bed."

"No," she said, unaware of the turn his mind had taken. "Put the dog on the floor, so he won't be grieved jumping doon from the bed. Here, let me make a comfortable corner for him." Shona yanked the coverlet off the bed and folded it up until it made a large square pillow.

She laid the folded fabric on the floor beside the bed. "Come here, boy," she called from atop the pillow.

The dog's tail started wagging, and Conall set him down. He walked toward Shona, dragging his encased forepaw behind him.

"You did a good job of bandaging him," Conall said. "His leg is nice and straight, the padding seems comfortable, and you've made it long enough so that he can't put any weight on it. A very resourceful field splint."

Shona scratched Dexter behind the ears. "Och. He may look silly now, but he'll be walking a treat in a few weeks. Mind ye don't let him outside. If his bandage should get even a little damp, his foot will rot."

Though he had seen his share of gangrenous limbs and necrotic tissue, Conall groaned at the thought of Dexter suffering any of that. "Well, I'm not sure the maid will appreciate having to clean up after him, but

I'm willing to make the sacrifice of living with him for a while."

"I'm glad. The company will do him good," she said as she rubbed the dog's head. Shona's mouth stretched into a smile, and Conall was amazed by the effect her expression had on him. He'd never seen her smile before, and when she wasn't busy being a demanding dairymaid or weapon-wielding warrior woman, she was actually very, very attractive.

There was a quiet knock at the door.

"Come."

"Your dinner, sir." Bannerman came in bearing a tray that he carried over to the table in the bedchamber's sitting area.

"Thank you. Er, Bannerman, would you please see if there is a dress that Shona could use? It seems she sacrificed her own for Dexter's sake, and we mustn't let her return to her room in only her shift."

"Very good, sir." The valet shot her a disdainful glance before discreetly closing the door behind him.

"Have you dined?"

Shona chuckled, and he realized he probably used the wrong word. After all, servants do not *dine*.

"No."

"Then please take your ease." He held out an upholstered chair beside the table.

She seemed embarrassed, and lifted one shoulder defensively. "I canna."

"I insist. The doctor deserves her rest. Besides, I'm not in the least hungry, and it would be a shame to waste all this food."

She smiled again, and rose from the floor. "Very well. If ye insist." She took the proffered seat, but remained with her hands in her lap. Her left hand concealing her right.

"Shall I serve or will you help yourself?"

She clearly felt uncomfortable doing so. "Allow me," he said, and heaped slices of roast mutton and potatoes upon her plate.

"Enough," she said, chuckling. "I do no' want to eat the lot. Perhaps Dexter can have the rest?"

He laughed. "Oh, don't worry about him. Dexter's going to have a feast." He heaped a pile of meat onto another plate and placed it in front of the pointer. The dog devoured it.

Shona was more reserved as she ate, though he suspected she was just as ravenous as his dog. She sliced the meat carefully with her knife and fork, and ate with an almost forced decorum . . . as if she were trying to impress him with ladylike behavior. Yet she almost purred with delight as the food satisfied her hunger.

Conall sat opposite her and poured himself some wine. "It took a lot of valor for you to stand up to the gamekeeper's rifle. I still don't know if it was a display of courage or foolhardiness."

The candle upon the table cast a glow upon her features. "Which do ye think?"

He sighed. "A bit of both, I expect. Your loyalty impresses me, especially considering how this morning we got off to such a disagreeable start. But why would you risk so much to protect my dog?"

She only shrugged, the response remaining locked within her.

He leaned one elbow on the table as he regarded her. A long finger curled in front of his mouth. "Bannerman thinks you ought to be disciplined."

She swallowed. "What for?"

"Insubordination. Defying the gamekeeper, disobeying Mrs. Docherty, and challenging the supremacy of Bannerman's own station."

"I was only trying to do right by the dog. No one else seemed to want to."

Her lips pouted prettily, and he marveled at the seductive way she had of pronouncing her vowels. Not "only," but "ooonly."

"Well, I happen to agree with you. And that is why I am prepared to overrule them all, and instead offer you a reward."

"Really?" She grinned, and wiped her mouth with the tips of two fingers. "What sort of a reward?"

The sensual way she touched her mouth ignited yet another flame in him. He wanted to taste the food from her own lips. "I don't know. What would you like?"

She retreated into a world of her own, her eyelashes fanning her cheeks. When she opened her eyes back up, the playful Shona had disappeared.

"Our freedom."

The smile ran away from his face. "Pardon?"

"Willow and me. Break our indentures. Let us go free."

It was not the answer he had hoped for. "I can't do that," he said.

"Why no'?" she asked, the fire returning to her eyes.

"Because . . . you're both underage. My duty as your master is to see you cared for—"

"No one has to know."

His duty had little to do with his decision. The simple truth was that he *would not* do it. Shona had sparked something in him, and damn it all, he wanted more of it. "I would know."

She cast her gaze down at her plate, and was silent for some time. "Then let me bed with my sister. Last night was the first time we slept apart. I dinna like being separated from her."

That was a simple enough request. "It shall be arranged."

"And one more thing. Ye wanted an apprentice, so make me one. A true and proper one. Not to work in the dairy at a job that anyone with a pair of hands and an uncomplaining back can do. An apprentice is supposed to learn a trade, so teach me what ye know. I want to be able to heal as well as ye can."

He chuckled. "I can't teach you to be a physician. It takes a great deal of schooling, and experience, and study . . . Plus, you're only a woman."

One eyebrow jumped into her forehead. "'Twas a woman who saved yer dog's leg. To say nothing of his life."

A sharp intake of breath admitted his defeat in that particular argument. "Touché. But even as a physician's aide, there's so much you need to learn. Even the most basic lessons in anatomy, chemistry, and biology require years of prior schooling in mathematics, physiology, Latin—"

"Och, man, I don't want to open a man up and poke around inside. I just want ye to help me know what to do in case I see someone hurt."

He smiled. "All right. I'll teach you about the preservation of life and rendering rudimentary medical care."

A great, broad grin returned to her face. Now *that* pleased him a great deal.

"Of course," he continued, "I won't have much time to devote to your training. I find myself under a training process of my own. I don't mind admitting that running an estate like this one is entirely foreign to me. I don't know the first thing about agriculture, and I'm quite in over my head."

"But why didn't ye say so?" she said, brightening even more. "I can help ye with that!"

"I appreciate the offer, but—"

"Truly! I've spent my entire life on a farm. At Miles' End we grew many different crops and raised all sorts of livestock. I know how to run a successful farm. And, by extension, a successful estate." She leaned over her plate. "*I* can teach *ye*."

He was intrigued by that provocative smirk. Very intrigued indeed.

"You can teach me about harvest prices? Crop rotations? Tenant disputes?"

"Oh, aye. And a great deal more, I'll wager."

Conall studied that wicked spark in her eyes. Suddenly, life in Scotland had become a lot more enjoyable.

"Agreed," he said, and held out his hand. Shona shook it . . . for once, making contact with her scarred hand instead of hiding it.

Bannerman returned with a nursemaid's dress, similar to the one that Willow was given, and made a quiet exit. Shona pounced gleefully on the simple blue frock as if it were an elaborate court dress.

"Turn round," she said.

"Why?" he replied with an amused frown.

"I want to put it on."

His head cocked to one side. "Very well." He picked up his chair and turned it in the other direction.

Behind him, he heard the rustling of fabric as she

took off his coat and slipped the dress over her head. The intimate sound was an aphrodisiac, and re-awakened long-dormant sensations.

"Are you decent?"

"Completely honorable."

"No," he chuckled. "I meant are you dressed?"

"Aye."

He turned around and was astounded by the vision that met his eyes. Gone was the common dairymaid with her coarse clothes and coarse mouth. Standing before him was a tall, slender lady in a fine blue dress. Except for the unpinned hair that tumbled chaotically over one shoulder, she was almost unrecognizable to that other person.

"Goolies! I can't fasten it. The bloody buttons are up the back."

He chuckled. Clearly, she was the very same girl. "Allow me."

He walked up behind her. She lifted her hair, sending a current of its scent up to his face. He inhaled deeply. Hay and sunshine.

His unrestricted gaze caressed her shoulders and upper back. As he buttoned up the bodice of her dress, he allowed his fingers to graze her skin. It was forbidden to touch a servant in such an intimate manner. Yet it was not *censure* he felt, but *sensual*—an erotic thrill snaking through his body. Shona was so unrefined, so untainted by social strictures, and he began to detect an allure to her that was both illicit and inescapable.

"That dress looks very becoming upon you."

She let down her hair and turned to face him. "Do ye really think so?"

"You look quite the lady."

His comment made her blush, something he found quite endearing.

"I have a confession to make," she said, dipping her head apologetically. "When I kept yer dog from being put doon, it wasn't out of loyalty to ye. I wasn't even sure he was yer dog. I would ha' done it all the same."

He felt a slight sting at her confession. But he learned two important things about her. First, he could trust her to do the right thing. And second, he could trust her to be honest.

"Thank you for your candor. My gratitude, however, is unchanged."

He opened the door to his bedroom, and waved to Bannerman, who was walking across the hall on the main floor below.

"You may not know this, Shona, but I too was an apprentice once. Every young man who desires to be a doctor must subject himself to an apprenticeship to learn the skills he needs. I know it isn't pleasant to feel obligated to someone else, but our relationship needn't be a contentious one. Need it?"

She shook her head.

"As for your education, we can start tomorrow. Because I have a confession to make as well."

"What's that?"

A lazy grin curled one cheek. "There's a great deal I want to teach you, too."

FIVE

Shona turned over in her bed and pressed her cheek contentedly against the pillow.

A smile drifted across her sleep-drenched face as her thoughts turned once again to the Englishman— Conall. She'd been dreaming about him all night. And even though the details of her dreams had evaporated, she remembered that he'd put a smile on her face during the night as well.

The source of that happiness: hope.

It had all started last night, in Conall's bedchamber. His attitude toward her had shifted, changed. He had gentled toward her. No, more than that . . . he had almost become *tender* toward her. She could never have imagined that rescuing Dexter would have such an effect on Conall. It pleased her to know he cared so deeply for animals. But she had no idea that he would take to her as keenly as he did.

It dawned on her . . . maybe her plan to marry him was not as foolish as she had thought.

Fortune enough that he had promised her she could sleep inside the nursery with her sister. But Conall also wanted Shona near, working alongside him—as his real apprentice! Her freedom—and Willow's—was once again within reach. Their wings might have to remain folded for the time being, but at least the door of their cage was opening.

The greatest challenge still lay ahead. She had succeeded in getting Conall to *like* her. But it was quite another leap to get him to *love* her. At the very least, that would call for a change in her demeanor. If she couldn't *be* the woman that Conall desired, she would have to *become* the woman that Conall desired.

Who that woman was would be one of the many things she would have to learn about Conall MacEwan. But discovering that would not be so disagreeable after all. For the Englishman was not as arrogant as she first believed. Shona had caught a glimpse of the man behind the hardness and bluster, and now she wanted to see more of him.

Dreamily, she opened her eyes . . . and bolted upright in the bed. The sun had crept way past the horizon, and light had flooded into the room through the pink and green drapes. Never had she slept this long into the morning. It must be past eight!

It would not do to be late for her duties. Not now, just when she was trying to make such a good impression upon him. Quickly, she put on her new blue uniform, buttoning it up as best as she could, and hastily laced up her ghillies. Grabbing her pinafore from the arm of the chair, she flew out of the door to the servants' quarters, and headed straight for the dairy.

But when she got to the dairy, someone else had taken her place. Seated on a milking stool beside Ivy the nanny goat was Kieran, the young lad who lived near Miles' End. He was industriously milking Ivy while she munched from the bucket of sweetened feed.

"Kieran, what are ye up to?" she asked.

"Up to? About three pails so far."

She rolled her eyes. "Psh! I mean, what are ye doing here?"

"Well, if this is the time ye decide to come doon to work, it's no wonder they want ye put out of the byre."

"Put out?" A flash of anger shot through her. "Who wants me put out?"

Kieran straightened up. "The laird sent a pony and trap for me early this morn. The driver brought word that I was to come by every day to see to the milking on the estate until the goats were sold off. Knowing how good ye are at tending to animals, my head was in a fankle over it. Aren't ye pleasing the new master?"

"'Course I am!" she responded archly. "Who do ye think cleaned oot this place afore ye came?"

The lad scratched his windblown hair. "Well, the master left word he wants to see ye aboot retraining ye. 'First thing in the morning,' he said." A smirk touched his smooth cheek. "But I guess now will have to do."

Their agreement the night before. She sighed, her anger vanishing. She had no idea he'd meant her to start so soon in the day. Conall MacEwan certainly moved quickly.

As soon as she entered the house through the servants' entrance, Mrs. Docherty zoomed in on her, all aflutter.

"Where have ye been, girl? I've been looking for ye everywhere but the attic. The master wants ye at table for breakfast."

"For breakfast?" Shona's green eyes rounded. She was being asked to *dine* with him? "Me?"

"It's not for ye to question, it's for ye to obey." Mrs. Docherty gave her a disapproving scowl. "My goodness, Shona, yer hair looks as if ye've been riding a horse at full gallop. Ye're not on a farm anymore. At the manor, all the women wear their hair up, ladies and servants alike. Why aren't ye wearing a cap? Och, come here."

Mrs. Docherty gathered Shona's long hair in a tight fist and tried to tie it up, but the heavy locks just fell down Shona's back again. "Well, there's nothing for it. But take that pinny off—it's soiled. The next time ye're called in to dine with the family, spruce yerself up. And for goodness' sake, be there before the family's gone in."

Mrs. Docherty pushed her through the corridor and stopped short of a set of double wooden doors. Mrs. Docherty motioned her to go through. Shona took a deep breath, and turned the doorknobs.

The room was like no other she'd ever seen. A chandelier hung from the double-storied ceiling like a large crystal spider from a single thread. A gleaming wooden table stretched along the room. Hanging upon the dark blue walls were gilt-edged paintings of MacEwan ancestors. The morning sun streamed in from tall draped windows, and bounced off the enormous mirror above the fireplace, setting the room aglow.

Conall MacEwan, seated at one end of the long table, rose from his chair. He was handsomely dressed in a dark brown coat and caramel-colored breeches. "Good morning, Shona. Please join us. There's someone I'd like you to meet."

Shona's shoes made no noise upon the carpeted floor. Two more men at the table also stood up.

"This is my brother, Stewart MacEwan. He's just arrived from London. Stewart, this is Shona Slayter, my new apprentice."

"How d'ye do?" she said, nodding curtly.

Stewart was handsome, just like his brother, but he wore a roguish leer. His thinning blond hair revealed even paler skin, but his startling blue eyes were instantly captivating. He never took them off Shona for a second, even when he bowed before her.

"My God. Two beautiful apprentices. To educate on all things worldly. May I have one?"

Conall rolled his eyes. "No, you may not. And Shona, I believe you already know my factor, Horace Hartopp."

"Aye. Good morning, Mr. Hartopp."

"Morning," he responded brusquely and sat back down.

Conall held out for her a beautifully upholstered chair that was covered in a brocade of cream and blue. Before her on the table were a gleaming gold charger and a crystal glass.

"Since Hartopp arrived early, I thought we could start reports over breakfast."

A footman silently placed a dish of sliced meats, a poached egg, and toast triangles upon the charger in front of Shona.

"How is Dexter?" she inquired.

Conall grinned. "In remarkably good spirits. I keep having to shout at him for trying to chew off his own dressing. The master barking at the dog."

Shona chuckled. She glanced up at Stewart, who had hardly taken those piercing blue eyes off her.

Hartopp wiped his mouth. "As I was saying, Dr. MacEwan, I've been making a great deal of headway on improvements to the land on the eastern part of the estate."

"I'm very glad to hear it," Conall replied. "That section has me greatly troubled."

Shona ate a bite from the thick slab of fried ham. "The eastern part . . . is that where the Hockney farm is?"

Conall nodded.

"Och! They'll be happy to hear that. The farms over there could really use a gentling touch. Especially auld Mr. Timoney's. He's gone frail these past couple of years. Hasn't been able to do much on his farmstead since the missus passed."

Hartopp began to butter a piece of toast. "That's why we feel that removing him will do the man a great deal of good."

The fork stopped halfway to Shona's mouth. "Removing him?"

"Aye. We'll be relocating the tenants to convert that land into grazing terrain." Hartopp turned to Conall. "I've already received three bids to rent that area, one of them quite generous from a man who wants a thousand acres to graze five hundred head of sheep."

Shona's mouth fell open. "Ye mean to clear those farmers off the land to turn it into sheep pastures?"

"Of course. They've been doing it in the north of Scotland since I was a boy. And it's made the landlords very, very rich."

Shona turned a furious face upon Conall. "Is that what ye've come here to do? Toss all the farmers off the estate so ye can populate it with sheep?"

Conall's lips pursed. "No. But Ballencrieff is in financial despair, and has been for some time. That is why I tasked Hartopp with finding a way to help me put the estate back on its feet."

"And ye think getting rid of yer tenants is the best way to do it?"

Hartopp spoke in Conall's stead. "There's no need for hysterics, Miss Shona. Just a few farms will be affected. A few of the less profitable farms. After all, we are not inflicting unexpected harm upon these people. There has never been any misunderstanding between landlords and tenants. Pay the rent, and ye can stay. Pay it not, and ye must go." He stuffed a thick slice of sausage into his mouth.

"And just where would ye have auld Mr. Timoney go? He's nearly seventy, and he's sweated and bled into that land for ages."

"Ballencrieff is not a charity, Miss Shona."

"No, but the tenants deserve yer consideration and respect. 'Tis the tenant farmer who pays the landlord, employs the laborers, and supports the Poor Laws that help the paupers, of which I myself have been a beneficiary. More importantly, 'tis the tenant farmer who provides what feeds the people of Scotland and England, and indeed what ye, Mr. Hartopp, are putting into yer mouth this very second."

Hartopp stopped chewing as all eyes turned to him.

Conall leaned back in his chair. "I appreciate your concern for these neighbors of yours, Shona. But the fact remains that the estate is in great debt. If we don't save it from ruin, we could *all* be out of a home."

A razor-blade smile cut across Hartopp's face. "Do ye have a better suggestion, Miss Shona?"

Shona's eyes scoured the table. She reached back into her memory, back through all she'd known, to find a way to save the estate—and the tenants who lived upon it.

"Aye, I do." She took a sip of tea from the china cup before her. "Whenever Willow and I would take our goods to market, it was always a slog to sell them. We always had to compete with the neighboring farms to sell our produce. When I brought potatoes, the Caird farm would also bring potatoes, and we'd each have to lower our prices to try to outsell the other. It dawned on me that if our farms could agree on what each would grow, there would be no fighting amongst us. If one year, auld Mr. Timoney would grow turnips, and the Caird farm would raise wheat, and at Miles' End we had carrots, then we could afford to sell the produce at town at fair prices, and each of us would benefit."

A furrow appeared between Conall's eyebrows as he considered this. "You mean, ask the farms to specialize in a crop."

"Aye, 'specialize.' And rotate each year. Instead of each of us growing five crops, all of us could grow a single crop. That way, when it came time to sell, there would be no competition, and at market the buyers would have to buy at the price we name."

Conall nodded slowly. "The idea has merit. Hartopp, what do you think?"

The white-haired man heaved a sigh. "I think it's impractical and simplistic, not to mention bordering on the tyrannical. Ye can't force the farmers to grow a particular product. As long as they pay their rents, they can grow whatever they damn well please."

"Aye, they can," she responded, swallowing her anger. "But it's worth the effort to try. I'm also aware of the other challenges. Farmers are resistant to try new ways. It'll take much talk over many glasses of whisky to get them into one accord. Also, this idea may take at least two years to rotate into practice. We'll be changing the configuration of the fields, and it'll take some doing to organize them so as not to ask the land to give more than two green crops or white crops in consecutive years. But in the end, each tenant will prosper all the more if they were to 'specialize.' It would allow them to pay their rents in full, and have a significant profit left over."

Shona glanced at Conall. She was unsure if he was convinced. But by goodness, he was *impressed*.

Hartopp's voice dripped with sarcasm. "While you were gossiping with the fishwives at market, did you by chance come up with any other ideas?"

"Several," she snapped back. "In their crop rotations, many farms follow a bare fallow field with turnip and barley. In terms of money, the yield is the same as if ye followed fallow with wheat—aboot eight pounds per acre. But the added manure and the labor required to ready the fallow field for turnips reduces the profit. Ye'd be better off beginning the new rotation with wheat after bare fallow."

Stewart began to chuckle. "Dear me! Hartopp, perhaps *you* should spend some time gossiping with the fishwives at market."

Hartopp glared at Shona with ill-concealed antagonism.

"And one more thing," she continued. "Ye must grant the tenants twenty-year leases. Most other estates in Scotland do so. But the previous laird of Ballencrieff never did permit it."

Hartopp threw his head back and laughed. "Now I can see yer true intentions. Ye want to get yer Hume Findlay a permanent situation here on the estate. Well, it won't work. If we start giving the tenants leases, we'll never be able to throw the wastrels off the land."

Shona stiffened. "If ye knew the people aroond here

as I do, ye would know that they are no' wastrels. Nobody in their right mind would make an investment in the land that another tenant'll benefit from. Why should they put any money into a property if they can be tossed off it at a moment's notice? But if the tenants felt the security of a long-term lease, they would be more inclined to make improvements upon their *own* land."

Conall scratched his jaw. "My uncle used to resist the measure of assigning leases. I have always perceived that to be a mistake. In my opinion, it's deepened the ravine between the landlord and tenants, and it pits us against one another instead of working together for a common good. And, as Shona says, it makes the tenants apathetic."

Hartopp poured some more tea into his cup. "Apathy is the least of yer worries at present, Dr. MacEwan. Half the tenants are in arrears, and few as bad as Hume Findlay. It would be preposterous to allow them a twenty-year lease. She'll be asking ye to reduce the rents next."

Shona felt like smashing the teapot over Hartopp's head. "Quite the reverse. I think it would be reasonable to add interest to back rent."

"Finally," he said, throwing his hands in the air. "A sound business idea."

Shona held back her disgust. She turned to Conall. "Kicking the farmers off the property won't get ye the money ye're owed. But if ye were to make an investment on their farms—supply some needed fertilizer, or add a purse from which to pay laborers—I think the tenants'll be happy to get ye the back rent with some added on. I know several farmers who would be overjoyed to pay interest if they could just have the capital to successfully bring in the crops *this* year. The Firley farm, for example . . . one of his fields is in desperate want of draining. Nothing will grow upon it. But he lacks the ready money to do that. The widow Jeanne Ryon has beautiful soil on her farm, but she can't afford the fertilizer to make her harvest come in plentiful this year. Invest a few bob in her farm, and it may just produce treble in the coming year."

"Once again, you've missed the point." Hartopp sneered. "Dr. MacEwan says he *needs* money. Ye're suggesting that he spend more of what he hasn't got."

Conall put up a finger. "Just a moment. Hartopp, how many acres is Mistress Ryon's farm?"

"About two hundred and forty," he answered.

"How much would it cost to buy this fertilizer?"

Hartopp touched the napkin to his mouth. "Er, I would need to consult my books."

Shona began to scribble imaginary numbers with her finger on the mahogany table. "Four hundred and eighty cartloads of manure at one shilling eleven pence per load is forty-six pounds even. And three men spreading it at two-and-six each for four days is one pound ten shillings . . . for a total of forty-seven pounds ten shillings."

Stewart threw back his head and laughed.

"What's so funny?" she said, scowling at Stewart. "It's accurate to the penny!"

"No doubt, my dear Miss Shona," he said, wiping his eyes. "But the look on Hartopp's face was *priceless*."

She turned to look, but Hartopp had already pasted a smile over his expression.

"Ye're certainly nimble with yer figures, Miss Shona. I salute you. May I ask where you acquired such vast knowledge of estate management?"

"I've been working Hume's farm for nearly ten years now. And my da used to be a landlord."

"Did he?" asked Conall. "So you come from a wealthy family?"

"No." She bit her lip. "Leastwise, I don't remember us being particularly wealthy."

Hartopp snickered. "Well, I've never heard of a *poor* landlord."

A crease appeared between her eyebrows. "Mayhap we weren't poor. But my da invested all he could into his tenants' property. He used to say that in his tenants lay his success, and in their ruin lay his own."

"Oh?" he asked, sarcasm dripping from his lips. "And how did that serve him?"

Shona's gaze went adrift. In a trice, she was eight years old, huddled under the sink in that kitchen, seeing that dagger embedded in her father's heart.

Hartopp leaned back in his chair. "I'd certainly like to meet this wondrous paragon of lairdship."

Shona's gaze jumped to Hartopp's face. "He's dead."

"Ho, ho! How very convenient for the purposes of your fictitious story. Did ye also make up a name for him?"

"'Tis not made up! My father is John MacAslan of Ravens Craig, and everything I say aboot him is true! What's more, he never had any need of a factor, for he knew what ignorant bullies they all were."

She thought that her words would wound him. She thought he would throw down his napkin and storm out of the dining hall. But he didn't. Instead, he blinked twice and stared at her, as if seeing her for the very first time.

"Ye . . . are of John MacAslan's brood?"

"Aye, and a more honorable man never lived!"

He hesitated. "Forgive me, Miss Shona. I meant no disrespect. There was no way I could know who yer father was." He subjected her to an assessing glance. "Would ye . . . do me the courtesy of passing the salt?"

Shona uncoiled. Finally she had made him understand that her father was a great man. She picked up the silver salt cellar upon the table and reached over to set it down before him.

Suddenly, her wrist was imprisoned in his. She tried jerking it away, but he held it fast.

A slow smile stretched across Hartopp's face. "Ye've the mark of the *slaighteur.*"

Shona cursed herself. How careless of her to leave exposed her damning brand. She yanked back her hand, but not before some perverse victory had crinkled Hartopp's eyes.

"So it's true," he said. "Ye are MacAslan's lass."

"What is it, Hartopp?" asked Conall. "Do you know what that mark upon her hand means?"

Hartopp smiled at Conall. "Ye mean she didn't tell ye? That doesn't surprise me."

A humiliated blush suffused Shona's face. "It means nothing," she insisted, desperately hoping Conall would drop the subject.

Hartopp chuckled. "That's the first thing ye've uttered that is entirely true. Those with the mark of the *slaighteur* are indeed *nothing.*"

She shot him an angry look.

"What is this all about, Hartopp? Tell me," demanded Conall.

Hartopp breathed a contented sigh. "It is Highland law, Dr. MacEwan. Those who are considered traitors to the clan are marked by the sign of *slaighteur*. Villains—or knaves—would be the nearest English translation. Though I don't think that those words convey the same repugnance that all decent Scots feel when they encounter someone with *that* upon his flesh."

"Why?"

"Because everyone knows that a *slaighteur* is not to be trusted. If they are traitorous to their own clans, then they are sure to be disloyal to others. Therefore, no other clan will claim them. Scotsmen know better than to marry a *slaighteur* woman—or even employ one."

Shona smarted under the sting of his words. In one simple sentence, Hartopp had destroyed any hope that she had of being Conall's apprentice. Or his wife.

Conall gazed across at her, a look of genuine concern printed upon his face. "Willow had it upon her hand as well. Why were you two branded, Shona?"

"It does no' matter anymore." She threw her napkin on the table and stormed out of the dining hall.

SIX

"Hoo soo!"

Baby Eric pointed a chubby finger at a spot on the nursery wall. The late morning sun was streaming in through the window behind him, sparking golden streaks in his soft brown curls. He turned surprised eyes upon Willow, who grinned excitedly.

"That's right, sweeting. That's yer shadow!"

He revealed tiny teeth as he smiled at the flowered wallpaper. Wildly, he waved his arms over his head, squealing loudly at the shadow, which mirrored his every move.

Stewart cringed at the shrill sound, but returned a grin to Willow. "The country air is certainly doing wonders for his lungs. Only two years old and he can already make the furniture rattle."

Willow chuckled, sitting on the nursery settee. "He's a good lad. So happy, he is. He's only cried once today, and 'twas only because of the medicine he had to take."

Eric stomped his feet on the floor in an attempt to dislodge his shadow. It wasn't working.

"What about you, Willow?" Lifting his myrtle-green coattails, Stewart sat down beside her. "Are you happy here?"

"Oh, aye, Mr. MacEwan! I love it here. 'Course, I miss

Miles' End Farm. And the Findlays. They're good folk, always kind to me and Shona. But ye and yer brother have been very kind to us, too." Her cheeks pinked.

"Tosh. It's hardly an effort. But if there's one thing you can credit us with, it is being able to discern who the good prospects are . . . er, I mean servants." He took a deep breath, and sunlight flashed off his gold brocade waistcoat. "Tell me, is there a gentleman waiting for you somewhere? A sweetheart or a suitor?"

"Oh, no, sir!" A hand flew to the front of her blue nursemaid's gown. "I would never keep a gentleman whilst I was made responsible for the bairn. I said as much to the laird. Ye must believe that."

Stewart's dimples deepened as he inched closer on the settee. "Of course I do. I just wanted to put my own mind at ease."

"One day, God willing, I'll marry. But never whilst I'm working here. Not without the master's permission."

Surreptitiously, Stewart took a whiff from her hair when her attention was diverted to the child. "Surely a woman such as yourself is deserving of *some* diversion. It would be a pity to waste all that . . . youth. Perhaps I might be able to convince you to grant me a tour of this lovely countryside."

"I thought ye hailed from Ballencrieff?"

He threw an arm on the back of the settee behind Willow. "I'm afraid not. It's Conall who was born here. In fact, this is my first visit to Scotland. And I'm already in love with the beauteous scenery of your country." As Willow watched the child, his eyes traveled down the front of her dress. "The mounded hills . . . the firm slopes . . . the bountiful natural beauty . . . A man could indulge himself all day long on your gorgeous splendors."

A figure appeared in the doorway. Conall MacEwan knocked on the open door. Willow rose respectfully—to Stewart's great annoyance.

"Pa-paa!" shrieked Eric, and raised his arms to his father. A toothy smile spread across Conall's face as he scooped Eric up and wedged him onto his arm.

"How's my little soldier?" he asked the boy.

Eric pointed to the wall and said, "Hoo soo."

He chuckled. "Hoo soo? Remarkable. Has he been a good boy, Willow?"

"The very best, sir," she answered. "He ate all his porridge in the morning, and a big glass of fresh milk."

"Excellent. Did you administer the tonic I gave you?"

"Aye, sir. I gave it to him in a spoon, but he spit it out. So I mixed it into some honeyed pears, and he gobbled it right up."

"Well done." He squeezed the boy tightly. "You're going to grow up big and strong!"

"Hoo soo!" said the boy.

Willow laughed. "He's just discovered his own shadow. Seems he's already given it a name."

Conall's eyes crinkled. "I'd like to take him out to the garden for lunch. Will you see to it that he's warmly dressed?"

" 'Course, sir."

Conall handed the child to Willow. "Stewart, what, may I ask, are you doing here?"

He threw innocent hands into the air. "Can't a man visit his own nephew?"

Conall flashed him an irritated look. "May I have a word? In private?"

"Oh, dear," replied Stewart. "You're going to say something dreadfully sensible, aren't you?"

Conall turned his back and walked out the door.

Once Stewart joined him in the hall, Conall squared up on his shorter brother. "What do you think you're playing at?"

"I'm sure I don't know what you mean."

"Don't play coy with me. I heard you chatting up Willow," he yelled under his breath.

"That's what healthy men do, Conall. They talk to beautiful women."

"Are you sure you were using words? Because it seemed to me your penis was doing all the talking."

Stewart stiffened. "All right, all right," he muttered. "There's no need to get cocky."

"That's it, Stewart. I'm fed up with your profligate ways. Father didn't mind rescuing you from sticky messes with your lovers, but I do not intend to be so magnanimous. If you get yourself into trouble, you'll have to get yourself out of it."

Stewart's lips thinned. "No one's asked for your help, Conall."

"And we shall keep it that way. I want you to choose a wife and settle down."

"Don't be absurd. I'm too young for the cosh."

"Young? You're a hairsbreadth from thirty!"

Stewart's face blanched and he swiftly shut the nursery door. "What are you trying to do . . . ruin my chances with that one in there?"

Conall's eyes widened. "For goodness' sake, Stewart, she's a servant!"

"Ha! If that isn't the donkey making fun of the rabbit's ears! I've seen the way you look at Shona. You're practically drooling after her."

He pursed his lips. "At least I'm not trying to seduce her. I mean, I enjoy the odd flirtation occasionally, but—"

Stewart's eyebrows drew together. "Really, Conall? Judging from your quasi-monastic lifestyle, I didn't know you enjoyed *anything* occasionally."

"Don't stray from the point of this conversation. Trying to defile and deprave that innocent girl . . . I'm not having it!"

"Unfortunately, I'm not having it, either. Not unless you stop bounding in upon me like a jealous husband."

Conall held up a cautioning finger. "I want an end to your escapades. I can't afford to support a bachelor whose only expertise centers around spending money and slaking his lust. Everything has changed, and the faster you embrace that, the better off you'll be. I had no intention of being the laird of anything, but I gave up my practice and a profession I slaved over to heal this estate. I've accepted the bonds of duty, and so shall you. You've got two choices. Get a wife, or get off my estate."

Conall shouldered past him and down the stairs, leaving the air pulsing with his ultimatum.

Once again, Stewart fumed with his sheer powerlessness. Second to all, master of none—his entire life was just one kick to the groin after another. Stewart MacEwan, second son of a second son. He may as well be a Gypsy rat catcher.

Conall. His brother had always been the favored one. Firstborn, first at school, first to inherit. First, first,

first. Conall was brighter, bigger, and better at everything. There was so little that Stewart was even permitted to do, let alone skilled to do. He wasn't nearly as
intelligent as Conall, so being a brilliant doctor was out.
Join the clergy? Stewart could only be a man of the cloth
so long as the cloth in question was a bed sheet.

He trudged to the library and poured himself a
drink. So what if he was a profligate? So what if he was
a drinker? At least he was good at something.

Somewhere behind him, someone cleared his throat.
If it was Conall prepared to chastise him for drinking
in the morning, he'd send him to damnation. Stewart
spun around.

Bannerman waited patiently at attention, holding a
silver salver. "Pardon me, sir, but this urgent letter just
arrived for you by special messenger. The messenger
will attend your reply."

Stewart's brows drew together as he tore apart the
wax seal and unfolded the lettersheet. His eyes went
from the emblem at the top of the page to the signature
at the bottom. Then he read the elegant but determined
script.

His hand flew to his mouth, as the blood drained from
his face. "Oh, dear. Oh dear oh dear oh dear."

"Alarming news, sir?"

"Yes. That is, no. Bannerman, do me a great service.
Tell no one about this letter. Least of all my brother. I'll
speak my reply to the messenger directly."

Unflappable as ever, Bannerman gave a curt nod. "If
you say so, sir."

Stewart stared at the letter, his eyes glassing over.
His own words burned acid into his gut. Stewart had
gotten himself into a world of trouble, and he had no

idea how to get himself out of it. How could he ask Conall for help now?

The brilliant sun lit up the lush emerald grass that blanketed the estate. The wind whipped Conall's brown hair as he climbed the rise toward the eastern field.

Standing behind a stone dyke and looking out onto the grazing sheep was Shona.

"I thought I might find you here," he remarked.

She glanced in his direction but said nothing, instead fixing her gaze to a cluster of sheep crouching in a sunny spot.

Conall squinted into the distance. "You seem to have a natural affinity for animals."

Still she said nothing.

"Why didn't you tell me about the brand?"

She turned to face him full on. "Stop beating aboot the bush, and come straight to the point. Ye'll be wanting me back in the dairy. Go on, say it."

His face was expressionless. "Perhaps. But first answer my question."

Shona cast her eyes on the ground. "How could I tell ye what it meant? Ye heard what Mr. Hartopp said. It's the mark of the *slaighteur.* Wherever I go, everyone will see this and know what I am."

"And what exactly is that?"

She winced. "A knave. A villain. A traitor."

"And are you such things?"

She harrumphed. "It doesna matter what I think. The mark says different."

"Of course it matters. Who you are, and who people say you are, are not the same thing at all."

She hesitated. "Ye dinna understand. No one will

bother to find out who I truly am. They won't be able to see past this." She held up her scarred hand to his face.

Conall fought the urge to flinch. He had seen many injuries far worse, but for some reason, it hurt him that such a disfigurement existed upon Shona's flesh.

"Ye've lived too long away from Scotland. Ye dinna know what this means. This mark makes us unwanted. For work, for wife. Look at Willow. I canna count the suitors who've come to call on her. But just as soon as they saw the mark, she never heard from them again. No one is going to love a *slaighteur.*"

Conall nodded slowly, absorbing the injustice of it all. "You've made it perfectly clear what others think. But I still have not heard what you think is behind that mark. So I ask again, are you a knave?"

Shona thought about it for a long time. "If I was no' before, I am now. I could never be kin to that band of brigands that killed my family right before my eyes. Every time I think on it, all I see is blood."

Conall inhaled deeply, shocked by the revelation. "When did this happen?"

"A long time ago," Shona said, but knew it to be untrue. No matter how much time passed, it would always be a fresh memory. "We were little, aboot eight years old. Mumma tried to hide us when the men broke down the door. They came for the blood of Thomas and Hamish, but Mumma and Da would never sacrifice their sons to quench their bloodlust. They tried to fight them off, but the men were stronger in number and might. Mumma and Da . . . Thomas and Hamish . . . and Malcolm. All of them slaughtered."

Shona closed her eyes to the vivid picture that splashed before her eyes every time she talked about it.

"I'll never forget the face of the man that slit my mother's throat. I hate him for killing her. I hate him for hurting Willow. But most of all, I hate him for making me remember him."

Conall winced at the image of that brutal scene. Five dead, a whole family all at once. God only knew what it must have done to an eight-year-old girl.

The knuckles on her hands turned white as they gripped the crest of the dyke. He reached out and placed a warm palm upon her scarred hand. "I'm sorry, Shona."

The sensation surprised her. She turned questioning eyes upon his face. There was a look of genuine concern upon his handsome features.

"Are there any more of you? Who survived, I mean?"

Shona blinked, unfamiliar with his extension of understanding. "Our brother Camran. He was five."

"Why do you suppose you three were spared?"

She shrugged. "Not a day goes by that I don't think aboot that very question. And try as I might, I canna come up with an answer."

"Where is he now?"

"I don't know. But I intend to find out. 'Tis why I wanted our freedom. I must try to find Camran. If he's still alive."

Conall heaved a deep sigh. "That means you would have to hunt down the men who did this in order to find out what happened to your brother."

"Aye. I mean to do just that."

Emotions battled within him. It was the height of foolishness for Shona to go off in search of murderers. By delivering herself into their hands, they'd probably finish their bloody deed by killing the surviving girls. And yet, Shona had a sound head on her shoulders. He was sure she had considered the risks. He'd give her that at least . . . she was certainly one of the bravest women he'd ever met. If she were cornered, there seemed nothing and no one she wouldn't stand up to.

But whether she was willing to accept the danger or not, he couldn't allow her to put her life at risk. And for the time being at least, he held the authority to protect her from her own headstrong intentions.

"In three years, perhaps. For now, you've got a great deal of work to do. You're responsible for making this estate profitable. And your duty to me comes before everything else."

"Ye mean, ye still want me to help ye? What aboot what Mr. Hartopp said?"

"Hartopp's been terminated. After he adamantly refused to follow your advice, which I considered to be quite sage, I found I had no more need of him. So it seems you've got your hands full at the moment."

"I . . . don't know what to say."

"I do. It means that I now have even loftier expectations of you. In addition to being to work *on time* and serving me with diligence and obedience, I also expect results and will hold you accountable for bringing them to me. Above all, I expect absolute honesty always. As your employer, I can teach some things, but I cannot teach character. That you must bring on your own. Is that understood?"

She narrowed her eyes at him. "Does this mean I'm now yer factor?"

"Yes. And as my factor, I will not pay you to stand about gazing at sheep. So come with me. There's something I'd like to show you."

* * *

Shona followed Conall numbly to the house. She had no idea what to make of this recent turn of events. She had thought for certain she would be expelled back to the dairy. For a few nerve-racking hours following breakfast, Shona had felt once again imprisoned by her circumstances. Instead, Conall was actually inviting her to remain in his circle of trust. Although they were still under their indentures, Willow could at least continue to serve in the nursery, which she seemed to enjoy, and Shona would get an opportunity to redeem herself from Hartopp's harmful slander. Relieved, her shoulders began to untense.

Shona climbed the stairs behind Conall, past the floor containing his bedroom, and to an upper level. He opened the door onto a room that burst light upon her eyes. The wallpaper was white and painted with tiny blue and yellow flowers. A long window cast squares of light upon the thick carpeting. A maplewood crib rested against the wooden wainscoting, and two beds were propped against the opposite wall. In the center of the room, a child swayed upon a rocking horse.

"Where's my soldier?"

"Pa-paa!" Clumsily, the boy climbed off the horse, and ran awkwardly toward Conall. He picked the boy up in his arms.

"Shona, this is my son, Eric."

"Eric," she repeated, and the boy smiled at her. "How sweet!" she giggled. "How old is he?"

"He'll be two a month hence. Eric, go and show Shona your toy soldiers." He set the boy down on the floor, and Eric spun his stubby legs as he raced to a shelf. Willow came to her feet and helped pull down the box he was jumping for.

"Please sit down," Conall said, waving her to the settee. He lifted his coattails and sat down beside her. He measured his words carefully as he spoke. "I know what it's like to lose a loved one. Eric's mother died just after he was born."

The boy carried the box to Conall's lap. Conall slid open the lid, and Eric reached in and pulled out wooden figurines, their little coats painted red.

"He's not known what it's like to have a mother. He's a lot like you two, I expect, having lost a mother at such a young age. But I try to give him much love and attention, to compensate for his missing parent."

Eric plopped down on the floor and began to stand his soldiers up.

"It's for him that I'm here. The estate will provide for him, now and when he grows, and I want to make sure that it thrives. This, then, is why you're here. You are going to make the tenants prosper, not just for their own sake, but so that Eric here will be provided for. Do you understand?"

Shona looked up at Conall. The tenderness toward his child warmed something within her. How fortunate his child was to have such a devoted father. It made her miss her own da all the more.

"I understand."

"Good. And by the by," he added, "I have fulfilled my end of our bargain. That bed over there, the one beside Willow's, is yours. I am, after all, a man of my word."

She glanced at the beds she had seen when she'd first come in. True enough, the nursery now had two narrow beds, separated by a low night table.

Willow watched Eric from the foot of one of the beds.

But something was wrong with her sister.

Though it was invisible to Conall, Shona could interpret the look on Willow's face. That glassy expression meant she was lost in unhappy memories.

Shona rose and sat beside her, placing her hands in her sister's. "Isn't this wonderful, Willow? We'll be resting together again tonight." She hoped to interrupt the stream of Willow's reminiscence.

Willow swung horrified eyes at Shona. Her voice was barely a whisper. "Look at the bairn. Who do ye see?"

Shona turned her gaze upon the boy. The child sat upon the floor, playing with his wooden king's men. Instantly, she could see through Willow's eyes. The two-year-old's blue velvet gown disappeared, and instead she saw a blue and red woolen kilt. The pale rosy cheeks of a toddler vanished, replaced by the darkened skin of a five-year-old boy who played outside the day long. Gone were the light brown curls of Eric, and instead she saw the soft black hair of Camran.

A sound like rushing water thundered in her ears. Instantly, she was transported to the happy, innocent moments in the kitchen at Ravens Craig—when Camran was a little boy playing with toy soldiers, Willow was shaping the bannocks for dinner, and Shona marveled at the way a spider could move both on the ground and through the air. *That* moment seemed centuries ago.

Shona blinked her eyes, dispelling the memories. Willow, however, remained locked in the nightmare.

The last thing Shona wanted to do was alarm Conall. So she patted Willow's hands and mustered as much cheer as she could.

"Ye're right, Willow! Eric *is* very like his father!"

Conall grinned. "You'll be able to play with him later. For now, there are some ledgers I'd like to show you. Willow, I'll be back at noon to collect Eric."

Conall rose, and Shona did, too. She cast a worried glance at Willow, who was talking herself through the panic as Shona had taught her to do.

SEVEN

The house at Ravens Craig had had a library, but it was nowhere near as grand as Conall's.

A gilt-edged tray ceiling crowned the oaken walls in the cavernous room. Long shelves groaned under the weight of so many books. Red brocade drapes dripped down the long windows, shaping the light that fell upon a long tapestry hanging on the opposite wall. A massive marble mantel arched over a brick fireplace.

The air inside the room smelled heavenly, scented with old pages warmed by the sunshine and seasoned with years. It was all Shona could do to keep from flopping onto one of the upholstered wing chairs that dotted the room and devouring each of the unloved books.

Conall lifted an oversized scroll from a cylindrical basket upon the floor. He unfurled it onto a long table. She came up alongside him, and was met with a new scent . . . the clean smell of soap upon him. The musky lemon perfume emanated from his hair and his face.

"Right. Here is a map of the estate."

Her eyes tore all over the surveyor's map. "Goolies! Is all this land yers?"

"Most of it, yes."

She traced her hand all over the bird's-eye view of the estate. "Goolies!" she breathed.

Conall shook his head. "Shona, your language leaves much to be desired."

Her eyebrows drew together. "What do ye mean? There's nothing wrong with 'goolies.'"

A smirk deepened in his cheek. "Not in its literal sense, no. But that is a word that doesn't sit well upon a woman's tongue, especially not when you are using it in that context. The anatomical nomenclature is 'testicles,' and unless I'm very mistaken, you're not talking about testicles, are you?"

She shrugged. "Oh, very well. How much land is this?"

"About five thousand acres."

"Gool—" Shona glanced up at Conall, who pursed his lips. "I mean, 'Mercy!' How much of that is arable?"

"Excellent question. About three-quarters of it, I would venture to say. But I can't be certain—Uncle Macrath's records are less than precise. The rest of the land—here, here, and here—is nonagricultural. It consists of forest, streams, the house, and so on."

"How many farms belong to the estate?"

"Forty-three. But I don't have an accurate representation of them on a map. And we'll need it if we are going to put some of your ideas for improving the land into practice. Therefore, I want you to take a survey of the land, and outline the farms on this map. I also want you to indicate who the tenants are and what their marketable crops can be, based on the quality of soil and irrigation."

"Survey the land? I dinna know how to do that."

He cocked his head. "The word 'apprentice' is derived from the French word 'apprendre,' which means 'to learn.' So that's what you are to do. Learn."

Shona grumbled. "When?"

"We can start this very afternoon. Be ready to ride out at half past one. We'll begin with the farms on the north side of the estate, and work our way down. We certainly won't be done today, but we'll try to cover as much terrain as we can before sundown."

Shona had hoped for some more of those English scones with the raspberry jam at teatime. "We'll be gone all afternoon? The sky promises rain, ye know."

"Half past one," he repeated as he walked out of the library.

She sighed as she rolled up the map. "Bugger."

He poked his head back in, an eyebrow jutting into his forehead. "And stop swearing, or I shall wash out your mouth with soap."

At the appointed hour, Shona was sitting astride the horse in the stable yard. She had inspected the bay to make sure he was up for a ride, and then seated him to get a feel for how her mount liked to be guided. The horse's hooves clattered upon the flagstones as she guided him into a canter.

Within minutes, Conall walked out into the stable yard.

"Punctuality. I admire that in my staff."

"I canna wait to survey the land," she said with a sardonic edge. "'Tis all I can think aboot."

"Glad to hear it. After this, I just may hire you out as a professional cartographer."

He watched her bounce gently upon the horse as she made wide circles in the stable yard. Mesmerized, his mind wandered as he regarded the sensual way her bottom connected with the saddle. A narrow leather strap hung loosely from her narrow waist, from which hung a sheathed knife. Though covered by the fabric of her ochre woolen skirt, the spread of her legs upon the beast created a stir in his loins.

A guilty blush made him turn the other way. "Do you not require a sidesaddle? I'm certain that my uncle must have kept one or two in the tack room."

She laughed as her hair flapped behind her like butterfly wings. "A sidesaddle is for auld women and Sassenach ladies. I am neither."

He grinned. "As you wish," he remarked, amused by her nonconformity to polite society. The groom steadied his horse as Conall climbed atop its back.

"Right. Are you ready?"

"Aye. The question is, are ye?" She dug her heels in the horse's flanks, spurring him into a gallop toward the north field. Conall squeezed the reins in his hands and took off after her.

The horses galloped over the fields toward the northern point of the estate. Within fifteen minutes, they reached the road that led them to the first farm.

The land was a patchwork quilt of greens and yellows. From a distance, Mr. Raeburn's many-colored fields undulated like waves on an emerald ocean. Blond wheat, golden barley, and knee-high grass waved in the breeze, beckoning them hither.

They were still a long way from the farmstead when Shona slowed her horse and dismounted. "Come."

Conall swung his leg off his horse and walked toward her. Fascinated, he watched as she dug her knife into the ground and pulled up a fistful of dark earth.

She held it up to him. "Have a keek at the soil that the Raeburn land has. See how rich it is? Hume's always had a green eye for Raeburn's land. This kind of soil is perfect for carrots or peas. But Raeburn won't grow them in great quantities because of the labor required to maintain the beds. His sons have all gone to war, ye see, and he has to hire all his help. So he mainly grows the easier crops to maintain, like wheat and hay."

Shona held the soil up to her nose and inhaled its perfume. " 'Tis truly fertile soil. If I had my way, I'd turn his land toward vegetables. His crops would make a fortune up in the Highlands where these foods do no' grow."

He crouched down beside her, charmed by her earthiness. Her hands were streaked black with the soil and her unpinned hair lashed about her neck. Shona seemed at one with the natural realm, like a wood sprite or a pixie from the childhood stories. As if a word from her could make the seeds grow and the trees bear fruit.

He drew in a deep cleansing breath. The smell was green and pure, and full of life. Birds sprinkled music in the trees, and the sweet sounds were carried to him on the wind.

He gazed upon Shona. Her young eyes still had not seen so much of the beauty of the world. And yet she delighted in the simplest things.

Or, perhaps, it was he who needed to see things through her eyes.

He handed her the handkerchief from his pocket. "Right. Let's go and find Mr. Raeburn. We'll get a full account of his crops and create a rough sketch of his land on the map. I'll also tell him that I wish to meet with all the farmers on the estate in a fortnight."

An hour later, they had finished speaking with

Mr. Raeburn, and were trotting toward the neighboring farm.

Conall had been thoroughly impressed with Shona. In addition to the jovial familiarity she shared with Mr. Raeburn, she asked more questions about the old man's crops than Conall had ever even considered were important. In one visit alone, Conall gained an appreciable understanding of cultivating crops.

"You have a very shrewd eye for farming, Shona. Given your youth, I'm quite impressed by how much you know. Sometimes I wonder which of us is the master and which is the apprentice."

"Och! 'Tis nothing ye canna learn. There's a book in yer library that I studied years ago. Since ye've a duty to know, 'twould be a good primer for ye."

Surprise flashed across his face. "You . . . can read?"

She blinked her eyes in disbelief. "Did ye think me such a dolt that I could no' read?"

"I just assumed that—"

"You thought that since I worked on a farm that I must be illiterate?"

He shook his head. "No. Well . . . yes. The thought had crossed my mind."

"Ye've a great deal to learn aboot me. I went to classes until I was fourteen. After that, I schooled myself with books. I've been reading since I was a wee lass. My father, God rest him, was never without a book, and he used to read stories to us at night by the fire."

"I apologize for my misguided assumptions."

"Apology accepted. But mind ye dinna make the same mistake again."

"Just a moment. Be fair. Had you made any untrue assumptions about me?"

"None that ye haven't disproven yet."

He smirked. "Come on."

"Well . . . behind yer back I may have called ye a name that implied yer parents were never married."

He chuckled. "I taste some vinegar in that sentiment."

"Well, ye were fairly vinegary to me."

"Perhaps I had cause," he said, cocking an eyebrow. "But I think I may have since discovered in you some compensating qualities."

"Such as?" she tossed at him saucily.

He grinned. "Let me think. Well, I like the way you talk—though not always what you say. I admire your courage—except when it's in defiance of me. I perceive how caring you are, and I believe that your husband and children, when you have them, will be very fortunate indeed."

A smile brightened her face. "Thank ye. 'Tis gentlemanly of ye to say."

By late afternoon, they had prospected three more farms. The sun began to sink in the western horizon, and gray clouds stained the sky, but Shona insisted they let the horses graze beside a brook. They walked over to a chestnut tree in blossom.

"You know, Shona," he began as he picked up a dried chestnut from the ground, "the tenant farms are in a state of disrepair far greater than I had at first surmised. I don't mind investing a small sum to improve their next harvest, but I'm concerned that the return on the investment won't be enough to continue running the estate."

A weight bore down upon Shona. "What does that mean?"

"I may be forced to sell some of the land." A look of

regret clouded his features. "I may be forced to sell Miles' End."

"What?"

He threw the chestnut into the forest. "It was one of the suggestions that Hartopp had made to bring in a fresh stream of money. He'd even located a buyer, the Baron of Bainbridge, who's offered to annex Miles' End and two adjacent farms to his own property, plus some of the hunting forest. Before you react—"

"Are ye oot of yer bloody mind?"

He sighed. "You should calm down first."

Shona gritted her teeth. "In the first place, ye must never sell off yer property."

"Sometimes a surgeon has to amputate a leg if he wants to save the patient."

"And in the second place, ye can't sell it to the Barren of Brains."

He chuckled. "It's Baron of Bainbridge."

She folded her arms at her chest. "Clearly ye haven't met him, because my name is better suited."

"I have no choice, Shona." He shrugged. "If I'm to improve some of my existing farms, I have to raise the capital. Money doesn't grow on trees, you know."

"It does for ye!" She threw her hands outward. "Ye've got orchards all over yer estate!"

He cocked his head. "Touché. But dribs and drabs of money won't go very far to buy what each of these farms needs. And you know that."

She sighed, calming herself down. "I ken that ye want to do what's best for yer estate. But carving off bits and pieces is not going to make ye any richer. Keeping the estate intact may mean ye'll have to do a bit of saving to stretch a farthing into a shilling. But the thrift won't have to last forever. Land, though . . . land is forever. There is nothing better to put yer money into than the land that already belongs to ye. Give it up now and ye'll never get it back."

Conall weighed her words. He was stuck between two very difficult options: becoming a pauper aristocrat, which Shona was asking him to do, or start dividing up the inheritance from his ancestors, as Stewart and Hartopp had recommended.

Shona looked up into his face. "I never promised ye it would be easy or quick. But it will be worth it."

His azure eyes gazed out to the horizon, worry creasing his brow. He was already bleeding money by taking on the arrears of the estate, but he wouldn't last long if he began to invest too much capital.

Life in England had been so much simpler. He worked and he got paid. And always discreetly. As a gentleman doctor, remuneration for his services was left inside his carriage or on a table in a silk pouch, which he collected after dining with the family. As a gentleman landlord, he could expect to collect rents only four times a year—and then only if the harvests were plentiful. And if they weren't, well, there was little he could do about it. Paying tenants were hard to come by. With the war on, there was a dearth of men to work the land. So if his tenants didn't prosper, then the one who'd be forced off his land by creditors would be himself.

He sighed. "Do you think I may actually turn a profit by the time Eric is ready for marriage?"

She smiled. "Aye. *That* I can promise ye."

"And if not, well, then I expect you'll have to teach me to become a farmer."

A twinkle appeared in her eye. "Ye? Become a farmer? With yer soft hands and yer London ways? I couldn't hold my breath that long."

He put his hands on his hips. "What calumny is this? I am hale and hearty yet! I've a strong back and sturdy arms!

"Psh! How old are ye, now?"

"I'm but thirty-five."

"Goolies! I thought ye halfway to a hundred."

A line deepened in one cheek. "That does it! It's high time we washed out that dirty mouth of yours."

Conall swept Shona into his arms, making her shriek in surprise. With grim determination, he carried her down the slope to the brook.

"No! Don't ye dare put me into the burn!"

"You asked for this."

Draped over his muscled forearm, her legs scissored helplessly. "Put me doon, ye great pillock! I'm warning ye!"

"Spare the rod," he said as he marched inexorably to the end of the brae.

She wound her arms tightly around his neck. He could almost read her thoughts. If he threw her into the brook, she meant to take him with her. As if he would let her do that.

Fearfully, she eyed the water below. "If ye get me wet, I'll—I'll—"

"Yes?" A determined chin dared her to make another threat.

She exhaled in playful defeat. "I'll not utter another swear word again."

He narrowed his eyes upon hers. "Have I your word? Your *decent* word?"

"Aye." She nodded eagerly.

Conall lowered his right arm, allowing her legs to slide to the ground. Shona remained adhered to him, her feet now mere inches from the edge of the freezing water. Nervously, her eyes flittered to his face as she unwound herself from his shoulders. But Conall found he could not let her go.

Waves of unspoken feelings washed across her face, feelings that mirrored his own. His heart beat thunderously in his chest, in rhythmic time with the hammering of his conscience. *Wrong, wrong, wrong,* it said, flashing a million reasons why it was so.

But Shona looked up at him expectantly, the pulse at the base of her throat racing. Her unadorned beauty dazzled his jaded sight. The freckles that dusted sun-kissed cheeks. The shoulders drowning in a sea of rook's wing hair. The luminous green eyes surrounded by thick black lashes, like the stained-glass windows in an ancient church. A whisper of musky earthiness breathed upon him, and it sent his senses spiraling out of his control. She was a thing wild and untamed, belonging only to this unfamiliar Scottish wilderness around him—and yet she hung pliant in his arms.

Since he'd met this creature, he'd felt an urge to possess her. Being her master was not enough . . . he wanted to own her desire. He lowered his head, bringing his mouth closer to her parted lips. As their lips touched, all warning voices in his head faded to silence.

His lips sank into the soft flesh of her own, and it lit something deep inside him. To his surprise, she didn't shrink from him, but met him right where she stood.

Feelings of sexual longing, long dormant since the death of Christina, surged anew. He cupped the back of her head gently, not wanting to frighten the trapped bird he had just caught. Slowly, his mouth smoothed over hers, beckoning—no, *begging*—her to open up to him.

Finally, her lips responded in kind, tentatively seeking a taste of him as well. A secret thrill warmed him all over. Her desire for him was set alight, and now he wanted to stoke it to a full-fledged burn.

She brought her arms back to his shoulders, and the added weight of her only made him feel stronger. Her body, pressed against his own, sparked hot yearnings in his loins. His mouth descended onto her neck, and he kissed the soft, sun-kissed flesh under her jaw. Her hot breath puffed onto his ear, and the warmth made his skin tingle all down his side.

Once again, his mouth opened onto her lips, this time with greater need as her hands splayed down his chest. At any moment, she could push him away. Instead, she moaned softly into his mouth, sending vibrations shooting straight through him.

At once, his mind was flooded with images of her in the stable. The memory of the curves of her naked body under the worn chemise, outlined in golden light from the lamp behind her, filled him with an intense sexual desire. He felt his manhood start to fill with long-neglected desire.

His hand spread across her back and caressed the strength beneath the woolen dress. She was strong and lean, so unlike the fragile, pampered ladies of his acquaintance. Of its own volition, his hand traveled down to her bottom and squeezed the firm roundness. Instantly, his mind was sparking with thoughts of thrusting into her lithe body.

"No more," she breathed.

He pulled away a little, the spell that had intoxicated him hanging in the air.

"I canna carry on," she explained to his closed eyes. "I'm sorry."

He groaned. He was caught in a war between his body's insistence to satisfy its carnal desire and his conscience's demand to do the right thing. Shona was his charge, his *responsibility,* and despoiling her would make him a reprehensible cad. But his body was still raging for her, and it would be a painful battle to make it give up.

"No," he rasped. "It is I who should apologize. Please forgive me. I forgot myself."

A callused hand stroked his cheek. "I think I like it when ye forget yerself. Ye become someone I'm very keen on."

He swallowed hard, wondering how many times he had wanted to do that very thing. "It's getting dark. Let's start back before it becomes too dark to navigate our way home. We could find ourselves marooned out here and have to spend the night."

To his surprise, her green eyes flashed a shared wish. Then she turned around before she divulged any more. But that alone was enough to put him in soaring spirits for the rest of the evening.

As midnight rain spattered on the nursery room window, Willow and Shona squeezed onto a single bed. While

Eric slept quietly in his crib, the sisters whispered to each other in the dark.

"He kissed ye? Just like that?" Willow's blue eyes became saucers.

"Aye!" Shona giggled. "One moment he was preparing to fling me into the burn, and the next, he pressed his lips again' mine and . . ." Shona closed her eyes to indulge again in the memory. "We kissed."

Willow bit her lower lip. "What was it like?"

Shona sighed deeply. "I canna describe it to ye. He's a very handsome man, to be sure, and he has a strong, braw shape to him. But there was something tender aboot him, too. He wanted me. He made me feel . . . beautiful."

"But ye *are* beautiful!"

"Och! Ye know what I mean. Not in the way Iona says . . . 'beautiful on the inside.' Beautiful in the way *ye* are. Desirable."

Willow cast her glance away, as if looking as she did were a curse instead of a blessing. "Ye had that lad in love with ye."

"Which one? Ye mean Dùghall?"

"Aye, that's the one. He was fair smitten by ye."

Shona tsked. "Dùghall was little more than a boy! And as thin as a stick. If he tried to make love to a woman, she'd barely need to spread her legs to let him through."

Willow let out a snort. "Shona! For shame! At least Dùghall was sweet on ye." She poked her sister in the shoulder. "And so, it seems, is the master."

A dreamy look descended upon her face. Conall MacEwan was sweet on *her*.

"What's he like?" asked Willow, yawning.

Shona stared over Willow's shoulder, as if Conall were standing in the room with them. "He's educated. And proper. And handsome." Shona looked deeper into the shadow of him. "Considerate. A man of principle. He's the perfect balance of gentleness and manliness. He touched me, Willow. In a way that's hard for me to name. But it felt so wonderful to be needed, to be wanted. Do ye ken?"

Shona glanced at Willow. Willow's eyes had closed, she moaned something unintelligible, and her breathing had steadied to a slow and even rhythm.

Smiling, Shona got up from the narrow bed, and adjusted the blanket over Willow's shoulder. Once in her own bed, Shona rested her head on the pillow and relived the events by the brook.

The memory of his kiss lingered, as fresh as if it had happened just a moment ago. The feel of his manly lips pressed against hers, his fingers threaded in her hair, his palms squeezing her shoulder and cupping her bottom. But her hands tasted of him as well . . . wide shoulders that stretched the fabric of his fine wool coat, a chest that was hard as Highland granite, and a face that softened at her slightest touch. She chuckled as she remembered trying to threaten him if he got her all wet. Faith, but that kiss really *did* get her all wet.

He had told her that he'd forgotten himself. So had she, and indeed, that had been the best part of it all. She'd forgotten she was naught but a parish apprentice, forgotten she lacked beauty and grace, forgotten she was a *slaighteur*. He saw beyond all these things, and held her in high esteem anyway.

She hadn't wanted to stop. She hadn't wanted it to *ever* stop. But to give of herself so freely would lessen her value in his eyes. And that she was *not* willing to let happen.

And as slumber overtook her, she marveled at the foolishness of trying to seduce a man who was clearly trying to seduce her.

EIGHT

A blood-chilling sound ripped Shona from her dreams. She awoke with a start, disoriented by the sound.

Willow was screaming.

Shona's heart pounded an uneven staccato as she scanned the unfamiliar room. The room was dimly illuminated by pink threads of dawn. Her sister sat up in bed, fists clenched to her eyes. Shona's eyes darted around the room for danger, but the room was empty.

Another of Willow's nightmares.

Shona flew to her sister's bed and hugged Willow from behind, the only thing that ever chased away the panic. Sloppy tears trailed down Willow's cheeks as Shona shushed the nightmare away. Willow finally quieted down, but Eric, woken by the screaming, bawled shrilly from his crib.

Then, over Eric's crying, she heard footsteps down the hall.

Shona's heart skipped a beat. Eric would wake up the entire household.

She pulled Willow out of bed, hastily wiping her sister's wet face. "Come, Will. Take the child and calm him doon. Hurry!"

Shona lifted Eric out of his crib and handed him to Willow—barely a moment before the door burst open.

Conall stood in the doorway with a lit candelabra, his dressing gown hastily tied. "What's happened?"

If Conall ever learned that his son's nursemaid suffered these occasional night terrors, he would dismiss Willow on the spot.

"I'm very sorry," said Shona. "I woke up and saw a shadow upon the wall. In my sleepiness, I thought it was an intruder. I screamed, and it woke the bairn."

"Is Eric all right?" Conall advanced upon his son.

"Aye. He's just afeard, that's all. Willow will settle him doon now. Ye can go back to bed."

Ignoring her, Conall took the blubbering child into his arms to soothe him. But the cooing words escaped him when he looked down into Willow's face. "Willow, why are you crying?"

Shona stepped between them. "My screams must have—"

Conall's hand sprang into the air, and Shona's explanation died in her mouth.

"Willow?" he repeated.

Willow cast her face downward as she wiped the unruly tears from her cheeks. "I had a nightmare, my lord. It frightened me. I'm very sorry for disturbing ye. Very sorry for waking the bairn. It won't happen again."

Conall turned his attention to his sobbing child. "Hush, now. It's all right. Big boys don't cry."

They each put on their dressing gowns as Conall bounced the child gently on his arm.

"All better now?" he asked the child. Eric's face was wet and his bottom lip jutted forward. "You go back to bed now, and Willow will get you some warm milk."

As Conall put the child back in the crib, Willow darted out of the nursery.

Shona turned to him. "Look, I ken what ye're thinking, but—" She bit off any protest when she saw the sharp scowl on his face.

"I'll have a word with you in the morning. In my study. Eight o'clock sharp."

It was bad enough she couldn't get back to sleep. But to have Conall's fury hanging over her head like the sword of Damocles was more than Shona could bear. The minutes ticked by painfully until in frustration she threw off the coverlet altogether.

She had done what she thought was right. Even Willow had expressed her gratitude to Shona for trying to cover up for her. But in the end, it proved pointless. Willow was incapable of bearing herself up under her betters. Just as a sheep becomes paralyzed with fear once it's been turned on its back, offering no resistance to a predator, so did Willow to the strength of those in authority over her.

Before her appointed meeting with Conall, Shona determined she would use all her advantages. She put on her best dress—a blue and white frock that everyone at church always said did her proud—and descended the stairs to his study.

Although she was punctual—she knew he liked that—Conall and Stewart were already there when she rapped on the open door. Their hushed conversation silenced altogether, heightening her nervousness.

"Come." Conall sat behind an imposing desk, his face lost in the morning sun that burned into her eyes from the window behind him. But when she approached, it was impossible to mistake the severe line of his mouth or his rigid posture.

He leaned an elbow on the surface of the desk. "You disappoint me, Shona."

The words punched her. "Why?"

"You deceived me last night. And I have no tolerance for liars."

Stewart's eyes brightened, a lascivious glee bubbling up from him. "Good Lord! Just what *did* happen last night?"

Conall swung irritated eyes at his brother, silencing him. "Now, Shona, why did you pretend to be the cause of the incident last night?"

"I had to. We would have gotten Eric to settle doon soon enough, but when ye burst into the room, I had to think of something."

Stewart turned to his brother. "You went into their room last night? You sly dog."

"Stewart, please. Shona, I put you in a position of trust. That means that you have an obligation to be completely honest with me at all times. Especially when it concerns my son."

"Yer son was in no real danger."

"That is not for you to decide. I expect to be apprised of all matters that relate to my household."

"All bairns cry. You mustn't get overwrought by it."

"Overwrought? He was jolted out of his skin by your sister's screaming in the middle of the night!"

Stewart turned to Shona. "Willow was screaming? What frightened her?"

"It was just a night terror. It does no' happen often. Now and again, perhaps . . . if she tries too hard to forget the memory of that Day, it'll burrow itself into her slumber. It only came upon her because Eric reminded her of Camran . . . the last time we saw him."

Conall hung his head. "I have every sympathy for what you girls went through. But I cannot allow my son to be contaminated by the distress of that episode."

Contaminated. That word shot an arrow into her heart. Indignation surged through her, just like when some stranger spat the word *slaighteur* at her. Against her impulses, she swallowed a retort. Right now, she had a mission to accomplish . . . she had to keep Willow from being dismissed. There was no safer place in this household than minding the master's son. If Willow was put out to work in the fields, there was no telling what might happen to her.

Conall rubbed his forehead. "I'm afraid I'm going to have to find Willow another situation."

Shona flew to the desk. "Ye must no' do that. She's sweet on yer son, and she loves looking after him. And Eric is safe with her. Truly, ye've naught to worry aboot. She'll no' have another night terror—no' for a long while, anyway."

"I cannot take that chance."

"Please don't send her to work somewhere else. She's so happy being Eric's nursemaid, and she is so grateful to ye for trusting her with that important station. Ye'll no' find a better maid in all the county, I promise ye. What's more," she said, measuring her words carefully, "I'd be grateful, too."

The weight of her meaning was not lost upon him. A momentary spark of lust skipped across his eyes before he returned to the matter at hand. "I'll consider it."

"Thank ye." Shona swallowed hard. "My lord."

The honorific made his eyebrow jump. She hoped it appeased him enough to keep Willow. Before she inadvertently said something to change his mind, she turned to go.

"I'm not through with you yet."

The voice echoed with authority, making Shona face him once more.

Conall leaned back in his chair. "There's still the matter of your deception."

Heat poured into her face. Only then did Shona realize that Willow was not the only one needing protecting.

Unsatisfied with being merely a spectator, Stewart decided to chime in. Hands clasped autocratically at the fold of his impeccable waistcoat, he faced Shona like a magistrate and clucked his tongue. "This is very serious indeed. You may shut your doors against a thief, as the saying goes, but not against a liar. I'm afraid we must punish you severely."

"Stewart . . ."

Stewart raised imperious brows. "Conall, I advise a half-dozen strokes of the cane, bent over the desk. I shall watch."

Aghast, she eyed Conall. "What?"

Conall pursed his lips. "I'm not going to do that, Stewart."

"All right, then. I'll do it."

Conall rolled his eyes. "No, you won't, either. My brother has a singular mind. Stewart, go in to breakfast. I want to have a few words in private with Shona."

A sly, knowing look came over Stewart's face. "A

private lesson, eh? Very well. I still think you would have fared better under my tutelage than under his."

The door closed behind him.

Conall leaned his tall frame upon his desk. "I apologize for Stewart. He's an unfortunate amalgamation of excessive drink, permissive women, and too little accountability."

"I'm sorry," she said.

"So am I."

"I meant aboot lying to ye. It was wrong of me. I only did it to protect Willow."

He reached out and took her hand in his. "On no account should you feel the need to protect yourselves from me. I hope you know that."

A hint of a smile touched her lips. "I'm beginning to."

His blue eyes warmed over. "Good." A half-smile lifted one cheek. It was utterly mesmerizing how expressive his face was. The gentle side of his character was always just under the hardened surface, and the more time she spent with him, the more he revealed it just for her. What delight there was in sharing a moment with this handsome, principled—and forgiving—man.

"And speaking of protection, you're not going to need this." He tugged at the sheathed knife that hung from a leather strap around her waist. "Take it off."

"But—" Like her shoes or her chemise, the *sgian* was an article that she never forgot to put on. She was unwilling to disappoint him any further—but equally, she was unwilling to be parted from it. "I canna be without it."

"I'm afraid I must insist. I have an aversion to

weapons. Their purpose is only to kill or maim, and as a doctor, I despise what they are meant to do. Besides, I don't want that thing in the same room as my son."

Reluctantly, Shona unhitched the clasp of her leather belt, and handed it to him. He placed it inside an ornately carved wooden box on top of his desk.

"Thank you," he said. "Now, can you learn to trust in *my* protection instead?"

"I'll try."

"Right," he began, changing the tenor of the conversation, "before you head out to continue surveying the farms, I've got a task for you to do." He went to one of the shelves and pulled out a polished wooden box. He placed it into her outstretched hands, and the weight of it nearly bent her over.

"As near as I can figure out, these rent receipts go back about five years. I want you to catalog them and document them into the main ledger. Here," he added, dropping a thick book on top of her load. "This used to be the most tedious part of my job, but no longer."

"Why is that?" she asked, trying to keep the book from slipping to the floor.

"Because I just made it the most tedious part of *your* job."

She gritted her teeth, illumination dawning on her that he was not about to let her get away without paying the consequences for her transgression. She dropped the box onto the desk, before it went crashing to the floor.

He strode to the door. "I'll have some breakfast sent in to you. And, I daresay, some lunch. By dinnertime, I expect you to have that ledger ready for my inspection."

She shot daggers from her eyes at his retreating back.

"Oh, and Shona?" he said from the doorway.

"Aye?" she replied with her most imperious countenance.

His head dipped as he shot her a warning look. "Lie to me again and I'll take Stewart's advice."

NINE

Summer faded gloriously.

Flowers spread across every untilled field, their fragrance filling the warm wind. Leaves shimmered in the trees, where myriad songbirds flittered. The land, like the people, came alive during this season.

Sunday was always a special day. No one on the estate worked, and after services at the kirk, the day was devoted to simple food and rest. Just after noon, Shona and Willow walked Eric across a field of thick, emerald grass. As the boy held on to both their hands, they swung him between them, making him giggle with glee. Conall carried the picnic basket, smiling at the spectacle.

At the crest of the hill, they found a sunny, warm spot, and Conall spread the blanket upon the ground. Tiny butterflies no bigger than a fingernail fluttered upon the lush grass, and Eric, fascinated, staggered after them while Shona arranged bread, cheese, and fruit upon the plates.

The four of them ate contentedly. Shona stuffed herself full, then lay on her side like a lioness overfed on gazelle. Eric knelt beside her as Shona popped blueberries into his mouth.

"Look up there, Eric," she said, pointing at the sky. "See that cloud? It looks just like a wee rabbit."

"Rabbit," the little boy repeated, gazing up.

Conall turned his eyes to the sky. "I can't see it."

"Up there . . . just in front of the sun."

He brought a hand up to shield his eyes. "That's a mouse," he said as he popped a piece of cheese into his mouth.

"Peculiar," she said, turning amazed eyes upon him. "You don't *look* like a simpleton."

"Shona!" exclaimed Willow, giving her a reproving smack on the leg.

He flicked Shona a sardonic glance. "Perhaps you could fight your nature and be pleasant for a change. Just for one day, mind. I wouldn't want you to strain yourself."

She smiled wickedly. "Very well. For the sake of the boy." She looked back up at the cloud. "Och, 'tis nothing now, it moved so fast. You know, that rabbit-cloud was probably in England this very morning, and in France before that. I would no' mind being a cloud, seeing the whole world so quickly from on high."

A crease formed between his brows. "Sounds a bit lonely."

"I shouldn't be."

"The trouble with clouds is that they're not connected to anything or anyone, and they never stay in one place for long. Is that what you desire?"

"I dinna know. I hold a candle to the hope that we'll find Camran one day. I've not given much thought to what will happen after that."

"Do you plan to marry, have a family?"

"Aye, I do. If I can make a bairn as bonnie as this one." She tickled Eric and he giggled.

Conall balanced his elbow upon the knee at his chest. "Well, you're young yet, I suppose. You've the comfort of years ahead of you. But appreciate them all, for one never knows how long they will last." His voice trailed off, and he grew thoughtful.

It was not hard to discern where his thoughts had turned. These past few weeks working alongside him had shown her what a disciplined and industrious person he was. And though they always enjoyed some friendly ribbing, he was seldom so reflective as he'd just become.

"Eric's mother . . . how did she die?"

His sharp intake of breath made his chest expand wider. It took many moments, as he amassed his regrets, before he spoke. "After Eric was born, Christina became ill. She developed puerperal sepsis." He must have seen her puzzled expression. "Childbed fever."

"I'm sorry," she said.

"I am, too," echoed Willow.

"How long did she live?" asked Shona.

"Not long. Four days. But long enough to have held her son, for which I am grateful."

Shona caressed the boy's soft brown hair. Eric was busy piling blades of grass upon her hip. How tragic that Conall's wife never got to know what a beautiful, delightful, intelligent boy her son would become.

"Time goes by quickly," Conall said. "With each tick of the clock, the years evaporate. Once, I was twenty-five and beginning my medical practice. Tick. Then I'm getting married to Christina. Tick. She gives birth to a son." His gaze disappeared into the horizon. "She's alive. Tick. She's dead."

Willow and Shona looked at each other, sharing in that knowledge. Shona silently communicated something to Willow, and Willow immediately understood.

"'Tis time for Eric's nap," Willow announced. "With yer permission, o'course, my lord."

He nodded, but he was still lost in memories long gone. A breeze gently ruffled the snowy cravat beneath his clean-shaven chin.

Willow stood, took Eric in her arms, and disappeared down the hill.

Shona sat up and poured some more wine into his glass. "I know what it's like to have someone ye love die. It feels like a part of ye has been ripped off, and ye think that the bleeding will never stop."

Conall's faraway gaze slowly focused on her.

"But in time," she continued, "it does. The wound will heal, though the scar will always remain."

He nodded stiffly, and took the glass.

"I suppose 'tis a blessing that the memories of the loved one become all the stronger. I remember," she said, a wistful grin emerging on her face, "when I was a wee lass, my father bought some japanning to blacken a table he'd made. I loved the look of the shiny black paint, so I used it to write curse words on the side of the barn.

He chuckled. "Now why doesn't that surprise me?"

"As luck would have it, at that moment, the parson rode up for Sunday lunch, and he discovered what I'd done before my da did. Whew! My da's face got fairly purple with shame and anger. Anger at me for drawing the dirty words, and at my brothers for teaching them to me."

She tossed back her head. "I thought I was going to get a thrashing. But I remember my da, he dropped to one knee and said, 'I want ye to know that I love ye very much. But I've no love for what ye've done. So now ye're going to fix it, and then all will be well again.' And he gave me a bucket of whitewash and made me paint over the bad words. But no matter how many times I whitewashed that barn, the damned black paint still came through."

He shook his head. "Clearly, the lesson didn't take."

A laugh, high and pure, burst from her. "So it didn't. But ye see, the memory of my da is like that. No matter how much time passes, no matter how much happens to try to obscure it, that memory is still there. And it's a memory I never want to go away. For even though I'd lost my father's favor that day, it made me happy to know that no matter what I did, I could never lose his love."

Conall's gaze faded into the distance again, the blueness of his eyes indistinguishable from the color in the summer sky. "The memory of my wife is a little different, Shona. Christina has become rather like the imagery in a stained-glass window. There are pieces of our time together I remember fondly, but the whole of it is disjointed and patchwork . . . and broken."

His words were puzzling, and she couldn't decipher their hidden meaning. Had they been locked in a loveless marriage? Did he somehow resent his wife for becoming ill and leaving him adrift with a motherless son? Had he tried to save her, only to discover that his medical skill was incapable of defeating death? There was an emotional charge to him, like the air just before a thunderstorm.

"After the death of my wife, I couldn't drink enough to drown out the thoughts of her. There is nothing in the entire canon of known medical science that can heal a broken heart." His eyes bored into hers, looking for answers. "Tell me, Shona, after all you've been through, how on earth are you able to go on?"

Shona's eyes trailed to the ground beneath her. "I don't know," she said with a shrug of her shoulder. "Perhaps it's because I have fallen so very far, there's only up from here."

He reached out a hand and brushed her cheek with his thumb. "My God, I've never met anyone so resilient . . . and yet so fragile. Despite all that's happened, there remains a wellspring of hope in you." A smile spread across his face. "You do me good, Shona MacAslan."

She didn't know whether it was the sound of her true name on his lips or the gentle caress of his fingers. But there was a powerful quickening in her heart that made the entire world diminish, leaving only her . . . and only him.

He stood and held out his hand to her. "Walk with me."

She put her hand in his, and he helped her arise from the ground.

Their stroll took them across the field, down to the tree-lined path, and toward the river. Since that kiss they shared by the burn, there had been no more. He'd been the consummate landlord, and she the dutiful factor. Yet though their relationship was mostly professional, they had grown very close. He spent more time with her than with anyone else—even his own family—and she relished both their conversations and their arguments.

But the memory of that kiss was never far from her thoughts, and every time she looked at his handsome face, she felt the ghostly sensation of his lips pressed against hers. Time and again she wondered if his kiss had been merely an impulsive reaction to their unintentional physical closeness . . . or if it had truly been a declaration of affection.

Now, as he wedged her hand in the crook of his elbow and they walked side by side, Shona began to feel it once again. The lightening of her steps, the breath catching in her chest, the silent trilling of her heart. This was not the way a man treats a lowly dairy maid or a competent factor, but how he treats a woman and a lady worthy of hanging on his arm.

The sound of the rushing water grew louder as they approached the old bridge. The gray and brown bricks were worn smooth where countless carriages had driven past. At the far end of the bridge was an abandoned tollhouse, a narrow structure built out of the same sixteenth-century stone. Moss painted the stone a bright green, and a heavy wooden door was held askew by broken black strap hinges. They walked to the middle of the bridge and watched the frothy water run underneath.

"Shona, I'm a man of science and study. The poetry of the fair sex has always eluded my understanding. But you . . . you're different from most women. I detect in you . . . I don't know . . . a kindred spirit. It's as if you're not really a woman to me after all."

Her mouth fell open as his words winded her. Shona gripped the edge of the bridge, unsteady. Gazing down at the white water speeding below, she could feel her own femininity washing away as well. Iona had always warned her of being too forward, too opinionated, too assertive, because these were aggressive masculine qualities. She had never listened, and this was now the result of her stubbornness. Foolish, foolish lass.

"Other ladies are so full of artifice and coyness. But you, you're the most genuine soul I know. And I can't get you out of my mind. I find myself desiring your presence, your company . . . and your embrace."

A thread of hope lifted her plummeting heart. "Embrace? Did ye say 'embrace'?"

"Yes. That kiss we shared . . . I find myself hungering for more. Because of one thing I'm certain. We are more together than each of us is apart."

"Ye mean, ye find me . . . desirable?" She bit her lip hopefully.

He smiled down at her. "I suppose that's the most decent word one can put to it, yes."

Happiness bubbled up from within her until she thought she would burst with it. She threw her arms around Conall's neck, strangling a surprised exclamation from him.

He chuckled. "Should I assume that you reciprocate my affections?"

"Aye. I never thought ye would feel as I do."

"Could you not sense it?"

His closeness, yes. His desire, never. "I would not have believed it if I had."

"Why is that?"

"It has always been the way. Wherever Willow and I are together, her beauty eclipses mine. Any man with a pulse desires to pluck her first."

His expression softened. "Then I am glad for my sake, since I believe I have the fairer flower in my arms."

She stood on her toes and placed a kiss upon his lips. He wrapped his arms around her and squeezed, until she could almost hang in his arms and not touch the floor.

Their kiss was no longer one of exploration, timid and restrained as the first had been. Now it was a declaration, bold and eager. Her lips slid over his, tasting the strawberries that still lingered upon them. Her heart was trilling again, beating a fast staccato that propelled her to show him how much she liked him. For the first time in her life, she felt as though who she was ceased to be a liability. He knew everything that was wrong about her, and he liked her anyway.

She felt free, wild, and her body was responding in kind. Her enthusiasm must have provoked him, for Conall gripped her by her hair and pulled her head to one side. He began to suck upon her neck, and his hot mouth made her skin tingle all down her side. Her hands splayed upon the stone wall of the bridge, their roughness scratching her palms. The extremes of his hot tongue upon her skin, followed by the cooling of the wind, maddened her beyond reason.

His mouth descended upon the base of her throat, and his thick hair feathered across her chin. His large hand came up from her waist and flattened itself upon her breast, sparking a deeper passion.

He straightened and kissed her fiercely upon the mouth. She felt him then. Upon her tummy, his passion had stiffened for her, and then all presence of mind was lost. The sun above, the torrential waters below, the song of nature all around . . . and now the powerful beast in her arms. Her body began a drumbeat march toward pleasure, and she had no power to stop it.

He pulled away, his eyes smoky with unfulfilled desire.

"Come with me," he said. Not waiting for her answer, he grabbed her wrist and pulled her in the direction of the abandoned tollhouse.

He tugged on the broken door and pulled her in. She was blind inside the dark, windowless room, but once her eyes adjusted from the light of day, she could see clearly. The space was little more than a kitchen and sitting room combined, with a stale fireplace against one wall and a spiral staircase leading to the floor above, which was no doubt a bedroom. The room was littered with the debris of forgotten furniture, like a long-neglected attic.

Conall began to lift some debris from a table. Shona came up behind him and wrapped her arms around his chest.

"'Tis a cozy nest for two."

He tossed an empty birdcage onto the floor. "It's a bit cramped, but it will do."

She smiled wickedly and let her hands wander downward, smoothing over the tented panel between his legs. "Nonsense. Plenty of room for a hen and her cock."

He stilled, and she could feel his chest expanding at her touch. "By God, you're a brazen wench. Come here."

He lifted her in the air, and plopped her down upon the table. Her legs fell open, and he wedged himself between them. She smiled into his face, his composure completely lost. His jaw clenched with steely determination, fighting to delay his satisfaction. Though she herself was humming with desire, she couldn't help smiling.

"What's so amusing?" he demanded.

"Ye," she answered. "I'm enjoying seeing yer animal instinct take over all that intellect."

The line deepened at his jaw. "If it's animal you want, it's animal you'll get." He tugged her hair back, forcing her neck exposed. His breath puffed on her neck, making sparks skip down her side.

She put her hands on his smooth cheeks and put a kiss upon his mouth. She drank in the scent of his breath, wine mixed with berries, arousing every sense she had. They spoke a common language now, each understanding the desire of the other. She could feel him thick and hard between her legs, his manhood urging to break free of the trousers.

He tugged at the ribbons lacing her bodice at the back. "I've wanted you since the moment I first saw you," he whispered in her ear, the warmth making her skin tingle. "Soaked to the skin, smudged from your tasks, all hiss and spit. No matter how you behave or what you wear, I will always see that spitfire in the rain."

That he could have wanted her since their first meeting, when she looked her worst, filled her with a dense happiness.

It had happened. Her heart was lost to him forever. And there was no way of getting it back.

He kissed her smile as her bodice loosened. He tugged it down over her shoulders, revealing a web-thin chemise underneath. His warm hand covered her breast, the thumb gently stroking the nipple.

The anticipation began to build between her legs. Her sheath ached for him, and her body moistened as if weeping at his absence. The table vibrated from the power of the rushing waters below, which she could hear just beyond the ancient stone walls.

He unbuttoned his trousers and freed his stiffened member. From a nest of dark, wiry hair, his cock sprang up, powerful and hungry. Even in the dark room, Shona was able to appreciate the considerable size of the plum-tipped cock.

"Is it going to hurt overmuch?"

"Is what going to hurt overmuch?"

"Our joining."

He chuckled. "I assure you it will not hurt me." Suddenly, his brows came together. "Is there a reason it should hurt you?"

"I have heard of such things. We shall see. Come to me, Conall."

He pulled back a little. "Wait. Is this your first time to . . . ?"

"Meddle with a man? Aye. And I'm glad 'twill be with you." Her smile dissolved. "Conall, what's wrong?"

His jaw clenched as he backed away. "I thought you were . . . I believed you were no longer a maiden."

"In a few moments, I shan't be," she said, smiling. "Come to me, love."

He began to button up his trousers.

"What are ye doing? Why are ye stopping? Did I do something wrong?"

"No," he said, shaking his head. "I did. I made . . . assumptions again."

"What assumptions?"

"That you had already been with a man."

She became indignant. "So what if I haven't? I've spent a lifetime on a farm. I assure ye I know how creatures fuck."

He chuckled, his cheeks flushing. "So you do."

"Is there something ye require of me? I will learn. Teach me."

"No." He sat beside her on the table, massaging the

hunger from his face. "It is a gentleman's code. A gentleman never takes a maiden unless she is his to keep. And unless a vicar says so, Shona MacAslan, you are not mine."

Shona did not know what she was supposed to do, or how she was supposed to soothe away the raging desire in her young body. But instinct spoke louder than protocol. "Perhaps soon we will be. Take me, Conall. Please. I have need of ye now."

He gave her a crooked smile as he cupped her face in one hand. "All right. As you already know how creatures mate, let me show you how *lovers* do it."

He kissed her, bringing them together once more. Here, in this forgotten place, it felt as if they were the only two people in the whole world. And yet she felt safe with him. Whatever code he professed, he could have broken it and no one would know—least of all her. But this remarkable man was true to himself, even when no one was watching.

Slowly, he pulled down her chemise. Her nipple came alive under the gentle scrape of the fabric. And when he finally exposed it, he took it into his hot mouth. She groaned. It was as if he had tried to douse a candle with kerosene. Instead of sating the vicious need, his ministrations fed it until she was on fire for him.

Once again, the heat between her legs began to roil. She began to pant, but that only seemed to fan the flame. She was ready to be joined with him. So she lifted her leg toward him, hoping to show her readiness and ease his passage. But once again he frustrated her by pulling back. She moaned piteously as she watched him kneel upon the floor, amid empty crates and discarded candle holders.

She watched in fascination as he kissed the arch of her slippered foot. Then he lifted the hem of her Sunday dress and kissed the inside of her stockinged ankle. His other hand slipped up underneath her skirt and slid over her other knee. None of this she could see. Her dress bunched upon her lap while his hands did their deeds in secret. But oh, what a delightful sensation!

She expected him to stand and bare his member once more, but that didn't happen. Instead his mouth kissed her knees, then her thigh just below her garter, and then he went higher—

She put a stilling hand upon his head. "What are ye doing?"

He smirked. "I mean to kiss you."

Her mouth fell open. "Doon there?"

His eyes crinkled in amusement. "Aye," he said, mocking her. "I promise you'll like it."

She shook her head, a thick tendril falling down over her exposed breast. "But that's not . . . how can ye . . . I do no' think—"

"Shh. Let me show you how it can be."

Shona's head swam with the strangeness of it. The woman's part was for the man's part. It didn't seem right that he would be able to see her private place up close with his own eyes. And to put his mouth upon it? She wasn't sure she had any liking for the idea. As he brought his face between her legs once more, she decided to tell him that—

"Oh!" she squeaked. His soft lips had connected with the very part of her that had been paining her with need. His hands pressed upon her inner thighs, locking her legs open.

"Um," she said helplessly as she did as she was

bid. It was strange, to be sure, but far from unpleasant. Suddenly, his lips closed around her nub, and she gasped.

Her whole body came alive, and only one thought came to her mind. *More*.

She leaned back upon the table, her nails raking the decrepit wood on its surface. Though her exposed back connected with the cold stone wall, no sensation could detract from the amazing feeling that he was giving her down there.

His tongue ringed around her nub as nimbly as if it had been a finger. Though she could only see the top of his sandy head, she marveled at what he was doing. But desire began to build up inside her, and the newness and wonderment of it diminished. Her body now demanded satisfaction. Her greatest pleasure came when his tongue flicked up the right side of her. Instinctively, she entwined her fingers into his soft hair and guided him in the direction she wanted him to go. And bless him, he knew just what to do. His tongue began to flick at the spot that rapidly pulsed fire throughout her body.

She panted at the sensation of his concentrated ministrations. Then he introduced a new sensation—his finger into her cunny—and she nearly swooned with the pleasure of it. His long finger pushed past the ring of her maidenhead, made slick by her arousal, and stroked her on the inside. The combination of sensations elevated her to new heights of intoxication. He pulled out, and then pushed in two fingers. Now she knew what it was like to be fucked, and it was Conall MacEwan who fired her blood this way. Within moments, pleasure splashed upon her in hot waves.

Her back arched as the spasms took control of her. Her fingers curled into his wavy hair.

He emerged from between her legs, and said one word. "Ouch."

She blinked at him as she gasped for breath, her throat parched. She was still blinded by a haze of desire. "Eh?" she managed.

"Would you do me the very great favor of unclenching your fingers from my hair?"

"Oh," she breathed as she let him go. "Sorry."

He smiled. "Are you contented now?"

She nodded dumbly, while he gently straightened her dress.

He sat down next to her on the table. "You taste absolutely delicious."

She smiled weakly. "That was . . . I feel . . ." She swallowed hard. "I like that very much."

He chuckled. "Good. If you're a good girl, I just may give you a command performance."

"What do ye call that?"

He put his coat back on. "I'll tell you what . . . as you love dirty words so much, I'll give you the pleasure of creating one for it."

Though her mind was still addled by the pleasure of his attentions, she regretted that he was as yet unfulfilled. "What aboot ye? How may I return the pleasure?"

He began to wind his cravat around his neck. "I shall be happy to give you that lesson—another day. I intend to take my time on that one, and teach you properly. Apprentice."

Apprentice. She didn't half mind learning more of *that*. She straightened her garments, growing excited about the anticipation that surged inside her at another such encounter. Perhaps they could return to this toll-house, which had just become her favorite place on the whole estate.

"Turn around," he commanded, and she stood facing away from him. He tightened the laces on her bodice, cinching her breasts decently behind the fabric.

"I despise secrecy. At the first opportunity, I want to make this relationship a formal one."

Happiness welled up inside her. Despite her misguided attempt to marry Conall only to make herself free of him, she realized that if he ever did propose, she'd probably never leave him.

She turned around. "I'm over the moon for ye, Conall MacEwan," she whispered.

"And I for you, Shona MacAslan."

Horace Hartopp's carriage climbed the steep roads through the mountainous Highland terrain. Being dismissed from Conall MacEwan's service stung his pride, and he never suffered these slights gladly. He contented himself with the knowledge that in the end, MacEwan would regret his actions.

He gazed out of the carriage window. He'd been on this tiresome journey for the last three days, and the last day and a half of it was spent traveling through McCullough territory. Duncan McCullough was one of the most powerful men in Scotland, whose wealth was derived from the countless acres and villages he owned throughout the country. He had an insatiable appetite for land, and when he saw something he wanted, he relentlessly pursued it until the deed bore his name.

The rocky trails now jarring his weakened carriage

wheels were McCullough's, and Hartopp cursed every one of them. But this trip promised to be a lucrative one, and he had to make sure that he delivered the news to Duncan McCullough personally. Before anyone else discovered the treasure he'd found at Ballencrieff.

Ramh Droighionn Castle reigned atop a high hill surrounded by thick forests on one side and green pastures on the other. Hartopp rode past a fold of long-horned Scottish cattle, their profuse shaggy hair obscuring their curious eyes. At the end of his journey was a fortress built at least four hundred years earlier, and it was still guarded by heavy stone walls that encircled a courtyard scattered with smaller buildings. Hartopp could sense the memory of Highland warriors of centuries past mustering here for battle.

Once Hartopp alighted, a kilted man came to greet him.

"Good afternoon, sir." A long beard, drizzled with white, dripped from the man's face.

"Afternoon. My name is Horace Hartopp. I'm here to see Duncan McCullough."

"Have ye an appointment, sir?"

"No, but I think the laird will be made very happy by the message I bring."

The man scratched his cheek. "I'll tell him. Wait in the hall if ye will."

Ramh Droighionn Castle was deceptive from the outside. The antiquated exterior belied the grandeur of the tasteful interior. Hartopp was led to a large hall, with veined marble floors unfolding toward sculpted wooden walls. Mounted upon the wall above a fireplace was what at first appeared to be a sunburst sculpture—but on closer inspection, Hartopp realized it was a circle of muskets.

On the opposite wall, fanning above an arched alcove, were dozens of metal-tipped spears, swords, and arrows, arranged like the tail of some warrior peacock.

Within minutes, he saw a man of about fifty emerge from a room beneath the elbow of the dark wooden staircase. He was wearing a kilt bearing a tartan that Hartopp had grown familiar with during his journey, as many people in these parts seemed to bear that sett. Behind him was a younger version of him, a handsome man about half his father's age, with the same brown hair and navy eyes. Both were exceedingly tall men, a trait common among Highlanders. Alarmingly, they were both armed with bow and quiver, and they each had a long musket slung over their brawny shoulders.

"Who the de'il are ye?" asked the elder.

"We have not met, my lord McCullough," he said, effecting a curt bow. "My name is Horace Hartopp. I am of late the factor to a gentleman laird in the Lowlands."

"Ye've come a long way." His voice rumbled within his massive chest.

"Aye. And a tiresome journey it has been. But I made all haste to meet ye, because I believe I've found the elusive treasure ye've been seeking for nearly ten years."

The man was intrigued, but his expression never betrayed it. "And what is that?"

Hartopp smiled. "The MacAslan lasses."

TEN

Duncan McCullough was a most insidious man. Though outwardly cordial and open, he fashioned his words carefully to elicit a desired response, and there was a motive behind every handshake and minute gesture of hospitality. Perhaps, Hartopp reasoned, it was how he was able to amass such a large fortune without much opposition—at least not from anyone who dared to be vocal about it.

"Ye're no doubt tired of being squeezed into that cramped carriage. My son Brandubh and I were just about to do some hunting. Walk with us."

Only two things would have relieved the ache in Hartopp's stiff joints—a good rest or a good walk. He nodded, and followed the McCullough men out of the house and into the forest. Trailing behind them were two servants who carried ammunition and bottles of whisky.

"The MacAslan gels," he said, staring straight out ahead of him. "I've been looking for that ragamuffin pair since they ran away from my man Seldomridge more than a decade ago. Where did they turn up?"

Hartopp knew better than to reveal his hand. The information he possessed had a monetary value. Once the information was out, there was no need to pay him for it.

"Down south, just north of England. I know precisely where they are, and where ye can find them."

"That's good news indeed," McCullough said. "I'll want to know. But how did ye find them?"

"Accidentally. I found them working on a remote farm."

"And how came ye to know that I was looking for them?"

Many had heard about the justice meted out to the MacAslan family. It served as a cautionary tale for anyone even considering not showing for battle. But Hartopp had learned of the slaughter directly from the chief of the McBray clan. One of the daughters of the chief was to be married to Hamish, the eldest MacAslan son. The McBray lass was so distraught at learning of her fiancé's murder that she took her own life.

Hartopp cast him a deferential glance. "Word spreads, McCullough. In the Highlands, everyone knows yer business."

He displayed a smile. "Glad to hear it."

They had quietly footed through the forest, careful not to step upon any twigs or brittle leaves lest they scare away any game. Finally, they spotted a pair of beautiful young does munching in a clearing. Stealthily, Brandubh braced the rifle against his shoulder and took aim. As the men silently watched, Brandubh pulled the trigger. The sound of the rifle exploded in Hartopp's ears, and a puff of smoke burst from the flintlock. Brandubh's shot found its mark, crippling one of the does. They bolted, one of them hobbling away.

"Did ye see? I clipped her in the flank," Brandubh crowed. "Let's go after her."

"Och! She'll get far before she'll tire. And my legs won't sustain me. Go on. Follow the trail of blood. Ye'll find her soon enough."

The younger McCullough took off running through the forest to finish off his quarry.

"I trained him well, did I not?" asked Duncan. "Do you have any children of yer own, Hartopp?"

"No doubt, but none that I'll claim," he quipped, to Duncan's rich laughter.

"Brandubh's an ambitious cur, more than his da was before him. He's just as keen to grow the McCullough holdings, but that boy has a head for politics. I canna wait to see what will happen to the Council when I turn Brandubh loose upon them."

It was not pride in his son that Hartopp saw in Duncan McCullough's eyes. It was bloodlust.

"Now," he burst, changing the subject. "I sense ye've come with a proposition for me. Let's have it."

"I'm a loyal man, my lord. The moment I laid eyes upon the girls, and realized who they were, I knew that they must be returned to ye. I remembered yer reputation for rewarding such loyalty."

"And how can ye be sure these are the right Mac-Aslan girls?"

"If ye're after Shona and Willow MacAslan, daughters of John MacAslan of Ravens Craig, then these are the right ones." Hartopp relished seeing Duncan practically drooling for the prize that Hartopp held. "And they bear the mark of the *slaighteur*."

Duncan licked his lips. "And where might I find them?"

Hartopp could almost feel his balls grow. "I'll be

happy to take ye to them, my lord. For a fee of ten thousand pounds."

Duncan nodded his head, which had only started to thread with white. He kicked at a loose stone on the ground, overturning it to reveal a swarm of slithering worms.

Hartopp watched him do it. And by the time their eyes met again, the end of Duncan's rifle was pointed at Hartopp's belly.

The blood began to pound thickly in Hartopp's head. His manic gaze flew from the muzzle of the rifle to Duncan's face to the servants who pretended to be absorbed in the study of their shoes.

"Do ye know what happens to men who try to get the better of me, Hartopp? Their satisfaction never lasts long."

Hartopp had two daggers on him, but he could reach neither one of them swiftly enough to defend himself against a man with a rifle. His only sure weapon was Duncan's own greed. "Shoot me and ye'll never get the information ye need."

Duncan's forehead dimpled with incredulity. "Shoot ye? I'm not going to shoot ye, man. Ye're the one that's going to take me to the MacAslan gels. For a fee of two thousand. Isn't that the bargain betwixt us?"

Hartopp let out a ragged breath. "Aye. That's the bargain."

"Good. Let's drink on it."

A servant immediately poured two goblets full of whisky and served them up. The two men eyed each other over the rim of their glasses.

At that moment, breathless from running, Brandubh returned. "The fucking doe got beyond me."

Duncan clapped Brandubh on the shoulder. "No matter, son. She'll not be able to run forever. Leave her to the wild dogs. She'll sate them for a while, and that'll spare the sheep. We've got ourselves a new hunting expedition."

ELEVEN

Stewart never saw the fist coming. One minute he was showing the letter to Conall, and the next he was crumpled upon the floor.

Conall stood over him. "You contemptible, misbegotten blackguard! How could you do this to me?"

Stewart cringed from the lightning pain that flashed from his mouth to the rest of his body. He touched a knuckle to the corner of his lips, and drew back a bloodied hand.

"I assure you, Conall. I never intended to injure you."

"Is that supposed to make me feel better? The fact that your reprehensible behavior was never meant to ensnare me?"

Slowly, Stewart straightened himself. He pulled a perfumed handkerchief from his coat pocket and pressed it upon the cut on his lip.

"Of course not. How can anything taint the perfection that is Conall MacEwan?"

Conall's eyes narrowed. "Don't you dare try to exact sympathy at a time like this! This is a young woman's life you've destroyed. To say nothing of mine." Conall flew to the window of his study. He gripped the wooden frame tightly, valiantly trying to keep himself from inflicting further violence upon his brother.

Stewart picked the letter up off the floor. The stiff, cream-colored lettersheet bearing the Basinghall crest had crumpled to the floor under Conall's anger—much as Stewart himself had done just moments before. In the duchess's elegant script was a message that was anything but cordial. He had already memorized the truly insulting portion.

> *I should have surmised by the frequent intersection of our paths that you had dubious designs upon my daughter. But hindsight offers only regrets, and had I known the indecent intentions you had upon the Lady Violet, I, and everyone in my circle, would have vehemently shunned you.*
>
> *I deplore the intimacy that arose from my daughter's association with you, a man without property or title, possessed only of an infamous reputation unbecoming a gentleman. This family has taken great pains to groom Lady Violet for marriage to a peer of the realm, as befits her station, beauty, and deportment. We are indignant that you have taken advantage of Lady Violet and sullied her virtue, rendering her wholly unmarriageable to anyone of noble birth.*
>
> *It is regrettable enough that you have imposed yourself upon our noble station—yet instead of honoring the trust reposed in you, you have callously besmirched the great distinction held by the Basinghall family. I am certain that even a man of your questionable character can appreciate that*

*our daughter's marriage to a man such as
yourself is beneath this family's dignity.
I have therefore designed reparation for
damages to our family thusly:*

*It is our understanding that your elder
brother, Dr. Conall MacEwan, a widower,
has recently inherited a sizable estate in
Scotland. I have received from all quarters a
good report of his character, and I am
heartened to learn of his education, manners,
and temperate ways. If your brother does the
honorable thing by asking for my daughter's
hand in marriage, I shall begrudgingly give
leave for her to marry into the family that
ruined her for nobler suitors.*

*I shall make arrangements to journey to
Ballencrieff upon the end of the Season to
discuss the terms of the betrothal. I expect
you to make our introductions to your
brother, and make our purposes plain to him.
Should he refuse to remove the dishonor from
my daughter's head, I intend to demonstrate
to you and to your family what it means to
make an enemy of Basinghall.*

Conall slammed his hand upon the window casing.
"Why could you not keep yourself from an unmarried
lady of nobility? Were there not enough widows and
harlots in London on which to slake your lust?"

Stewart dusted himself off. "You may not believe this,
Conall, but Violet seduced me."

Conall turned incredulous eyes upon his brother. "An

innocent maiden seduced *you*? My God, man, have you no honor?"

"Why is that so incredible? I mean, the chit has been pursuing me for ages. She's had calf's eyes for me since her coming-out. And you can't ignore a woman like Violet. She's beautiful, gracious, demure . . . a man can only hold out for so long before his baser nature is provoked beyond restraint."

"I would have assumed that by now you would have the presence of mind to keep yourself under control. You're a man of mature years, Stewart."

Stewart flung the letter onto the massive desk. "Regrettably, I am also a man of flesh and blood. I am not made of marble—as you seem to be."

Conall jabbed a finger in the air. "If you think you're going to worm your way out of this by crying self-pity, you're sadly mistaken."

Stewart backed away from him, and crossed over to the tray of brandy resting on a hundred-year-old table. He poured the amber liquid into a glass until it almost spilled over.

Conall rubbed his sore knuckles. "Let's reflect for a moment. If she pursued you so relentlessly, is it possible that she had already been deflowered? When you bedded her, had she already been plucked?"

Stewart could say that she had, and it might allay his brother's fury for the moment. But as soon as the duchess arrived, there would be little escaping the truth. "No. She was a virgin. I'm certain of it." He took a long swallow.

"Dammit, Stewart. Just what am I supposed to do now?"

"You heard the duchess. She won't have me for a son-in-law. And I might add that you could do worse than Violet. She's a very beautiful woman. Her mother has pots of money. The old duke's stroke turned out to be the duchess's stroke of luck." He pocketed the bloody handkerchief. "Despite her disapproval at this turn of events, the duchess is not about to let her only daughter live in penury. Violet will no doubt come with a generous dowry or a healthy annuity—certainly enough to get Ballencrieff out of arrears and to pay for all those improvements you and Shona have started."

"That's not the point, Stewart. This whole situation unmans me. You've robbed me of my ability to choose my own wife."

Stewart's arguments gathered momentum. "You could not have made a better choice. Violet is an only child. When that gorgon of a mother finally pushes up the daisies, you'll be one of the wealthiest men in England *and* Scotland. Think on it, Conall. You may see this now as a curse, but this could very well be a godsend."

"A godsend? Stewart, have you no natural revulsion for this situation? The knowledge of having shared a woman carnally with my own blood brother—it turns my stomach to have crossed swords with you."

Stewart shrugged. "That is easily remedied. Do not bed her."

Conall looked aghast. "Do not bed her? You would doom us both to a frigid marriage bed for the sake of your own convenience? You *are* a selfish bastard!" He threw himself into the chair behind his desk.

"All right, then. Don't marry the girl. What would the duchess do if you were to simply say no?"

Conall rubbed his forehead. "I don't know. I know

what she *could* do. She could accuse you of raping her daughter. She could prefer charges against you and have you thrown in prison. She can bring a lawsuit upon the estate, demanding financial redresses that we simply don't have."

Stewart sat across the desk from him. "No one in Society desires such public disgrace. I daresay she wouldn't bring the affair to light."

Conall grabbed the letter and shook it. "Does this sound like a woman who is afraid of public scrutiny? My God, she committed all this to paper on her own stationery! I think she cares more about exacting retribution than quietly putting the matter to rest. God help us if the girl is with child."

A child? Something stirred within Stewart in a way he'd never felt before. A child of his own . . . the thought of it brought a smile to his lips. He gazed into the etched glass in his hand, and the fleeting pleasure that the idea brought was quickly drowned out by his own self-recrimination. How careless of him it would be to engender offspring that he could never care for, provide for, or raise in the way it ought to go. God forbid the child should turn out just like him. A wayward miscreant, flouting all correction and instruction, devoted only to his damnable self-destructive impulses. In moments such as these, Stewart took careful stock of how much he truly loathed his own weaknesses.

"I'm sorry, Conall. Really, I am. I never once suspected that what I did behind closed doors would somehow entangle you. I cannot undo the damage I caused. But if there is anything I can do to pull us back from the precipice, you have but to name it."

Conall looked into his brother's distraught eyes.

Though few and far between, Stewart had moments when he finally landed from his flights of recklessness and self-indulgence. And Conall was always there to tell him what to do. But right now, Conall had no idea what to do, either. All he knew was that his future had suddenly darkened.

And Shona's presence in it was fading.

TWELVE

Shona jumped onto the seat of the cart and flicked the reins. Conall would be pleased today.

Market day had been long, but very profitable. The farmers on the eastern side of the estate had done well, even though her newest reforms would not show fruit until the spring harvest. The tenants handed over their quarterly sums—plus ten percent for those who'd received a subsidy from Conall—all of which was safely ensconced in a wooden box under her seat. Kieran and his cousin Fergus, a stout man who easily weighed three of Kieran, rode with her to safeguard the cache.

Conall had been so inexplicably distracted these past few days, and she knew he'd been laboring under financial concerns. She desperately wanted to put a smile on his face, and she was certain that the rent monies would do the trick. But she was especially thrilled to bring news of a discovery she'd made on the way to market. There, in Conall's own park lands, were some large burls growing upon a smattering of larch and beech trees. These large growths upon the trees create a beautiful swirled grain to the lumber, used for artistic wood veneer. In London, this wood would undoubtedly fetch high prices from furniture makers and wood sculptors.

Shona was excited to tell Conall that he had a cache of green gold growing right on his land.

Ever since that vulture Hartopp had been discharged, the farmers had become acquainted with a different picture of Conall. Conall had been trying so hard to be the honorable sort of landlord, the kind that tries to collaborate with the tenants as a partner, rather than as an overlord. She had been with him a few days ago when they stopped in to the pub for refreshments after overseeing the delivery of shovels, picks, and bone dust to drain Firley's field. The pubkeeper himself bought a round of drinks for Conall and Shona, and within minutes, their table was littered with glasses from the rounds that men at the neighboring tables bought them in gratitude for either giving them employment or helping their neighbors. He laughed as he saw the collection of ales and whiskies upon their table.

"Let this serve as a warning to ye," she'd told him. "This is what happens when ye become well liked in the village." Conall was beginning to remind her of her father, who had been a much-admired man among his people.

The carriage rumbled up the southern approach to Ballencrieff House, its once derelict landscape now beginning to green with newly potted plants. The moistened ground gave off an earthy smell, offering the delightful promise of the coming harvest.

As the carriage came to a halt, Shona jumped off the perch, her loose hair floating down her back. She reached under the seat and took the box clanking with the sound of coin. "Farewell, Kieran. Farewell, Fergus. Send my love to your mother, now."

"Good-bye, Shona," answered Fergus, his deep baritone booming across the stable yard. "Will ye be needing me tomorrow then?"

"Aye. We'll be doing the Stonekirk market in the morn. Come and collect me at six o'clock sharp."

As she ran through the stable, she noticed several unfamiliar horses munching on hay. Two unhitched carriages crowded inside the coach house.

It appeared that Ballencrieff House was entertaining visitors.

Her Grace the Duchess of Basinghall

Conall rubbed his thumb across the lettering on the calling card that Bannerman had just handed him. Like her letter, the duchess's card was terse and snappish, and communicated in just six words a centuries-old arrogance that demanded to be knelt before.

He expelled a labored breath, and cast a meaningful glance at his brother. "They've arrived."

Moments later, a footman announced the duchess and a second woman into the drawing room. Conall and Stewart rose in greeting.

The duchess herself was a beautiful woman, with striking Gallic features and a narrow waist. Dark hair was collected in curls at the crown of her head, revealing earrings of pearl that almost matched the paleness of her smooth skin. Her emerald dress draped handsomely down her lithe figure, and from the bodice shone a diamond and pearl brooch connected to a rope of pearls that encircled her high waist.

"Greetings, Your Grace," Conall said, bowing before her. "I am Dr. Conall MacEwan of Ballencrieff. You are happily met. I hope your journey was not too unpleasant."

"Quite uneventful, Ballencrieff. Please accept my gratitude for your gracious hospitality."

It was not arrogance she wore, but eminence—as if a mist of regal distinction surrounded her at all times. The duchess waved to the woman beside her. "May I present my daughter, the Lady Violet."

The other woman was a young doppelgänger of the duchess. Beautiful in face and form, with milky skin and shiny brown hair. Like her mother, she had wide, almond-shaped eyes that were distinctly alluring. Her dress, aptly enough, was a pale violet in color, and, although cut a bit low, set off her sylphid waist and high bosom to advantage.

Conall bowed. "Lady Violet, it is an honor to meet you."

Lady Violet curtsied gracefully. "Dr. MacEwan."

"You remember my brother, Stewart MacEwan," he said, gesturing behind him.

Stewart effected a stylistic bow. "A great pleasure to see you both in good health."

The look of pique upon the duchess's face did not escape Conall's notice.

"I've arranged for some refreshments. Won't you please take your ease upon the settee?"

The ladies situated themselves next to one another, appearing like a couple of gemstones in a crown. Conall and Stewart sat opposite them in wing chairs.

The duchess placed her hands neatly in her lap. "Forgive my directness, Ballencrieff, but I am a candid woman, a fact for which my late husband Frederick often chided me. Therefore, to prevail over any lengthy awkwardness, I shall come straight to the point. You've no doubt been apprised of the reason for my visit."

"I have read your letter, Your Grace."

"The first thing to say is that I will not excuse my daughter for forgetting her good breeding and position of responsibility, both socially and morally."

Violet's eyelashes fell upon her cheeks as she blushed hotly. Her poise cracked ever so slightly at the reproof, but to her credit, she maintained her composure. Clearly, this was but one of the many times she had heard this remonstrance.

The duchess continued. "Children in this day and age are famously in want of strictness and restraint. Nevertheless, it is inherent to the conscience of every good mother that any fault found in her child is a fault in herself. While I do not condone the impropriety of my daughter, I must share in the blame for her failures."

Conall glanced at Violet. Her back was straight, her legs were folded demurely at her ankles—yet despite the sting of the invective, she was enduring it graciously. He began to feel a need to defend the girl.

"Who among us has not fallen short of perfection, Your Grace?"

"It is not perfection I expect, sir. It is duty. Requirements are made of all of us, and she must comply with hers, just as we all must. Her dalliance with Mr. Mac-Ewan ill befits a lady of her station."

An unsettling thought was beginning to take shape in Conall's mind. "May I ask what Your Grace specifically finds fault with? Is it the fact that your daughter has fallen from grace, or that in doing so she has landed in my brother's arms?"

"My daughter has been instructed in every one of the social graces—piano, singing, dancing—as well as having been tutored in history, French, Latin, and dozens of other subjects that would strain the intellectual capability of most men. She is capable of masterfully organizing a masked ball for five hundred guests at a moment's notice, and can speak on a variety of subjects to a person of any class, from a member of the clergy to His Royal Highness. Let us be perfectly candid with one another. How many masked balls do you expect your brother to hold?"

Conall shifted in his chair. "Surely that isn't the measure of a man's worth in your estimation?"

"Not if we're discussing humanity, Ballencrieff. But we are speaking of practical matters. Now that she is damaged, I cannot in good conscience give her hand in marriage to a man of equal breeding. Neither, however, does one indiscretion make her fit only for dogs."

Stewart leaned forward. "Dogs? You do me a great disservice, Your Grace. Although I am no prince, I cannot allow you to slander me—"

With the quiet dignity of an elder statesman, the duchess halted Stewart's argument. "Please contain your protestations, Mr. MacEwan. While I can certainly appreciate your sordid interest in Lady Violet—my daughter is a pearl after all—it is beyond the pale that a presumed gentleman should take advantage of a girl of such tender years. My daughter has defended you by claiming you did not force yourself upon her, but I think I can say without contradiction that you and I know better than that. We are worldly people, you and I, and we know that in moments of passion, the sword will demand its sheath. You've behaved reprehensibly, and I regret that my daughter did not realize earlier on that you were nothing but a common lothario. To my knowledge, your only known achievement is having seduced scores of women, and that is a shabby accomplishment indeed. You would do better to become a chimney sweep, sir, for then you can claim to have done some good in the world."

Stewart reacted as if he'd been slapped. He ground his teeth and gripped the arms of the chair until his knuckles turned white. Although Conall reluctantly shared the duchess's opinion, he felt sorry for his brother. The duchess seemed to possess the cruel skill of exploiting people's insecurities. But Conall was surprised to notice the pained expression on Violet's face. Once the duchess's ammunition turned upon Stewart, Lady Violet seemed prepared to jump out of her seat to protect him.

"Your Grace," said Conall, "as reasons for the liaison between these two, you've cited the moral decline in our society, the laxness of your maternal guidance, and the recklessness of my brother. There is one reason that you did not mention. Had you stopped to consider that Lady Violet and Stewart might be in love?"

Without a moment's hesitation, the duchess answered. "Does that matter?"

Conall searched her face. He had never seen a countenance so beautiful, yet so cold.

The duchess continued. "People of noble birth do not have the luxury of love, Ballencrieff. Matches must be made to the advantage of both families. This is as it has been for hundreds of years, and how it always shall be done. Empires rise and fall on alliances made at the altar. And for peers of the realm, a good alliance makes the bloodline stronger, while a bad one ends in disgrace."

"An alliance to the bloodline of MacEwan is the same whether your daughter is wed to my brother or to myself."

"Let us not quibble, Ballencrieff. I think you understand precisely the point upon which I stand."

He cocked an eyebrow. "Yes, I believe I do." He'd say one thing for her. She was venomously direct. "Nevertheless, I do not believe that a woman should be dragged to the altar. What, may I ask, does the young lady opine about all this?"

The duchess turned gracefully toward her daughter. Not a single perceptible change in the duchess's expression had occurred, but Violet seemed able to read her mother's face a great deal better than Conall.

"I . . . am receptive to becoming better acquainted with Dr. MacEwan, er, Ballencrieff, if he'll do me the very great honor of paying court."

The duchess returned a triumphant look at Conall. "Are we then in agreement?"

He glanced at Stewart. His brother's face dissolved from offended pride to sullen rejection to . . . jealousy?

Conall cleared his throat. "I would consider it a very great privilege to become better acquainted with Lady Violet. I find her delightful and charming, and I am certain that her heart is as pure as you claim. But I am a recent widower, as you know, and it has been a challenge to overcome the feeling of loss I had when my wife departed this world. I would like an opportunity to get to know Lady Violet at leisure, and allow her equal time to consider me. Perhaps then, in due course, she may choose—"

"There is no due course, sir. The banns must be published immediately."

"Your Grace, this is beyond tolerable. I will not be marched down the aisle at the point of a rifle—"

"There is a child."

The last word seemed to echo in their ears.

The silence stretched tight. Conall's eyes darted from the duchess to Violet. Violet's gaze was riveted upon Stewart.

"Lady Violet, are you quite certain?" asked Conall.

The younger woman's voice was barely above a whisper. "I missed my monthly courses, sir."

"A fact she confessed to me only last week," the duchess added with a clip of irritation. "So you see, we also do not possess the luxury of time. My grandchild may have been conceived a bastard, but I will not have it born as one. We can have the wedding at Basinghall within the month. On the wedding day, I will bestow upon you a dowry of fifty thousand guineas, plus her goods and a house in St. James Square. You should also know that Violet is the sole heiress to the estate of Basinghall, and upon my death, it too shall proceed into your hands."

Conall began to squirm under the pressure. There was no denying that marriage to Violet would reverse his financial woes. And indeed, Violet herself was a very beautiful and well-mannered young woman. Not to mention what a blessing it would be to the poor girl to take her out from under her mother's dictatorship. But every single one of his instincts screamed that marrying

Violet would be a colossal mistake. The reasons could not be put into words, because there was only a face: Shona's.

"That is . . . a very generous offer, Your Grace. And your daughter is worth marrying even without all the added inducements. But I regret to tell you that I am not the right suitor for her."

For the first time, the duchess's expression lost all serenity.

Conall leaned forward. "We will, of course, take full responsibility for the child. You may stay at Ballencrieff for the duration of Lady Violet's pregnancy and confinement, with full assurance of our discretion. Should you determine that the needs of the child are best served by giving it over to the parish authorities, then I will of course deliver the child personally without naming its mother."

Lady Violet whimpered, drawing Conall's eye to her. She merely wrung her hands in her lap.

The duchess looked up at him from under her delicate brows. "I am sorry to hear that you will not be co-operative. I must therefore tell you that if you do nothing to protect my daughter, I shall do nothing to protect your son."

At the mention of his beloved child, Conall's body tensed. "What do you mean?"

"I have it on the very best authority that your wife did not die of childbed fever, as you have so often asserted."

The ground disappeared beneath him. "I beg your pardon?"

The duchess spoke with complete equanimity. "Christina MacEwan may have met her fate in bed, but it was not a disease which claimed her life."

His vision clouded over with rage. He never thought to hear these words outside his own head, but it infuriated him that they were carried on the tongue of such a ruthless serpent.

"Well, Ballencrieff?" she asked. "What is to be your answer?"

THIRTEEN

Shona bounded through the house looking for Conall. She had a small fortune in a case under her arm, and maybe, just maybe, it would earn her another trip out to the tollhouse.

He wasn't in his study, and he wasn't in the library. Just then, she saw Mrs. Docherty emerge from the kitchen with a large tray of tea and scones. Shona reached over the housekeeper's shoulder and swiped one from the dish.

Mrs. Docherty turned angry eyes upon her. "Those are for the guests, Shona! Put it back!"

But Shona had already taken a huge bite of the warm, buttery cake. "Sorry. I haven't eaten in ages. Who's here? And why are there so many coaches outside?"

Mrs. Docherty walked toward the end of the hall. "I haven't got time to gossip idly about the guests. I'm as behind as a cat's tail. Look at the time, and I've just got the tea prepared."

"Where is everyone?"

"In the drawing room."

"I'll get the door for ye." Shona jumped in front of her, and swung the doors wide open on the drawing room. "Greetings, all! I bring good news of—"

The cheer she brought with her was quickly sucked

out through the door. A pall of moroseness hung about the room like a thick winter fog rolling over a dark loch.

Conall stood. Though he was dressed handsomely in a burgundy-colored coat, a doomed expression weighed down his features. "Er, Shona, this isn't a very good time."

Worry gripped her. "Is everything all right? What's happened?"

"There's no need for you to be alarmed. We just need a few moments to sort things out."

The two beautiful women on the settee stared at her in polite curiosity. Dressed in emerald and amethyst, they looked as if they belonged in a painting.

The older of the two subjected her to an inquisitive assessment. A wave of self-consciousness splashed over Shona. Shona's hair was unpinned and tossed about by the fierce winds outside, and her new bluebell-print day dress, though presentable, was leagues beneath the elegance of the ladies'. Although there was no expression of disdain on the woman's face, Shona could sense her contempt.

"Will you not introduce us, Ballencrieff?" the duchess asked.

Conall's lips thinned. "If you wish it. Your Grace, may I present Shona MacAslan, my factor. Shona, this is Gwendolyn, Duchess of Basinghall."

Shona dipped down, as she knew she had to before a peeress. "How do ye do?"

A fine eyebrow arched into the duchess's forehead. "A *female* factor? How very novel."

Shona smirked. " 'Tis only because his first one was as useless as a two-legged horse."

"I see. Miss Shona, may I present my daughter, the

Lady Violet." The duchess focused her full attention on Shona. "Ballencrieff's fiancée."

Shona's eyes grew wide as saucers. She turned to Conall. "Fiancée?"

Conall's face flushed to the color of his coat. "Yes. It's just been arranged. You're the first outside the family to know."

She cast a glance at the young woman in question. Her pulse throbbed thickly in her veins as she regarded Lady Violet. They were close in age, but Lady Violet was prettier even than Willow. Pale skin, elegant features, gorgeous clothing, sparkling jewels. And a title. Every single thing Shona lacked.

"Well, thank ye for the honor. Glad I wasna the last." She spun around and flew past Mrs. Docherty out the door.

She got halfway down the hall when Conall gripped her by the elbow.

"Slow down, Shona. Let me explain," he said.

She jerked her arm from his hand. "No need. I can see plainly. Ye exhorted the truth from me, but here ye are, a black-hearted liar. What was I meant to be? A little distraction to while away the hours before she came to be yer wife? Or did ye actually intend to make me yer official mistress?"

"Shona—"

"If ye had to be two-faced, the very least ye could have done is shown me the good-looking one."

At that moment, Mrs. Docherty walked past them with the empty tray under her arm. Her eyes never lifted from the floor, but she left with an earful.

Conall ground his teeth. "Dammit, Shona," he muttered hotly, "I will not have you insulting me in front of the servants."

"All right then." She tossed her head back. "Who shall I insult ye in front of?"

Irritation pinching his face, he pulled her by the hand into the empty library and shut the door. "Listen to me. I have no liking for this betrothal. But this marriage is being thrust upon me."

"Alas! Poor man to have to marry *that*. I don't have enough tears to cry for ye."

"It's true. I've only just met the girl this very day."

Shona crossed her arms. "Then why do ye have to marry her?"

He wiped his hands across his face as if trying to erase his thoughts. "I can't explain that to you."

"Well, I'm no book-learned gentleman like yerself, but I may understand if ye use really simple words."

He heaved a weary sigh. "Can we discuss this like civilized people? It does us no good for you to give me the sharp edge of your tongue."

Her finger poked him in the chest. "Ye're lucky I don't give ye the sharp edge of my blade." She turned around, blinking against the hot sting of tears.

"Shona, Lady Violet is not the woman I would have chosen to be my wife. This is simply a marriage of convenience. She will get a husband, and I will receive her dowry. And you know how badly we need that flow of capital into the estate. All the major improvements you wanted to make on the farms can now be done." He put a hand on her shoulder. "I know that's a small comfort to you, in light of the romantic moments we've shared, but—"

A knot in her throat strangled her words. "Ye needn't worry aboot me. They meant nothing to me."

He turned her around. "They meant something to me. Look, I've not been a stellar landlord. I can't figure out how to get us out of this financial muck. Perhaps marrying a woman with money is the only way out, I don't know. But one thing I do know, Shona. I don't want it to end between us."

A tear escaped down her cheek, just before her anger exploded. "Oh, ye are a selfish ape! Ye would have me be your Scottish bit of stuff while ye take Lady Whatsit on yer arm as your missus. Iona warned me aboot Sassenach masters. Now I see she was right. Well, I won't be yer parlormaid paramour!"

She stomped toward the library door, but then spun to face him.

"And if it's money ye be after, then here's yer wedding present!" She threw the box on the floor, exploding coins and notes all around his boots.

FOURTEEN

For the first time in her life, Shona had run out of bad words to say.

After ten full minutes of smearing Conall's character, befouling his parentage, and cursing the unmentionable parts of his body, she had exhausted her supply of swear words. But for just this occasion, she was firmly resolved to make up some new ones.

Willow sat upon the bed, rocking Eric in her arms, trying to soothe the pouting child back to sleep after Shona slammed the door. "Are ye done blackening the man?"

Shona slumped on the bed. "For now. How could he have agreed to marry another woman after he and I . . . after we pledged ourselves to each other?"

"If ye ask me, Shona, ye shouldn't have behaved so naughty. Iona always told us that a man won't buy the cow if he can get the milk for free."

"I did no' get round to giving the man any milk."

"Ah, but ye let him handle yer udders."

Shona rolled her eyes and buried her face in her hands. Giving in to her passion was her doing—and as it turned out, her undoing. She felt cast off, like an old shoe—only less attractive. "What difference does it make? No gentleman wants a cow in his drawing room anyway."

"I don't hold to calling ye a cow, mind," Willow began as she laid the now sleeping child into his crib. "But the reality is that ye're a servant and he's the master. Perhaps things would be different if ye both were of equal station. Were it not for the miss's money, I daresay he would marry ye instead."

Marry! Dear God, if that woman married Conall, Shona would be trapped in this house for three more years. Lady Violet would become mistress of the household, and Shona would be forced to do her bidding. It was bad enough having to endure watching the two of them live as husband and wife, but she'd be damned if she was going to be Conall's bit of skirt as well. Shona was simply not willing to *have* a mistress and *be* a mistress.

"I don't know what Conall stands to gain from that woman, but she's no' going to get him."

"What are ye planning to do?"

There was only one thing she could do, only one way she could free herself and Willow from the hold Conall MacEwan had over her.

"I'm going to win him back. I'm going to marry Conall, no matter what it takes."

"It's back to that, is it? Marry the laird to get out of our indentures?"

"Aye. I've come this far with him, haven't I? Just a wee bit more and we'll be home free."

Willow's expression sobered. "But I feel at home here, Shona. I thought ye did as well. I thought ye had a real tenderness toward the master. Has all that gone away?"

The words cut a hole in her insides. These past

weeks had been the happiest of her life. Conall had revived feelings in her she would have sworn had been carved out of her heart. He had shown her love, in spite of her imperfections, and she had reflected it right back at him. To use him now seemed wrong, felt wrong. How would she be able to turn her heart of flesh into a heart of stone? How was she going to be able to look at Conall and see only a key to unlocking her cage . . . and nothing more?

"My home is not with Conall. Not anymore. Having that woman in the parlor says so. He chose her over me, but I'm no' going to let him get away so easily. Even if he wants her more, he's going to have to marry me first. Lady Violet can have him when I'm through with him."

"Do ye think ye can get him to propose to ye, then?"

"Aye, I can." She had discovered the possibility in his respect for her, in the honor of his character. And aye, in his kiss. The affection was there. But it was just not enough—yet. "Even though right now I'd rather see him on his knees writhing in pain than proposing marriage."

"That's hardly the right attitude to take if ye're trying to win the man's heart."

Shona went to the small table, where they kept a hand mirror. "First thing I've got to do is get rid of that witch and her mother. If he thinks I'm going to give up my place at the dinner table, he's got a surprise headed his way." She glanced at Willow. "Do I look pretty enough?"

"For what?"

"For dinner tonight."

"To eat it or serve it?"

Shona's hands dropped to her sides in frustration. "Willow—"

"Well, ye can't go like that, can ye, in that dress and with yer hair as mussed as a horse's mane. Here, let's tidy ye up some. Then ye can go doon and show that milkwater English miss what kind of women we Scots are!"

Shona descended the staircase feeling as awkward as a ewe wearing a petticoat.

Willow had been making a new Sunday dress for herself, but for this occasion, she gave it to Shona to wear first. Dainty ruffles graced the sleeves and hemline of the print muslin, lending it a beautiful French flair, and a pink ribbon adorned the high waistline. But the dress had not been finished—there was supposed to be a chemisette to preserve modesty from the low neckline—so Shona had to be incredibly daring to wear the thing as it was. Willow had also collected Shona's hair at her crown, cleverly creating a mound of petals blossoming around the knot. The coif was quite stunning.

Of course, the result of all this tarting up meant that Shona was nearly late in to dinner.

Bannerman was in the hall. "The family and guests are in the drawing room, miss, partaking of an aperitif." A gentle smile touched his lips. "If I may say so, Miss Shona, you look quite fetching."

The comment brought a smile to her lips, but a strange sense of foreboding to her heart. If after all this she failed, then there really would be no hope. She clutched her roiling stomach as the urgency and importance of her mission weighed heavily upon her.

"I was on the point of announcing dinner," he continued, "but I shall delay it by a few moments." Bannerman opened the door and let her through.

Her eyes scanned the room. Conall was on the settee talking quietly with Lady Violet. He looked handsome in his navy blue tailcoat, the same one he was wearing when she first set eyes upon him. The sight of him took her breath away once more.

Did he feel the same way about her? Would he consider her more appealing than the beautifully arrayed Lady Violet, who outshone her in a sheer white organza-draped gown tied with a shiny silk scarlet ribbon? Would her less-Scottish clothes tonight at least turn his head in her direction?

He rose, and so did her hope. Amazement swam upon his features, and he almost smiled.

"Shona, you're—" He swallowed hard. "You've decided to join us."

Censoring himself for Lady Violet's benefit. That made her mad all over again.

"Aye—I mean, yes. I hope I'm still welcome at table."

Stewart walked up to her and bowed over her hand. "Of course you are. And may I say that you look ravishing tonight."

"Thank ye, Stewart. Ye're quite handsome yerself."

Lady Violet turned away, her cheerless eyes glinting in the firelight.

The duchess approached, the diamonds at her throat winking at Shona. "Good evening, Miss Shona. I had no idea that Ballencrieff dines with his factor."

"He likes to receive daily reports on how his holdings are doing."

The duchess turned to Conall. "And do you require this report tonight, Ballencrieff?"

Conall's gaze never left Shona's face. "It is . . . most important to me."

The duchess's dark eyes appraised Shona's form. Shona was several inches taller than the duchess, but the older woman had a way of making a person feel much smaller.

The door clicked open, and the footman announced dinner. Per proper form, Conall walked the duchess into the dining room, and Stewart held out his arms for both Lady Violet and Shona. Shona could hardly take her eyes off Conall's broad back. As he walked in front of her, it pained her to think that he might walk out of her life forever. She flicked a jealous glance over at Lady Violet, hanging on Stewart's other arm. If she too had been gazing at Conall, Shona just might have to scratch those beautiful almond-shaped eyes out. But surprisingly, it was Stewart who commanded her full attention.

Gracing the long mahogany table in the dining room was a new set of dishes, one that Shona had never seen before, of white porcelain and blue filigree edged with gold trim. Etched crystal goblets sparkled in the candlelight. A warm fire cast a reddish hue on the blue walls, giving the room a violet tinge.

Conall turned to the duchess, seated on his right. "I've asked Cook to welcome you to Ballencrieff with some of our delightful Scottish fare. Although I sometimes find myself missing England, I must say that I overwhelmingly prefer the food grown in the northern climate."

The duchess glanced at her daughter, seated across from her on Conall's left. "Violet and I spend most of our time in London. After the Season, we'll repair to the country for the distractions of Basinghall. Do you know Buckinghamshire, Ballencrieff?"

"I'm afraid not," he said, as the footman served a refined version of cock-a-leekie soup. "Our home in

London was our place of residence throughout the year. I hadn't even been back to Ballencrieff since I was five. But I rather enjoy it now I'm here."

He tossed a momentary glance at Shona, which no one witnessed.

Except the duchess.

"Then allow me to acquaint you with the home you will one day own." The duchess began a lengthy description of the estate of Basinghall, from the enormous stables housing prized Thoroughbreds to the gallery displaying gifts from England's monarchs.

Shona eyed Lady Violet. She wanted to hate Lady Violet—for her pretty organza dress, for the exquisite ruby around her neck, for her prized Thoroughbreds. Even for that demure loveliness that she wore so artlessly. But the hatred kept slipping away. The truth was that the girl was not at fault for being blessed with beauty and wealth. Making her an enemy for that was akin to despising Willow—neither deserved blame just because men naturally gravitated toward them. If blame was to be flung, it had to land on Conall. It was he who had betrayed Shona's affection for him, he who'd proposed marriage to Lady Violet. It was he who deserved her displeasure.

The cock-a-leekie was delicious, the best Shona had ever tasted. But Lady Violet just kept moving her spoon about the bowl, shifting the bits of chicken about. At first, Shona thought that the girl was doing it for appearances—after all, some ladies liked to give gentlemen the impression that they would rather eat their napkins than the food on their plate for fear of getting fat. But it soon seemed clear that Lady Violet really didn't care for the soup.

By degrees, Shona returned her attention to what the duchess was saying.

"So you see, Ballencrieff," continued the duchess, "it was easy to keep those holdings within our purview, as my husband, Frederick, died intestate."

"Poor man," exclaimed Shona. "What happened to them?"

The duchess blinked her lashes. "Them? Them what?"

"His testicles."

The duchess's lashes drew back in shock. Stewart laughed outright. Even Lady Violet giggled behind her uneaten napkin.

Conall held back a chuckle. "No, Shona. To die intestate means he passed away without having prepared a will."

"Oh. Sorry."

Shona felt her cheeks redden, but inexplicably, it gladdened her heart to have elicited a smile from the wistful Lady Violet.

The footman delivered the marinated Solway salmon to the table, served on a bed of sautéed kale. It smelled heavenly to Shona, and she was glad of the distraction. But the look on Violet's face changed. She began to look quite repulsed by the dish, and leaned back in her chair with her napkin to her face.

"Are ye feeling aright?" asked Shona.

"Quite well, thank you," she replied nervously, perspiration breaking out on her upper lip.

Shona could detect Violet's quiet suffering. "Ye're not! 'Fact, ye're looking a touch green. Mayhap ye'd like to lie doon a wee while?"

"I think I'd like that very much. With your kind indulgence, Ballencrieff? And your permission, Maman?"

Conall rose from the table. "Of course. I'll have Mrs. Docherty take some fresh lemons to your room—inhale their scent to reduce the effects of the *nausea gravidarum*. I'll also have some puree of strawberry sent up. That will help settle your stomach."

"Thank you," she said before sprinting out of the room.

As the seconds ticked by, Shona became increasingly concerned. She got up from her chair. "I'm going with her."

The gentlemen rose again.

"I'm sure that won't be necessary," declared the duchess.

"Actually, Your Grace," interjected Conall, "I think it will be a great comfort to Lady Violet. Thank you, Shona. Truly."

She should not have wanted to help the woman who was trying to steal Conall away from her. But all she could feel was that relentless impulse to ease suffering, regardless of whose it was. She accepted his knowing nod before making her way through the hall and up the stairs to the guest bedrooms.

When Shona burst in through the door of Lady Violet's bedroom, she found the girl vomiting into her chamber pot.

Shona grabbed a towel and moistened it with water from the ewer on her washstand. She sat down next to Violet on the bed and dabbed at the girl's perspiring forehead.

The wave of nausea had passed, and collapsing upon the pillows, Violet was now nothing more than a limp memory of her former beauty.

Shona dabbed the wet towel at Violet's cheeks,

which were now pockmarked with red from the effort of her upheaval.

"Are ye better now?"

Violet nodded weakly.

"What's the matter with ye? Did ye eat something unpleasant?"

"No. You're very kind to worry. I should be fine soon enough."

"Ye don't look fine to me. Ye look like a cat that's just swallowed a sickly mouse."

Violet groaned and gripped the chamber pot once more.

"Sorry," said Shona, cursing her own insensitivity. "Let's just chat aboot lovely, cheerful things."

Violet nodded, spent from the effort of fighting the sickness. "You love him, don't you?"

Shona's hand stilled. "Eh?"

"Dr. MacEwan. You love him. I can tell."

Those almond-shaped eyed saw a great deal more than Shona had wanted to show. She felt as if she were falling apart inside. Shona shrugged, unable to trust the confidence in her voice to answer.

"If it's any consolation to you, Miss Shona, I don't wish this marriage to take place any more than you do. Oh, I'm fond of Dr. MacEwan . . . he's a kind gentleman, and a very handsome man. But my heart already belongs to another."

"Does it? To who?"

She closed her eyes. "Ballencrieff's brother. Stewart MacEwan."

Shona's heart lifted. "Ye . . . love Stewart?"

Violet's eyes misted over. "With all my heart. Even though I fear he doesn't love me."

Shona was nonplussed. It was happy news that Violet was not a rival for Conall's affection. But the tragedy of Violet's unrequited love for Stewart leached all the joy out of it.

"I'd no idea that you even knew him."

Violet sighed. "We know each other quite well. Ever since the year of my debut into Society. We met at the opera. He was so dashing, so charming. And forward—he approached me directly, without a care or concern for my chaperone. As if we were the only two people on earth. And when he spoke to me, it was as if he could see straight into my heart, and I into his. Even though he had a lady on his arm—one of questionable repute, mind—I knew then that he was just as crushingly lonely as I. And whenever we met, no matter how many people surrounded us, he and I seemed to understand each other as no one else could ever do."

A lone tear streaked down Violet's temple. Instinctively, Shona dabbed at it with the towel.

Violet's lip trembled. "Thank you. You're so kind. I'm so sorry for having to be a part of this terrible injustice that my mother has orchestrated against Stewart and Dr. MacEwan. And, it seems, against you." She put a hand on Shona's. "I'm so ashamed of myself. When I saw the way Stewart's face lit up when you came into the drawing room, I wanted to hate you so much. It was wrong of me, and I'm sorry."

If it wasn't so tragic, Shona would have laughed at the irony of it, having felt the same way. "Och, ye needn't worry aboot Stewart falling for me, Lady Violet. He's got a rogue's eye, to be sure, but he knows better than to lay a finger on me. Anyway, it's foolish for us women to hate each other. Far more effective to just cut his bollocks off."

Violet chuckled halfheartedly before the smile dissolved. "I just don't think he comprehends how much it shatters me when he looks at another woman."

Shona tried to imagine the two of them together. "I know ye've the coddlin' for him, but quite frankly, he's as insatiable as a tomcat. How can ye lose yer heart to a man who gives himself to every woman he meets?"

Violet raised herself on her elbows, new tears glistening in her earnest eyes. "You don't understand him, Miss Shona. No one can. I know that there is a great man in him—I can see it! But deep inside him, he feels unworthy of love—least of all, from himself—and it eclipses any extension of love from others. He sabotages his own happiness by choosing to find his own value in the passion of women. I hate the fact that he makes so little of himself. How then can he appreciate the love I bear for the same soul that he so despises? I pray that he would only let me show him all the good and glorious things I see in him. Then he shall truly be the man he was destined to be."

Shona sighed in amazement. "'Tis more than just coddlin' ye feel for him then."

"A good deal more." Violet shrugged, surrendering to a grin. "Also, I can't resist a man with dimples."

The girls giggled. Consequently, neither of them heard the door open. Or saw the duchess walk in.

"I see you're already feeling better," declared the duchess.

The glee ran away from Violet's face. "Not really, Maman. I was just—"

"Violet, please compose yourself and return to table."

"But Maman, I only just purged—"

"Then there should be nothing left inside to sicken you. Please rejoin Ballencrieff at table. They're holding dessert in abeyance for us. I believe it is some Scottish thing called cranachan. Whatever it is, I expect you to eat it all. I shall be along shortly."

"Yes, Maman." Violet flicked Shona an apologetic glance, and smoothed out her dress before walking out of the door.

Shona started after her, but was halted by the duchess's indomitable voice. "Miss Shona, may I have a word with you in private?"

It was phrased as a request, but her tone offered little choice for Shona to decline. She turned to face the duchess.

"Close the door, if you please."

The duchess waited to hear the click of the door before speaking. "Forgive me for being so abrupt, but I have no wish to prolong this conversation unnecessarily. Do you have designs upon the house of MacEwan?

"Designs?"

She closed her eyes, rephrasing the question as if she were addressing a mere child. "Let me be even more direct. Are you having sexual relations with Conall MacEwan?"

Shona's mouth fell open. "Ye've a bloody cheek! What business is that of yers?"

"I assure you it is every bit my business when my only daughter is about to marry him. I would like to know what sort of people he associates with. And what sort of women shall be surrounding him."

"Then ye'd do well to ask him that question."

The duchess smiled weakly. "I think I already have

my answer." She took a bold step and brought her face to within inches from Shona's. "You are a very unique sort of woman. There is a great deal of strength in you, even if it is obscured by your total lack of finesse. But allow me to do you the very great favor of sparing you some private agony. Strictly *entre nous,* a man like Conall MacEwan is intrigued by women of low birth, especially those that serve at his pleasure. You are a mere plaything to him. It hardly seems reasonable that a man of his conspicuous beauty should be wont to embrace a mere servant girl . . . unless it is to make sport of you. Therefore, I advise you to be on your guard against harboring the regrettable hope that you will somehow win his heart and become mistress of all this. Many a fellow-fond servant girl has fallen into that trap, sometimes at the lord's encouragement, only to find themselves broken by heartache and covered in shame. Perhaps yours is a love that *should* be, but it is not a love that *will* be. Conall MacEwan is destined to marry a woman with noble blood or a grand fortune. You cannot think he will marry some Scottish miss, least of all something he clearly scraped off the street. So I advise that whatever designs you have upon Conall MacEwan, you abandon them forthwith. Do we understand one another?"

Shona felt winded. Her heart beat loudly, as if to drown out any truth there might be to the duchess's words. Yet there was nothing Shona could say with certainty that would dispute what the duchess had just told her.

But there was one thing that Shona knew to be absolutely true.

"When I was working at Miles' End Farm, we once had a very proud mule who thought she was too good to pull the plow."

The duchess's neck stiffened. "Yes?"

"Yer breath smells just like the back of that mule."

FIFTEEN

Shona's triumph was short-lived.

It was the duchess who had the final word, but Shona was not around to hear it. Because the next day, Shona's duties took her out into the field, leaving her to contemplate what mischief the duchess could be planning with Conall's future.

She heaved a profound sigh as she walked up the hill on the southern part of the estate. For as long as she could remember, two of the tenants had been arguing about the other encroaching on his property. Conall—after listening for hours to Grady and McKie recite tales of animals grazing upon the wrong owner's land, relive decades-old harassments, and dispute over inches here and there—decided to build a stone dyke to separate the farmsteads at his own expense. It was now Shona's responsibility to make sure that his decision was carried out.

But while she was supervising the hired hand who was told to dig a shallow trench to embed the dyke, her mind kept wandering back to the library. At breakfast that morning, Conall had promised to show Lady Violet a rare volume in the library. Even though she knew that Lady Violet had no interest in marrying Conall,

Shona couldn't help feeling a stab of jealousy. He never showed Shona such a volume.

She could see it all now, as clearly as if it were happening before her eyes. Conall escorting Lady Violet to the library, now warmed by the morning sun. The duchess also following, but wanting to encourage their attraction, would find an excuse to discreetly remove herself from the room. Conall ascending the ladder to retrieve a dusty book from a high shelf, leaving Lady Violet to finally appreciate the length of his legs beneath the polished Hessian boots, the toned sinew of his thighs, and the height of his square buttocks.

Conall pulls down an ancient book of love and seduction, and they look at the illustrated pages together. A tendril of hair falls from Violet's perfect coif, and he reaches out to pull it away from her face. His touch sparks a feeling of desire in her, and she leans in close. Her hand splays flat on his chest as he lowers his head to put a kiss on her mouth.

"That's mine!"

The shout pulled her from her uncomfortable reverie. She glanced up. McKie was shouting at the hired hand digging the trench.

Grady, who'd been seated upon a felled tree trunk on his own property, bolted upright with a finger pointed at a boulder. "Don't ye listen to him! The laird's already agreed it becomes part of my property."

"The hell it does! This boulder's been a landmark on my property for ages. It's even got m'name carved on it. See? It says 'McKie.'"

"Bah! Ye put that there t'other day."

Shona advanced upon them. "What fresh hell is this?"

McKie pointed at Grady. "There! See the cheatin' kind of man he is? He waits until the laird is gone to take what doesna belong to him."

Grady shook his aged fist at his neighbor. "Ye're the one who's cheatin'! The laird said that this rise belongs to me, and ye get the footbridge over the burn."

"I canna feed m'flocks on a fuckin' bridge. It's the land I want, and it's the land I'll keep!"

Shona pinned her fists to her hips. "Shut yer pie-hole, McKie! And ye, too, Grady. I'm sick to death of the quibbling between ye. Ye're like children fighting over the same toy."

"Toy?" cried McKie. "This boulder's defined the end of my property for ages."

Her patience shattered. Shona squared up on McKie, and though he was a burly man and outweighed her by at least seven stone, he backed off.

"Fine! Ye want the boulder? Ye can have it! Horner, dig the trench as I instructed ye, and roll the fuckin' boulder onto McKie's property. See there, McKie? It'll still define the end of yer property!"

A satisfied grin marched triumphantly across Grady's face.

"And Grady?" she said, facing him. "As ye'll be the new owner of this eighth-of-an-acre strip, I'll be tacking on the two shillings sixpence to yer annual rent. I expect full payment on it in January."

Shona stomped down the hill, leaving silence in her wake. Though she'd finally gotten the two men to stop arguing, she was unhappier than ever. She wished Conall were as easy to divide as the land. But the truth was that he could not belong to both her and Lady Violet. And even if Shona could win him over just long enough to be free of her indentures, she would not be satisfied if she didn't also have his heart.

The way he already had hers.

As the afternoon died, a dense fog rolled in on the Ballencrieff estate.

Shona gazed out the nursery window at the thick soup gathering at the foot of the hill. Usually, fog made her happy. The world lost its sharpness, the flapping of birds' wings became muffled, and time seemed to still while a web of water was spun over everything. A person could even gaze upon the sun when the heavenly veil was thrown over its face.

But this evening, the fog reminded her how unclear everything had become. Her future was as murky as the gray mist outside. She gazed at the haunted moon, gnarled and yellowed like one of Mr. Seldomridge's teeth, and a terrible sense of doom fell upon her. No matter which way she considered it, Shona could see no happiness for herself.

The duchess had not wasted any time. The vicar of the local parish had been asked in to tea, and arrangements were made to publish the banns in the kirk on Sunday. And in two days, Conall, Lady Violet, and the duchess would set out for Buckinghamshire, where the wedding was to take place within a month.

It felt as if she were standing on the edge of a great precipice. And the rocks under her feet were beginning to give way.

The house was curiously silent.

Mrs. Docherty was lighting the candles in the hall, illuminating the house in the premature darkness.

"If ye be looking for the master, he's in his study," she said.

Shona's eyebrows curled in puzzlement. "How did ye know—"

"Go on," she whispered, flashing Shona a knowing look. "He's alone now." She returned to her task, as if she'd never been distracted from it at all.

Shona approached the study quietly. Her mind was tormented by the imminent loss of him. There was so much she wanted to say, but words were lost in a jangle of emotions.

The door was ajar, and she peeked in. He was absorbed in the study of a large book in his hand, its pages open to face the candelabra upon the desk. Soft light was cast upon his handsome profile, and Shona was mesmerized by his manly beauty. Shadows pooled in the recesses of his cheeks and in the hollows below his brow. But the candlelight danced upon the golden speckles in his chestnut hair, twisting and turning in the waves until his hair began to look like warm rushing water.

She glanced at the page he was so intently scrutinizing. Upon it was an illustration of a naked woman's body.

Shona's mind immediately jumped to her jealous imaginings of that morning—the ancient book of love and seduction, and Conall and Lady Violet kissing over a shared secret. Except it no longer made her mad to think on it. It made her heartsick.

With effort, she adopted a lighthearted tone. "Staring at naughty pictures? You dirty sod."

He turned around and his expression lit up.

"Shona! It's good to see you. Come, sit down."

She did so. Suddenly, she felt happy again. It was alarming how much her mood was dependent upon his.

As if his good graces could direct the flow of her happiness.

His expression became mischievous. "I have a surprise for you. Wait here."

Her eyes followed him out the door, which he closed behind him. She didn't know what he was going to give her, but there was only one thing he could do that would lighten her mood forever. Stay at Ballencrieff and marry her instead.

Her eyes drifted to the book on his desk. She slid it toward her and spun it around. It was a line drawing of a naked woman. Of a naked *pregnant* woman.

She glanced at the title on the cover. *The Practice of Physic, Surgery, and Midwifery on the Human Female.* Once again she looked at the diagram of the woman with a child in her womb. Lines radiated out from the drawing, showing the names of all her parts in Latin.

Why was Conall so engrossed in this book? Was this the book that he was so eager to show Lady Violet that morning? Shona flipped through the pages. There were chapters covering how to treat any ailment, from the vapors to hysteria to twisted limbs to incontinence.

She heard the door open behind her. Conall peeked in through the opening and smiled.

"There's someone here who'd like to say thank you."

He opened the door, and Dexter bounded in. On four healthy legs.

As soon as he sensed Shona, Dexter squealed in happiness, and raised himself up on her lap to lick her face.

Elated to see him well and happy, Shona hugged his spotted torso. Dexter's high-pitched squealing spoke the joy in the dog's heart.

"It gladdens my heart to see you, too! I see yer pointing arm is back up to snuff!"

Conall chuckled. "Thanks to you. He owes you his life. And the use of his legs."

"'Twas the least a feelin' heart could do."

"If that is true, then I would very much like to see the most your heart could do."

She smiled halfheartedly. *Marry me, and I shall show you.*

Conall sat down in the chair behind the desk. "Shona, you know how fond I am of you. I shudder to think where I would be if not for you being my trusted friend, and my factor, and my . . . companion. I just want to tell you how much I wish things had turned out differently between us."

She nodded, the desperate words in her heart somehow getting tangled in her throat.

"I know that your birthday is in a few weeks, but I doubt I shall be here to celebrate it with you. Therefore, I wanted to give you your present early." He opened a drawer and pulled out a sheaf of papers. He took out the paper at the very top of the pile, and looked at it with something like trepidation.

Apprehensively, he held out the paper, and she took it from his hands.

"Those are the articles of your extended apprenticeship, the ones that Hartopp drew up when I took you over as my charge. As you can see by the lack of stamp, I never had the articles validated with the parish overseers." He took a deep breath. "I know how much you desire your independence, so take it. Your freedom is my gift to you. Upon your twenty-first birthday, you are both free to go."

Free. It was a word she had wanted to hear all of her life. In a matter of days, she would become her own woman. She could go wherever she liked, work wherever she liked, do whatever she liked. She held in her hands a ticket to be free, and not just her, but Willow, too. It should have been the happiest moment of her life. If it were not for that other word. *Go.*

"Of course," he hastened to add, "it is my wish that you remain here at Ballencrieff. I would have you stay on . . . as an appropriately paid factor. Goodness knows you've earned it. And Willow, too. She has shown herself to be an excellent nursemaid for Eric. And because . . ." He swallowed hard. "Because I don't want to live without you."

He couldn't say it. He couldn't say he loved her. Was it because he didn't? Or because he knew loving her to be futile?

She opened her mouth, but nothing came out. She never had problems speaking her mind—until now. She longed to say the words that she felt, but like him, she could not express it. Though she had no doubt that he cared for her, her love would not be enough for a man like him. He needed a wife with money, prestige, and enviable beauty. And these things she could not offer him.

She had to let him go. She had to let him build a life with Lady Violet. He had given her her freedom. Now she had to give him his.

But God help her, she couldn't. She had lost too many people she loved. She was not about to give up another.

There was a knock on the door.

"Come," he said in exasperation.

Bannerman opened the door. "Excuse me, sir. But the

ladies have descended for dinner. They're in the drawing room, awaiting your company."

"Very well. Do me a favor, Bannerman. Take Dexter up to my room, will you?"

"Certainly, sir." Although Bannerman did not appreciate animals of the four-legged kind, he performed his requested duty with aplomb.

Conall held out his hand to her. "Let's go in to dinner."

Shona looked at his hand. It pained her to think that would be the only way he could offer her his hand.

She turned away, unwilling to face the pain any longer. She had always been so attuned to the suffering of others, and would swiftly come to another's rescue. Now it was her own heart that was screaming for rescue. She had to do something.

And when her gaze landed on the book upon his desk, something snapped into her mind. It was a desperate idea . . . but then again, this was a time of desperation. Time was a noose around her neck.

"No. Thank ye. I've no wish to dine tonight. I want to share the good news with Willow. Ye go on in."

It took all the courage she had to look into his eyes. And then he bent over and gave her a kiss on the cheek.

How wonderful was that kiss! Chaste as it was, she'd have taken that over losing him forever. Even after the door closed behind him, the memory of that kiss was imprinted there upon her face.

Until a tear washed it away.

She wedged the book under her arm before dashing upstairs.

SIXTEEN

"You're not eating, sir. Is the dinner not to your liking?"

Conall glanced up at Lady Violet. Worry marred her otherwise beautiful features.

"Forgive me," he said as he set down the fork beside the untouched plate of roasted lamb. "I seem to be off my food tonight."

"I hope you are not unwell."

His eyes darted to the empty seat beside the duchess where Shona would have sat. "Not at all, Lady Violet. Just a trifle distracted. Thank you for your concern." He decided to change the subject. "And you? Have you had any more discomfiture?"

"No, sir. Thank you. A touch queasy this morning, but it has since left me in peace."

Suddenly, there was a commotion outside the dining room. Raised voices warred with hushed voices. Finally, Bannerman opened the door and shut it quickly behind him.

"What's happening, Bannerman?"

"Forgive me, sir, but Miss Willow is outside and she is most insistent on seeing you."

"Bannerman, I've told you before. You are never to censor Miss Willow. While she cares for my son, she is allowed full and immediate access to my attention. Let her in this instant."

"Yes, sir." Bannerman opened the door, and Willow ran in out of breath.

Immediately, Conall became alarmed. "Willow, what's wrong?"

"It's Shona, sir. She's fallen doon. I think she might be hurt!"

He bolted out of his chair. "Where is she?"

"In the garden. Come quickly!"

He ran out of the dining room without so much as a by-your-leave. "Where's Eric?" he called out to her as she ran behind him.

"In the nursery. Mrs. Docherty's looking after him."

He sped to the rear of the house and threw open the French doors. Darkness hid all but the flagstone walk along the middle of the square knot garden. The tall bushes and hedgerows surrounding it were only silhouettes in the twilight sky.

"Where is she?"

Willow skidded up behind him. "Over there," she panted. "Behind the rhododendrons."

Conall ran down the steps and across the walk. The gloaming cast the ground in shadow, but he could just make out a long form lying upon the far garden path.

"Shona!" Conall flew to the form.

Shona raised herself up on her hands. "I'm aright."

He knelt on the ground beside her, and took her in his arms. "What happened?"

Willow came up behind him. "We were oot here taking a walk. Next thing I know, doon she went."

"Are you hurt?" he asked her.

"I'm no' sure. I think it's my foot. I canna stand up."

Willow clutched the mantle tighter around her chest. "Poor, brave thing. She was screaming in agony a moment ago."

Concern clouded his features. "Let's get you inside. I want a proper look at you."

He lifted her effortlessly in his arms. Swiftly, he walked back up the garden path and up the stairs to the house.

In a trice, he had negotiated through the house to the drawing room. Willow opened the door for them.

Gingerly, he laid her down on the settee by the fire. Shona grimaced as he did so.

"Which foot is hurt?"

"The right one," she said.

He sat down beside her feet. He wrapped his hand under her calf and raised her foot in the air. Gently, he slid off her slipper. Shona groaned in discomfort.

He laid her stockinged foot upon his muscled thigh. "Is there any numbness in your toes?"

She shook her head.

"That's good. There doesn't seem to be any deformity in the ankle . . . most likely, you haven't broken it. Tell me if this pains you."

He pressed the ball of his thumb upon the arch of her foot.

"Ouch! Dammit, Conall!"

He cracked a smile. "Sorry. What about this?" Between his thumb and forefinger, he gently squeezed the hollows around her ankle.

"Gah!" She whacked him on the shoulder. "Are ye doing this on purpose?"

"Ow," he exclaimed. "You're not supposed to strike your doctor."

"Then stop torturing me!"

He smiled. "All right. One more examination. I'm going to move your foot to ascertain if there really is anything broken. Try not to hit me as I do this."

He lifted her leg up, and slowly moved her foot up and down. Shona groaned and bit her lip.

"Right. It seems you have sprained your ankle."

"Before or after you jostled it aboot just now?"

He shook his head. "Pity you didn't sprain your tongue."

She hit him again, prompting a chuckle from Conall.

"All right. Let's have a look at the skin. Take off your stocking."

"Ye do it. Ye've done it before."

He cast a sidewise glance at her. "Shona, behave yourself!"

"It pains me to bend that far. Go on. Have a heart."

He shook his head. "Er, Willow? Could you tear Bannerman away from his duties and tell him to fetch me some bandages?"

"Straightaway, sir," she promised before sprinting out of the room.

"Right. Let's have a closer look at that ankle, shall we?" Conall slipped Shona's skirt and petticoat up to her knee. His smooth hand slid up her leg, enjoying the feel of the firm contours. Midway up her thigh, her stockings ended, leaving exposed the baby-soft skin of her upper thigh. He couldn't help himself. His fingertips drew a lazy circle around her inner thigh, making her close her eyes in remembered ecstasy. He played with the ribbon garter holding up her stocking. With just one hand, he deftly unbuttoned it. Shona sighed as he trailed the tips of his fingers along her skin just above the stocking—all the way around her thigh. Her skin was so sweet, so smooth, that the touch of it sent desire rushing down to his cock.

He could still remember the sweet smell of her virginal musk, and how copious her desire for him had been. Between her legs, all had been warmth. The pink folds of her inner womanhood were plump on his tongue and tight around his finger. Many times he had relived that moment in the tollhouse, when he introduced her to a new form of pleasure. How he yearned to teach her more, and to bring her to fulfillment by joining his body to hers. And giving his penis the thrill that his fingers had enjoyed.

He curled his fingers over the top of the cotton stocking and pulled the fabric down. His knuckles stroked the skin down her knee, and then rolled the stocking all the way to her ankle.

The door opened and the duchess walked in. "Ballencrieff! What is the meaning of this?"

Conall, jolted out of his reverie, looked down at what the duchess saw. Shona was reclined upon the settee, the hem of her dress to her knee. Her calf was exposed, and her stocking was curled around her ankle, in his hand.

He faced the duchess. "I am in the process of examining Miss Shona's ankle, which has just suffered a very bad sprain. To what are you referring, Your Grace?"

"Ballencrieff, surely you can see the impropriety of examining a single woman's naked leg alone in a room, can you not?"

"I am a doctor, Your Grace. There is no indecency in what I do."

"Correction. You *were* a doctor. Now you are a landed,

titled gentleman, sir. It ill befits a gentleman to hold a profession of any kind."

"Madame, medicine is more than just a profession. It is a calling, one achieved through many long hours burning my eyes in focused study. And having acquired the skill to heal, I will not now withhold it from someone who is in dire need of medical attention."

The duchess's jaw tightened. "For the life of me, I cannot comprehend how such a learned man could be so naïve. Can you not see that this chit is merely trying to lure you away from marrying my daughter?"

Conall became incensed. "How can you be so narrow-minded? Does nothing in the world exist beyond your daughter's marriage?"

"Certainly there does. And that is why I am endeavoring so diligently to ensure that scheming vixens like your 'factor' over there do not conspire to subvert my arrangements."

To Shona's groans, Conall shifted her foot from his lap and eased out from under her. "Madame, I am mortified by your callousness. Have a care not to push me too far, or else there shall be no wedding."

"And if there is no wedding, sir, you shall push *me* too far. And I think we both know what that will mean for you."

Conall ground his teeth, fury blurring his vision. He took Shona into his arms once more, regretting the distress that the dangling of her foot caused her.

"I think, Shona, that the drawing room is not a fitting sick room for you. Come. I shall take you upstairs to your room where I can tend to you *unhampered and in my own manner.*"

* * *

Shona wrapped her arms tighter around Conall's neck as he climbed the stairs up to the nursery. He wore a scowl, but it was certainly not from the exertion of carrying her up the stairs.

"Are ye aright, Conall?

"I'm fine."

"Ye don't look fine."

"Shona," he replied in exasperation, "I'm fine. You're the one who's injured."

It seemed to her that he was the more injured, but she held her tongue. They finally reached the nursery, and as Willow said, Mrs. Docherty was there with Eric.

"Oh, dear! What's happened?"

Conall shouldered past her, bearing Shona in his arms. "Shona's had a nasty fall. She's injured her ankle. Bring those candles over by the bed, won't you?"

Conall put Shona down upon her bed. "Mrs. Docherty, I will need some medical supplies. Will you do me the very great favor of fetching the brown valise in my study?"

"No, please," exclaimed Shona. "You get it, Conall. I need to relieve myself, and I'll need Mrs. Docherty here to help me."

His mouth pursed in worry. "Of course. But have a care not to put any pressure on the foot. I'll return shortly."

Shona waited until Conall closed the nursery door . . . before she leaped off the bed.

"Did ye get it?" she demanded of Mrs. Docherty.

"Aye. It's right here." Mrs. Docherty opened a drawer and pulled up a bowl covered by a cloth. "Beet juice. Just like ye asked."

Shona flew to the desk and pulled out an unused quill feather. "Bring me the book."

While Shona yanked off her stocking, Mrs. Docherty pulled *The Practice of Physic, Surgery, and Midwifery on the Human Female* from under the bed and opened it onto the mattress to the bookmarked page. "Here ye go."

"Right. Now let's see . . . the diagram says that the foot discolors here, here, and here. Bring the beet juice!"

Mrs. Docherty held out the bowl. Shona dipped the top of the feather into the red liquid and dabbed at the outside of her heel. She also brushed some on the top of her arch. Immediately, the beet juice began to absorb into her skin, and the reddish stain made her foot look as if she had hurt it quite badly.

"How's that?" she asked the housekeeper.

"Looks convincing enough to me. Do you think the master will believe it?"

"I certainly hope so," she said, fanning her foot to speed the drying. "Because if he marries into that snobby family with their estates all over England, ye can be sure he'll have no more need of Ballencrieff."

Mrs. Docherty bit her lip. "God forbid it. I canna afford to lose yet another position."

"Aye. We'll all be losing something important."

The housekeeper placed an understanding hand on Shona's shoulder.

Shona exhaled. "I just need more time with him. Seeing how well he looked after his dog, he's bound to do as much for me. If I can just keep him here long enough, maybe I can get him to change his mind aboot Lady Violet."

"Let's hope this works," said Mrs. Docherty. "By the

by, ye do know that bruise will have to turn blue on the morrow, don't ye?"

"Aye," she said. "I've already got some indigo ink on the desk. It'll turn my skin blue enough, don't ye worry."

A voice came from behind the closed door. "Shona, it's me, Willow."

Mrs. Docherty went to the door and let Willow in.

Shona held up her foot. "What do ye think?"

Willow's eyes rounded as she set down the cotton bandages on the bed. "Looks ever so painful!"

Shona giggled. "Aye. It'll buy me a few days out of the fields, at least."

Another knock sounded on the door.

"I've returned with medicines," said Conall behind the door. "May I come in now?"

The smile ran away from Shona's face. "Just a minute!" she yelled at the door. "Here!" she shouted in a whisper. "Hide the book. And the feather! Quick!"

The two women snapped into action as Shona adjusted herself on the bed. When all was safely hidden from view, Mrs. Docherty opened the door.

"Thank goodness, sir. She's in terrible pain."

Conall's brows knitted as he glowered at Shona. "You stood upon it, didn't you?"

"I—I had to," Shona replied.

"I knew you should have waited until I've properly bandaged it. Right, let's have a look at it."

He crouched down beside her bed as he peered at her foot. The three women held their breath.

"Hand me that candle on the table."

Shona did so and waited. She watched as he puzzled over her heel, which was now stained dark pink. He compared it to her other foot, and shook his head.

Shona's heart started hammering in her chest. She hadn't even contemplated what she'd do if he discovered her deception.

"It's quite an injury," he said. "The ligament is either very strained or partially torn. But I can't understand why there hasn't been more swelling in the foot."

He glanced at Shona. Shona glanced at Willow. Willow glanced at Mrs. Docherty.

Mrs. Docherty shrugged. "God only knows, sir. Must be the chill outside that's kept it doon."

He blinked. "Perhaps. Well, the warmth in here will not serve you as well. So let's get your injury properly dressed, shall we?"

She watched him as he went to the washstand and poured a little water from the ewer into the basin. The sight of so large a man in a child's room filled with dainty furniture was curiously fascinating. Then he opened his valise on Willow's bed, and Shona peeked in. One side of the valise was lined with small wooden compartments, and the compartments were filled with bottles and jars of varying sizes. On the other side, strange-looking metal instruments were affixed to the inside of the valise. She hoped he wouldn't have to use those torture devices on her.

He lifted a small brown bottle from one of the compartments and poured some into the basin of water. Completely unmindful of his elegant shirtsleeves, he dunked a cloth in the mixture and wrung out some of the water. He stood at the end of Shona's bed and leaned over her foot with the wet towel.

"Wait!" she exclaimed, surprising him. "What the de'il is that?"

His hand froze in midair. "It's perfectly harmless, I

assure you. Just some water mixed with Goulard's extract."

Harmless to other people, perhaps, but a wet rag on her painted ankle would be disastrous. "What kind of piss-water is Goulard's extract?"

He shook his head. "It's an astringent. It'll keep down the swelling."

"I don't have any swelling. You said so yerself."

"True, but the tissues in your ankle will soon inflame. And the swelling will worsen the pain."

"I don't want any of that. It's got a funny smell."

"Don't be such a child. It'll do you good."

"I don't want it, I tell ye!"

"All right," he said. "Would you prefer a wet compress of hot vinegar? It's not as effective but a good astringent nonetheless."

She'd not have a *wet* anything. "No. Just the bandages. It worked for Dexter. It'll work for me."

"Shona, if you're going to be difficult, I shall have to tie you to the bed."

Panic began to bubble up. "N-no. I'll take the funny-smelling stuff in yer hand. Just let me apply it. I'm ticklish," she added with a shrug.

He handed her the cloth. "Suit yourself. Make sure you get it all over your foot."

Gingerly, she applied it onto her ankle, trying as best she could to give the *appearance* of moistening her foot. If any of her bruises began to erase before he bandaged her leg, it would be catastrophic—not just for her, but for Willow and Mrs. Docherty as well.

Then Conall took one of the strips of cotton and held it in place above her toes. He wound it around the ball of her foot and continued up her foot.

"Is this too tight?"

Shona shrugged. "It isna comfortable."

"I mean, do your toes feel numb? I don't want the bandage to occlude blood flow to the rest of your foot."

"No."

"Let's make sure." Conall brought the candle closer. He pressed his thumb into the flesh beside her toenail. Shona noticed how the skin blanched, but quickly turned pink again.

"It doesn't appear too tight, but let me know if your skin begins to tingle."

She watched as he wrapped a second strip in a figure eight around her ankle and under her foot, effectively immobilizing it.

Finally, a third strip went up her calf. She loved the feel of his hands on her bare flesh. She should have considered faking an injury to her hip instead.

"There," he said as he tied off the end of the strip. "How does it feel?"

"Better," she said. "Thank ye."

He smiled. "As it's you, I'll waive my usual fee. Now, let's tend to your other injuries." He took one of her hands and turned it palm upward. Puzzled, he looked at her other hand. "That's strange. There are no scrapes on your knees or your hands. How did you stop your fall?"

"Oh," she said, her mind racing. "I fell on my arse. Plenty of cushioning there. Didn't feel a thing."

"I see," he said with a smile. "Well, it's very important you keep your foot elevated and at rest for the next seven days at the very least. Willow, please fetch some pillows for your sister, and place them under her foot. I'll check on you in the morning."

"Don't go." She gripped his hand, then tried to erase

the desperation from her expression. "Won't ye keep me company a wee while longer?"

He grinned benevolently. "Certainly." He went to the desk and dragged the chair closer to her bedside.

"Mrs. Docherty," began Shona, careful to convey her meaning clearly, "would ye mind terribly bringing me some supper? It's a bother, I know, so ask Willow to help ye. We'll look after the sleeping bairn in the meanwhile."

Mrs. Docherty nodded knowingly, and closed the nursery room door behind her.

It was only after they were left alone that Shona seemed to struggle for words. There was so much she wanted to say that she didn't know where to begin.

"I canna pretend to be happy that ye're marrying Lady Violet. But I suppose a man such as yerself must choose a lady of quality for a wife—"

"Shona . . ."

"—and Lady Violet is very beautiful—"

He pinched the bridge of his nose.

"—and I'm glad after all that she's a sweet-natured lass—"

"She's in love with Stewart," he blurted out.

Shona's eyes widened. "Ye know?"

"Of course. She doesn't want to marry me any more than I want to marry her."

Shona was aghast. "But . . . then why?"

"Her Grace wants her only daughter to marry a titled man."

"But there are lots of titled men in England. Why ye?"

He heaved a profound sigh, and she could see how much this weighed upon him. "Lady Violet is carrying Stewart's child. The randy fool deflowered the girl and got her with a belly. Consequently, the duchess can't bear the sight of Stewart, and I can't say I blame her. But such is the hatred she feels for him that she'd rather condemn her daughter to perpetual shame and ignominy by letting her give birth to a bastard than allow Stewart to inherit the dukedom of Basinghall."

Now she knew why the poor girl's stomach had been so unsettled. And her mother offered her no comfort! "Och! That woman is a heartless banshee."

"Yes, she is. But she's also a very powerful banshee. One with the ability and disposition to inflict great damage."

His words were pregnant with meaning. Suddenly, she could sense the hidden suffering in his heart, just as easily as if it had been a full-throated shout. "The duchess threatened ye in the drawing room, didn't she? What did she mean when she warned ye against pushing her too far?"

He placed his elbows on his knees and stared at the floor. Immediately, she became alarmed. She had never seen him so conflicted.

She put a reassuring hand upon his head. The soft waves curled around her fingers.

"I wasn't entirely honest with you when I told you my wife died of childbed fever. The truth is much more salacious. And something I've been forced to keep a secret."

It was many moments before he spoke. Shona's breath caught in her throat.

"My wife . . . was murdered."

The word brought flash upon flash of images on her mind. Her family's dead bodies strewn on the kitchen floor. The haunting screams—theirs and hers—echoed in her ears. "How?"

"She was poisoned. By her lover."

Shona tried to wrap her mind around what he'd just said. Which was the more terrible—that Conall's wife was murdered, or that she had betrayed him?

He looked up then, guilt etched upon his forehead. "I don't know precisely how long their affair had been going on. I was away a great deal. The practice was thriving. My patients were numerous, and wealthy—very demanding upon my time. Christina . . . was a young woman, not much older than you are now. I suppose I neglected her needs. I left her alone too often, and . . . I imagine she determined that she was not going to be lonely all by herself."

He rubbed his palms together, as if he were trying to erase some invisible spot on them. "One day, a patient I was treating made a swift recovery, and I came home a few days earlier than expected. I found them . . . in our bed . . . asleep in each other's arms." He closed his eyes against the visual memory.

"I'm sorry," she said, but he shook his head against her offered consolation.

"It was bad enough that she had cuckolded me," he continued. "But that blackguard actually refused to give her up. He told me in no uncertain terms that I was a disappointment as a husband and that I didn't deserve her. That Christina had sworn her life to him, and he intended to run away with her. I don't mind telling you it gave me a great deal of pleasure to beat that man to a pulp before he was able to run out of the house. Christina, however . . . she never apologized for taking a lover. In fact, she seemed relieved that her affair had finally come to light.

"I should have divorced her. But I couldn't bring myself to do it. I did love her. A few weeks later, though, Christina told me she was pregnant. I didn't know what to think. And she couldn't make me any assurances about whose baby it was. But she wanted us to be a family, and . . . I wanted that, too. So she rededicated herself to me and promised to be faithful. For my part, I vowed to make her happier. And we consented to leave our marriage bed untouched while we began to rebuild the trust between us.

"But that man . . . he would not let her go. He pestered her whenever I was called away. Sometimes he sent her gifts, and sometimes he wrote angry, vitriolic letters. If she had only told me about it at the time, I would have been able to protect her. But she hid the truth from me.

"Four days after Eric was born, some teacakes and chocolates were delivered to her. The note was felicitous, but unsigned. She must have assumed it was from one of our friends, or from one of my well-wishing clients. Neither of us imagined it could have been from *him*. I found her in bed, her tongue—"

Conall's face twisted into an expression of heartsickness. The breath backed up in his throat.

Shona raised herself to her knees and poured her body over Conall's quaking shoulders. A futile gesture, perhaps, because what pained him came not from without, but within.

"I'm sorry. I shouldn't be burdening you with this," he said.

"Of course ye should." She would give anything to protect Conall, and never had she felt the instinct to defend so keenly as now. Whatever it took to make his silent suffering go away, by God, she would do it. "We're friends. Ye must tell me the grief. I'll understand."

"No," he said, wiping his eye with the heel of his hand. "I feel a complete fool."

She took his sodden face in her hands. "Listen to me, Conall MacEwan. The grief . . . it's like broken glass. Ye must no' keep it inside, or it'll just keep making ye bleed all over again. Ye've got to let it out. Preferably to someone who knows what to do with all the pieces."

His eyes shone from the tears that still pooled in his reddening eyes. "I tell my son that big boys don't cry. And look at me now."

"Tears are special things, Conall. They're no' a sign of weakness. No other creature can cry. Tears are a mark of yer humanity."

He nodded a mute thanks, distrusting the emotion in his throat. Guiltily, he laid her back down on the bed, and adjusted a pillow under her bandaged ankle.

"Whatever happened to him?" she asked. "The man that poisoned yer wife?"

He resumed his seat on the chair and sighed deeply before answering. "I let him go."

Shona's eyes rounded. "Ye what?"

"What else could I do? I had no proof it was he who did it. And even if I had, what good would it have done Christina to have him brought to justice? Her infidelity would be brought to light. Her memory would be tarnished—in the eyes of her friends, her family, her child. If I'd brought accusations against her lover, it would have ruined Eric's future. Even I can't be certain that Eric is mine. The doubt of his legitimacy would pursue him forever. I couldn't let him live with that. So yes, the man who killed Christina walks free. She pledged him her life, and when she wouldn't give it to him, he took it. Losing Christina was enough. I was not about to give him my whole family."

Things started to fall into place in Shona's head. "Is that what the duchess threatened ye with? Exposing yer wife's unfaithfulness?"

He nodded slowly. "And my son's potential illegitimacy."

Simultaneously, Shona and Conall turned toward the crib. Eric slept quietly, his full pink lips a perfect *O*. The long eyelashes curled over his round cheeks, and his breath came in quick bursts.

"Even if he isn't mine," Conall continued, "I couldn't love that boy any less."

Shona was touched deeply. Conall was indeed a special man.

"How did Her Grace learn about yer wife's bedmate?"

Conall made a throaty, frustrated growl. "I don't know! And she won't tell me. God knows she has little enough motivation to do so. If she does, she might lose the hold she has over me. At this point, I can only speculate. There was an inquest following Christina's death, but there was never any suspicion of poison. I was a doctor, and no one questioned my observation that Christina had died of childbed fever. In fact, the coroner was a friend of mine . . . I did my medical studies with him. But maybe he had ascertained the truth about Christina's death and covered it up for my sake. Maybe the duchess paid him to learn the truth so that no one would ever give credence to my medical opinion again. Maybe Stewart had become such a thorn in her side that she did everything she could to show her daughter what a loathsome family we are." He rubbed his forehead. "All I have are maybes. But the only thing I know for certain is that the duchess has extraordinary power to cripple us. If she reveals what she knows, it will not only make Eric a bastard in the eyes of the world, but it would taint his memory of his mother once he's old enough to understand."

He took her hand in his. "So you see, Shona, I'm not marrying Lady Violet for her money. I have to marry her because if I don't, whatever happiness my son can enjoy will be destroyed. Do you understand?"

"Aye, I do." She squeezed his hand. "But what aboot yer happiness? To marry a woman who does no' love ye . . . won't ye just be reliving that which ye had with Christina?"

"That doesn't matter. When a man becomes a father, his own well-being falls miles behind that of his child."

And, it seems, that of the woman who loves him.

Conall began to pack up his medical valise. "I'll talk to Her Grace. We'll postpone our journey a few days until I'm certain you're fit enough to be back on your feet."

Shona watched him collect the vials and adjust the implements. She had accomplished her purpose—to keep him near her a wee while longer. But in light of all he had confessed to her, it seemed pointless now. To make him love her now would only make his inevitable separation even more painful. And even if Shona could get him to propose to her, their marriage would cost him his child's future.

"So ye'll be marrying the Lady Violet, then."

He stood over her. But his proud shoulders were now stooped from the weight of his cares. "Get some rest. I'll check on you in the morning."

SEVENTEEN

Stewart gazed out at Lady Violet, who was seated upon his glossy black mare, Charybdis. Violet walked the horse into a trot around the enclosed paddock, the sun shining on her perfectly straight back and her feathered hat.

He cupped his hand around his mouth. "How does she handle?"

"Stunningly!" she called back. Her dark blue riding habit draped becomingly over the horse's flanks. "And she's so beautiful, too."

You both are. Stewart smiled from behind the gate, perching a polished black Hessian on the lowest rung. Oh, how he envied that saddle. He knew precisely how it felt. Violet's bottom was a veritable masterpiece of flesh—high and rounded with barely a fold underneath it. Those pert nether cheeks were beauteous to the eye, but the sensation of them curving in his palm and bouncing upon his hips were without equal.

One stolen afternoon. That was all they'd had together, after more than three years of eyeing each other over champagne glasses and circling each other on the dance floor. Yet their pretend courtship made the anticipation of her surrender all the sweeter. That afternoon, she was tremulous in his arms, wanting to love him but afraid to do so. He gentled his tack for her, slowly coaxing her until her desire clamored louder than her reluctance. Finally, she became a willing participant in her own seduction—not just offering her breasts to his kisses, but dangling them for his mouth; not just spreading her legs for him, but wrapping them around his waist. The first time he made love to her, her pain kept her from reaching her climax. But he found that he derived far more enjoyment from watching her reach her pleasure at his fingertips than he had merely thrusting inside her.

He closed his eyes to better relive the memory. She had kept her shift on, a beautiful lace-trimmed garment, as conciliation to her modesty. But by the time they were ready for the second lovemaking, she herself shrugged it off, along with her other maidenly inhibitions. A most assiduous pupil she was, and when he asked her to ride him, she demonstrated—naked—what a spectacular equestrian she truly was. He opened his eyes once more, watching her bounce upon the beast and imagining all her naughty bits under that royal blue riding habit. Violet looked eminently regal riding sidesaddle, but she was so much more bewitching when she rode astride.

He sighed. Since that one glorious afternoon, he hadn't been able to get her out of his mind. And if that were not self-imposed torture enough, he realized that his mind and body craved no other but her. Of all the women he knew—and they were legion—only Violet ever seemed to want him for who he truly was, and not for who he often pretended to be. Other women relished his faults, even taking advantage of them. Violet, however, accepted his shortcomings but always expected better of him. She was warm, charming, and tenderhearted. And he enjoyed her company not just in his bed, but on his arm. His eyebrows lifted in self-mockery. That afternoon . . . who, he wondered, surrendered to whom?

From the corner of his eye, he caught a flash of yellow. He turned to look. It was the duchess walking up the path to the paddock, a gold-colored parasol open above her head and an abigail walking behind her.

"Good morning, Your Grace," he said, effecting a deep bow.

"Good morning," she replied archly. "Do have the goodness to tell me why my daughter is out here unchaperoned and why she is riding that horse."

"Ah. Well, Charybdis is to be my wedding gift to Lady Violet." He returned his gaze to horse and rider. "Just look at her out there. Those long, beautiful legs. The curve of her rump. That soft, tender mouth. She almost begs to be mounted. I can tell you that she was a bit wild at the first, but once I broke her in, she is the best ride a man could ask for."

The Duchess of Basinghall leveled her quickly devolving composure upon Stewart. "I beg your pardon!"

Stewart wrinkled his forehead, confused. "Oh, I see! How carelessly vague of me. Of course I was referring to the mare, not your daughter."

The duchess glanced distrustfully at Stewart before signaling to Violet with her parasol. "Mr. MacEwan, on behalf of my daughter, I would like to thank you for your wedding gift. But I'm afraid we must decline it."

Stewart was pained. "But why, Your Grace? Charybdis is the finest thing I own, and I love that mare dearly. Even so, there would be no greater pleasure for me than to give her to Violet."

She offered him only her profile. "I believe, Mr. Mac-

Ewan, that you have had quite enough pleasure at my daughter's expense."

Stewart narrowed his eyes upon her. He was not as good as Conall at keeping his emotions in check. "Your Grace, you ought to have a care. If not out of respect for the fact that we will, after all, be family, then at least consider that being mean-spirited also makes a woman extremely unattractive."

The duchess didn't flinch in the slightest. "Mr. Mac-Ewan, I would consider that horse a member of my family before I do you. Do not insult me by pretending that you care for my daughter's happiness. If you had, you would have asked for my daughter's favor in the proper manner, not making away with it like a thief in the night. You injure my daughter's honor and then ask me to simply forget the defilement, even as it grows in my daughter's belly. Family indeed! You have no regard for me whatsoever. What you have done is filled a wooden box with rotting rubbish, wrapped it with a bow, and placed it upon my lap—calling it a fragrant gift. Please ask my daughter to come down off that animal. I will have nothing more from you."

There was nothing more she could do.

Shona turned onto her side on the bed. Dejectedly, she watched the dust motes swirling in the ray of sunshine streaming from the window. In the light of the sun they sparkled and danced. But once they left it, they were adrift and in the dark. Like her.

She tried turning her thoughts toward finding Camran. Imagining their excited reunion always used to bring her joy. But not this time. Her heart craved a different happiness, and the loss of it eclipsed any other emotion.

Conall was to marry Lady Violet at month's end. It was little comfort to her that neither wanted this marriage. Because in the end, Violet would become his wife and not Shona. It was Violet who would receive his smiles, grace his arm, fill his bed. Even if he did not love her now, Conall would eventually succumb—there was little of Violet not to love. And then Violet would not only be his wife, but the love of his heart. A lone tear wended down her temple and disappeared on her pillow.

Mrs. Docherty came to the nursery door. Motherly sympathy filled her voice. "I brought ye some tea, hen."

Shona didn't even face her. "I don't want anything."

She put the tray down on the desk. "The master keeps wanting to come up and see to yer ankle. I've put him off all morning. I don't know what else to tell him."

Shona was supposed to have risen early to feather some blue India ink onto her ankle, aging the appearance of the bruising. But she had neither the desire nor the willpower to keep up the deception.

"Tell him I lopped it off."

"Shona, ye've got to be sensible. Get up. If ye don't paint up yer ankle, he'll know we all tricked him. Ye don't want that kind of trouble. And quite frankly, neither do Willow and me."

She didn't care—not for herself, at any rate. As soon as his carriage departed for England, she intended to leave Ballencrieff House with Willow.

Mrs. Docherty sat on the edge of the bed. "And ye don't want that uppity duchess thinking she was right about ye all along."

No, she didn't want that. The Duchess of Basinghall already had too much control over other people. She wasn't prepared to give her any more.

"And ye've got one more day with the master. Don't spend it here in bed when ye can spend these last precious hours with him."

One more day. It wasn't enough time. What she wanted to do with Conall could fill a thousand lifetimes. She closed her eyes. One day long ago, her life had changed in just a few minutes. There was power in a moment's time. And she was now being given a whole day of moments.

Mayhap her life would change once more.

Conall could not focus his attention on the papers on his desk. Though they were orderly and well categorized, all he could think about was that it was Shona who had made them that way.

It wasn't difficult to guess that their conversation last night had something to do with why he wasn't being let in to see her this morning. He knew it wasn't just her ankle that was hurting; her heart was hurting, too. He wanted more than anything to comfort her. But he could not give her the solace she wanted.

He grew restless in his chair, feeling as if the walls were pressing in on him from all sides. Twice in his life, he had had the sensation that he was about to make a monumental mistake—once, when he took a woman back. And now, when he pushed another away.

He was a man of science. He relished the inflexibility of evidence, and the indisputable reality of facts. One could always build a path of thought or deed upon the stepping stones of facts. Empirically, he knew he was making the right choice by marrying Violet.

But his gut was telling him something altogether different.

A knock at the door sounded before Bannerman stepped in. "Pardon me, sir, but some visitors have just arrived."

He pursed his lips in irritation. "Bannerman, can't you see I'm trying to prepare for a month's voyage?"

"I beg your pardon, sir, but the gentlemen are not here to see you. They're asking to see the Misses Shona and Willow."

"Oh?" His brows drew together. "Are they tenants?"

"No, sir. They've given their names as the McCullough and his son Brandubh. And sir? Mr. Hartopp is with them."

A warning sounded in his head. "What the hell does that man want?"

"I could not say, sir."

"I'll see him. But say nothing to the ladies just yet. Just explain to the men that Shona is indisposed."

"I do apologize, sir, but they intersected in the hall as Miss Shona was coming downstairs. She's escorted them into the morning room. I came to alert you to their presence."

"Blast! What is that woman doing out of bed?" *And yet refusing to see him.* He dropped the portfolio onto the desk and bolted out of his chair. Conall got that doomful sensation again, the same one that penetrated his life the moment he first laid eyes on his wife's lover.

He practically ran to the morning room.

EIGHTEEN

Conall flung open the door to the morning room, trying to quell his rising fears.

Three men stood up as he came in. The oldest was a burly man, heavy about the shoulders and chest. His brown hair had begun to silver, lending an air of experience and wisdom that his eyes already boasted. He and the younger man, who was a head taller but with a similar worldly expression, wore the same green and red checkerboard tartan on their coats and kilts.

The elder held out a beefy hand. "Good morning, Ballencrieff. I am the McCullough of McCullough."

"How do you do, sir?"

For a moment, the corners of the man's mouth twitched. "May I present my son, Brandubh McCullough."

Conall was met with proud, unflinching eyes as he shook the younger man's hand.

"I believe ye already know Hartopp."

Conall cast him a leery glance. "We've had dealings."

Hartopp acknowledged him before sitting down, a strange smile painted on his face.

Shona was seated in an upholstered chair, one foot shod and the other still bandaged.

"Good morning at last, Shona. May I ask how you got down the stairs?"

"Carefully."

"You should be resting that ankle. I'll ask Bannerman to help you back up the stairs."

"Ballencrieff," interrupted McCullough, "with yer permission, I'd like Miss Shona to stay. What I have to say concerns her."

"I see," he said, reluctance gnawing at his belly.

"And Willow, too. Is she at home?"

"No, I'm sorry," responded Shona. "She's gone in to Thornhill with Dr. MacEwan's little boy to collect some new shoes she'd ordered for him."

Conall felt uncomfortable letting these men into his confidence as Shona had just done. "Please sit down, gentlemen, and tell me to what I owe the surprising pleasure of your visit."

There it was again, that curling at the corner of McCullough's mouth, as if he were trying to contain his laughter.

"Did I say something amusing, McCullough?" Conall asked.

"Er, no. Forgive me. I . . . did not expect ye to be English."

Conall sighed in irritation. "I assure you, sir, I am as Scots as you are."

The elder man's gaze scoured Conall's linen cravat, brocade waistcoat, fawn breeches, and black boots—and his smile widened. " 'Course ye are. Just that I know of so few Scotsmen that would willingly masquerade as a Sassenach."

The sarcastic remark made the other men chuckle. Everyone in the room was Scottish—including him—but somehow, Conall felt like an outsider.

"Perhaps that's because they would never be able to pass themselves off as articulate enough to be English."

A flicker of rage flashed in McCullough's eyes, but he masked it well. "'Pon my word, ye've a quick wit, haven't ye? I like that in a friend and ally. Ye must call me Duncan."

Conall immediately became suspicious. "Is that why you've come? In the hopes that we'll be allies?"

"Aye! And we soon shall." He turned to Shona. Duncan had a habit of breathing wetly before each sentence. "Miss Shona, I tell ye first that I'm aware what happened to yer people. My condolences for yer loss. John and Fiona MacAslan were good folk, and are well remembered up our way."

Shona acknowledged his sympathy with a curt nod.

"Ye were just a wee lass at the time they were killed, so ye couldn't have known. But John MacAslan and I made a pact with each other. When ye came of age, one of ye gels were to be married to my son, Brandubh."

Conall watched as Shona's gaze flew to the handsome young man sitting beside Duncan. There was a steeliness to him, an innate pride that came from the comfortable knowledge that he was a man with wealth, power, and good looks. It would not be difficult for a beautiful woman like Shona to fall in love with a man such as he.

"Wait," she said. "Ye knew my parents?"

"Of course!" exclaimed Duncan. "Yer father and I were old friends. We fought side by side in our youth. And we wanted to bind our two families forever by making an alliance of matrimony. Even after yer parents were killed, 'twas always my intention to fulfill that pact.

But then ye and Willow ran away, and we lost ye. And Brandubh has been waiting for years for his intended bride. 'Twas happy news indeed when Hartopp here told us he'd found ye."

Brandubh leaned forward over his knees. "I know ye've been caught unawares with this news. If yer parents hadn't died, ye would ha' grown up at Ravens Craig and we'd have come to know one other well these past twelve years. We canna recover that lost time, but we can start afresh." Brandubh turned his blue-black eyes upon Conall. "With yer permission, sir, I'd like to visit Ballencrieff House and pay court to the ladies."

Conall was taken aback, aware of an imminent feeling of loss. Rationally, he knew that it should not concern him once he married Violet. But the thought of Shona belonging to another man was something he found exceedingly distressing.

"I'm afraid that's impossible, sir. I shall be setting out for England."

"Oh?"

"Yes, I'm being married."

"Congratulations," Duncan said.

Brandubh's eyebrows threaded together. "Is Miss Shona going as well?"

"Er, no, but it would be highly improper for her to receive guests without a supervisory presence to safeguard her reputation."

Brandubh and Duncan glanced at one another. Duncan's maddening smile reappeared. "I was under the impression that Shona and Willow were servants in yer employ. I can appreciate yer protectiveness of them, but the lasses are of age. Surely they can see whomever they like."

Conall was caught off guard. "Yes, well, I am very cautious where it concerns the female members of my staff. And these ladies are my apprentices until they turn twenty-one. I am therefore legally responsible for their well-being and for the formation of their character."

Brandubh made a face. Clearly, he was unaccustomed to being declined anything. "Well, when *may* I pay court?"

"I shall let you know." Conall stood up to indicate that the meeting was concluded.

Shona looked up at him, daggers shooting from her eyes. "May I not be permitted to give answer first? After all, this is aboot me."

If there was ever a time that Conall wished she'd hold her tongue, this was it. "If you must."

Shona clasped her hands in her lap before addressing Duncan. "Thank ye for wanting to honor the pact that ye made with my father. But now that he's gone, I am not beholden to it. As ye say, I am of age, and I can marry whomever I like."

Duncan smiled broadly. "Aye, ye can, lass. But before ye turn my son away, ye should know that marrying him will make ye one of the wealthiest women in all of Ross-shire, Cromarty-shire, and Inverness-shire combined. I own land in the hundreds of thousands of acres. Businesses, farms . . . even a few villages named after me. Castles, carriages, clothes . . . whatever it is, ye will want for nothing. And Brandubh here," he said, slapping his son on the back, "has just been given a seat on the Scottish Council, one of the youngest men ever to be named to it. Mark my words, he's going to be leading the nation of Scotland in the years to come. And he's handsome, too. Just like his da."

Shona smirked at Duncan's playful chuckling.

Conall did not feel like sharing in the joke.

"Och," continued Duncan, "I could go on and on aboot my son. I'm a proud father. But I'd like for ye to get to know him as I do. Welcome his suit, and learn for yerself what a good man he is." He leaned in conspiratorially. "Besides, lass, ye're a Highlander. Ye don't belong doon here in the Lowlands. May as well be North England. Ye must return to the sweet grass of Ross-shire, and the land that birthed yer father and every generation afore him. E'en if ye don't do it for the sake of Brandubh, at least do it to honor the memory of yer da."

Conall could swear on the Archbishop of Canterbury's Bible that every word Duncan was saying was a lie. But again, it was not the facts speaking, but his gut. And that was a language he was just beginning to understand.

"Gentlemen," interrupted Conall, "speaking as the lady's doctor, I really must insist that she rest. She had a very nasty fall yesterday, and I must tend to her right away."

Duncan shot him a withering glance. "Mayhap she fell because she is being ill used. A lady is too delicate a creature to be serving as a factor."

Shona spared Conall a response. " 'Tis a lie! I've been the laird's factor since Hartopp here was discharged, and I've been doing a first-rate job. Ye can ask him yerself. In fact, we've already gotten some of the tenants paid up—something Hartopp could never do for all his bullying and threats."

"My apologies, Miss Shona. I didn't mean to imply that ye *couldn't* do the job. I just meant that a lady such as yerself ought to be benefiting from the estate's wealth, not building it."

Brandubh turned to Conall. His voice was deep and his words determined. "Which reminds me of something else that Mr. Hartopp mentioned to us. He said that yer estate has been struggling of late. That the previous laird, yer uncle Macrath, had nearly bankrupted the estate, and his death has left the tenants adrift."

Anger welled up inside Conall. "This is outrageous, Hartopp! You have no right to discuss my private affairs with anyone!"

Brandubh held up a steadying hand. He wore a confidence that was unusual for a man who was only a few years past twenty. "Ye may be glad he's done that, my lord Ballencrieff. Because I have a proposition that ye may find pleasing. Knowing ye to be unaccustomed to managing such a large estate, I am prepared to purchase the land from ye."

"What?"

"Hartopp tells me that it's a worthy investment for someone with the experience to manage it. Unlike my father, I choose not to limit my residence to the Highlands. I would like to own a home in Dumfriesshire, and having seen Ballencrieff with my own eyes, it pleases me." At Conall's hesitation, he continued. "And you needn't worry about yer servants. I'll retain them all. Yer tenants, too. And yer apprentices," he added with a nod toward Shona. "Name yer price."

Duncan put an elbow on one knee, arrogance emanating from him. "Is that *articulate* enough for ye?"

With each passing moment, Conall grew increasingly suspicious of these men. He'd stake his life on the notion that they were up to no good. But he could not imagine what their motives could be. Whatever it was, these men gave him the sickening feeling that they brought disaster.

"Ballencrieff is not for sale, gentlemen. I may not have arrived with extensive familiarity with running an estate, but experience comes by doing. And I hope to get better at it as the years progress. I will, of course, make note of your interest, should the occasion to sell ever arise." Conall rose from his chair. "And now, with your kind indulgence, I should like to return to my arrangements. Good day to you."

Duncan lumbered out of his chair. "A pity. I wish ye a safe journey, Ballencrieff. And our felicitations on yer upcoming nuptials. Miss Shona, it was a pleasure to make yer acquaintance. Give my regards to Miss Willow."

A sense of relief washed over Conall as the men walked toward the morning room door.

Suddenly, Duncan turned around. "One last question, Miss Shona. Which of ye is the elder—ye or yer sister?"

She shrugged. "Willow is. By aboot three minutes."

Duncan smiled broadly. "Thank ye. Good day to ye, now."

"Good day."

Conall turned them over to Bannerman, who returned their hats and walking sticks to them before showing them out the front door.

A sense of foreboding weighed upon him as he closed the morning room door.

"Shona, I've been thinking . . . perhaps you and Willow ought to make the journey to England with us."

She narrowed her eyes upon him. "Really? Is that an

actual invitation to yer wedding, or did ye want us to wait outside in the carriage while ye speak yer vows?"

"Don't be so acerbic. I'm worried about you. Those men," he said, pointing at the empty settee, "are not what they pretend. I'd stake my life on it. I don't know what their intentions are, but I'll swear that their motives are nefarious."

"Why? Because that handsome Brandubh McCullough wants to marry me?"

"Yes." Immediately, he realized the way his answer sounded. "No! What I mean is—"

"So! Ye think it's too fantastical that someone like me could be desirable as a wife, is that it?"

"No, that it's not it at all—"

"I ought to put my good foot right up yer insufferable arse. Here ye are, aboot to marry a beautiful, wealthy woman, and yet ye canna bear me to attract the attentions of a good-looking wealthy man. It doesna content ye to have all the sweets on yer own plate—ye have to begrudge what's on mine as well!"

He held up his hands defensively. "Listen to me—"

She stood up in anger. "No, ye listen! If ye think I'm going to wither away for want of ye, ye're sadly mistaken. My life shall not be over just because ye choose to give yers up. Go. Marry Lady *Violated*. See if I care."

Against his will, he chuckled. "I never said that was what I wanted from you. I'm just asking that you not entertain Brandubh McCullough. He's after you, Shona, and not in the way that should flatter a woman." Conall began to pace the carpeted floor. "The McCulloughs want to possess you, no matter what the cost—glorify Brandubh's accomplishments, appeal to the love you bear your father . . . even offer to purchase you along with this estate. They'd do anything to get their hands on you."

Her mouth became a grim line. " 'Tis a pity ye won't do the same."

Her words sliced him right through the heart. "Shona . . ."

She turned away, staring out the window at nothing. He came up behind her and put his hands on her shoulders. She was shaking.

He smoothed his hands down her arms. The skin was soft, but cold. "I despise myself for what I've put you through. I hope you will find it in your heart to forgive me. Because I do love you so."

Shona inclined her head. "There was a time when I desperately wanted to hear those words. But now I realize they are not enough. Spoken love is worth its own weight—nothing. I want a love that can be seen, Conall. I want a love that I can depend upon."

She was right. He'd meant what he said, but he had failed to prove it.

And she deserved it from him.

She deserved it from someone.

But she would not find it in Brandubh McCullough.

He kissed her ear. "One day, I will prove it to you."

NINETEEN

Stewart leaned his back against the trunk of the tree, a scowl on his face. He gazed down into the valley where a swollen river laughed along the rocky brae.

"What's wrong with me?" he shouted to nobody.

Charybdis craned her massive head in his direction, giving him a perplexed look before returning her attention to the patch of high grass she was munching on.

He felt like a complete ass. Why was he allowing that medusa of a woman to rob him of his child? Of his future?

He knew that the answer to that did not lie with the duchess. It lay within himself. He could not offer Violet a future. He had no money, no prospects, no character—only an insurmountable string of vices. She was better off with Conall. And so was his child.

His child. For the first time, he understood why Conall had made the decision to acquiesce to the duchess's demands. Nothing was more important than Eric. He was willing to sacrifice his own happiness to ensure that Eric would never suffer from his mistakes. Now Stewart understood why Conall had agreed to marry Lady Violet. It certainly wasn't to save Stewart's hide. Quite frankly, he wasn't surprised. His hide wasn't worth saving.

Ever since he'd left London, he felt renewed. After wallowing in the underbelly of London's vices for so long, he'd begun to lose sight of himself. He'd felt drained and hollow, like an empty wine bottle. It seemed as though he didn't enjoy the pleasures of London so much as the pleasures of London enjoyed him. Putting some distance between himself and his old life had given him a new perspective on things.

And on people. Upon much reflecting, he realized that only one person in the world would give two farthings to save his miserable hide. Only one person in the world thought the world of him.

"Mind if I join you?"

He recognized the voice instantly, but its nearness startled him. He turned around, raising a hand to shield his eyes from the sunlight.

There, haloed by the rays of the late morning sun, was Violet. She was as lovely as ever, her dark hair pinned up under a pink and green silk bonnet, while her light green dress was flattened against her trim figure by the strong breeze. She looked like a rare flower.

"Good Lord!" he remarked as he stood up. "I must have just conjured you with my thoughts."

Violet grinned. "That gladdens my heart, for you are never far from mine."

Stewart felt a quickening in his heart. "Is your mother not with you?"

"No. She's abed with one of her debilitating head-aches."

Probably bitten by one of those snakes growing out of her hair. "Would you care to sit down?" Stewart looked about for something she could sit on to keep her beautiful dress from getting smudged. The only thing he'd brought with him was his sketchbook. "Here, sit upon this."

Stewart placed it on the soft grass, but Violet picked it back up again. "What are you reading?"

"Nothing," he said, taking it from her hand. "It's just my sketchbook. I hash in it from time to time."

"May I see?"

His heart started pounding as he gazed into her expectant eyes. It shamed him to let her see those pages. He should have torn them out weeks ago, but he hadn't the heart. Now, they were about to be opened up to the eyes of the only woman who had any regard for him.

Tensely, he nodded. She opened the cardboard cover, and beheld page one.

She stared at it, her expression inscrutable. Was she appalled? Ashamed? Angry?

"This is . . ."

He held his breath. He didn't care what anyone in the world thought of him. But this woman . . . it mattered enormously what she thought. If he ever lost her esteem, he may as well chuck it all in.

". . . quite magnificent."

His breath returned, relief washing over him. She turned to the next page, and the next, and the next—and at each one he suffered a small death of expectation.

"Stewart, I had no idea you were so talented."

He shook his head. "You must have been misinformed on what constitutes talent."

"I mean it. These drawings are quite masterful."

Embarrassment stained his face. "You're too generous in your praise."

Violet sat upon the grass, completely unmindful of what it might do to her frock. She studied one page for some time, and it made him increasingly nervous.

"Who is she?" she asked.

He sat down beside her. Humiliation crept up his face once more. "A woman I once knew. A long time ago."

Violet traced her gloved finger around the woman's bare breasts. Her back was draped against the arm of a settee, one arm dangling down alongside her cascading hair. The woman's eyes were half closed in desire, her breasts offered up like an erotic gift. A plump thigh folded down over the other one, revealing only a peek at the dark curls at the nadir of her abdomen.

"She's very sensual."

Stewart remembered that woman well. She was a lady's maid, a woman he'd met in Covent Garden while she bought fabric and ribbons with her mistress. It had been a brief affair, but a particularly memorable one.

Now, in light of Violet's perusal, he realized what a mistake it had been to have sex with this woman. She was so different from Violet, so much more base. She had given herself freely, swiftly, without any consideration for her own worth. Or his.

Violet turned the page. This sketch was of a woman in the bath, her breasts bobbing above the water and her legs folded over the lip of the tub. Water cast a sheen upon the woman's curves, and her blond hair dripped over the cast-iron edge.

Stewart flushed, torn between desiring her artistic critique and fearing that she would ask him who the subject of the portrait was.

"And her?"

Stewart pinched the bridge of his nose. "Violet . . ."

"It's no secret to me that you are enamored of beautiful women." There was only the tiniest catch in her voice, but it spoke volumes to Stewart. "I just didn't know you had memorialized them in this book."

It was like having all his sins open for her perusal. He hated them being exposed to the light, let alone to the eyes of the woman he loved.

"I had affairs with these women. But they mean nothing to me."

She turned her almond eyes upon him. There was no condemnation in them. But there was pain. Oh, so much pain.

"Am I in here?"

He wanted to lie to her. It would be so easy. But he had shown her so much of his past. Best to have done with it, and lay out all of the ugliness of his character before her once and for all. If she hated him, then it would be for good reason.

He reached over and flicked through to the end of the filled pages. There. It was a portrait of Violet, kneeling on the bed. Her bottom was lovingly drawn, softly shaded, even to the tiny dimples on her lower back. He had traced the gentle curve of her back all the way up to the graceful column of her neck, with an errant tendril of hair escaping from her flawless coif. Beside her slender arm was the gentle slope of one breast, its nipple small and dark upon the white paper. Her face was in profile, but as he looked at the lady sitting next to him, he realized it was indeed a poor likeness.

"But I don't understand," she said. "I never posed for you."

"Nor did any of these others. I drew them all from memory. You were by far the easiest to remember." He turned the page, revealing other drawings of Violet. Her flirtatious eyes. Her grinning face. Her gloved hand from which dangled the reticule she wore to the opera the first time they'd met.

She flicked through to the subsequent pages, but there were no women after her. All she found were a couple of rough sketches of Charybdis, and then blank pages.

"Look," he began, "I know I'm a nobody. A donkey with a cravat, nothing more. You deserve a better man than I, I don't deny that. But I can't help but love you, Violet. I'm certain I've loved you from the moment I met you. I just didn't know how to show it."

He swallowed hard, trying to put into words what he'd been thinking since they'd made love. "Never, in my most hopeful fantasies, did I believe there was a woman out there for me. And because I couldn't have *her,* I would have them all. Do you see?"

His gaze fell on the stetchbook. "I wish to God I'd never met any of those other women." He ripped the book from her hands and tore out the pages containing the sketches of Violet. Then, with a mighty swing of his arm, he flung the sketchbook into the rushing water. It fell into the burn with a splash, and then floated out of sight. Stunned, Violet covered her open mouth with both gloved hands.

Stewart fell to his knees in front of her.

"I've mucked up everything I've ever touched. But I couldn't bear it if I muck up your life as well. Or *his,*" he said, nodding at her belly. "Even though I don't deserve you, I would do anything to be your husband. And to be a father to *our own* child. I couldn't stand it if you became my brother's wife. And I certainly don't want your mother regarding our child as a 'defilement' and an injury to her honor all its life. Marry me, Violet. You'd have to sacrifice your houses, your parties, your posh friends—but I swear I'll find myself a respectable position and be the devoted husband and father that our family needs. Marry me. Your mother will have an apoplexy, to be sure, but I will bear all of her wrath. In time, perhaps she'll forgive you. But I swear I won't ever let you regret becoming my wife." He held out his hand to her. "Will you take a chance upon me?"

The horse was lathered in sweat as it sped at full gallop through the forest. Its eyes were wide and crazed, driven both by the lash of the whip—and the child screaming inside the carriage.

Once on the driveway in front of the house, the driver yanked on the reins. The horse's hooves locked, spraying gravel all around. The driver grabbed the child, still bawling shrilly, and ran up the stairs as fast as his old legs could carry him.

"Ballencrieff! Ballencrieff!" The man pounded on the door.

Bannerman came to the door, alarmed. The man began to jabber incoherently while Eric cried.

At the sound of his son's wailing, Conall rushed to the door. He took Eric into his arms, and the boy's cries diminished to whimpers.

"What in blazes is going on?" he demanded.

"Sir," said the rail-thin man, his white whiskers trembling with dread, "my name is Kincaid. I run the linen draper's shop in Thornhill. A lass came into my shop—tall, flaxen-haired, very bonnie—and she had the bairn with her. While she was looking at fabric, a couple of men came in and began to talk with her. She didn't seem to know them, so I came out from behind my counter . . . just to be ready to send them away in case they began to bother her. Sure enough, they were up to no good, for I saw when they grabbed her by the arm, shoved her into a carriage, and sped off like the de'il was chasing 'em."

Shona pushed Bannerman to one side, her face pale. "That's my sister!"

Kincaid swallowed hard. "Oh, miss! Heartless they were, to take a woman and leave the child all alone. I would ne'er have known who he belonged to if it weren't for her, sir. For as they hauled her away, she shouted yer name."

"What did they look like?" she asked.

"Och, I could pick 'em out in a dark room! Tall as trees, both of 'em. One old, one young. Wearing the same tartan, green and red. Highlanders, I'll wager."

"Which way did they go?" Conall asked.

"North. Up the high street, my lord."

"Oh, no!" cried Shona, dissolving into sobs. "Willow!"

Conall handed Eric to Mrs. Docherty, and took the distraught Shona into his arms. He had never seen her cry before, not even at her most distraught. "Listen to me, Shona. They can't be far. We'll find her. Do not fear." Despite his assurances, worry lined his forehead.

He held his hand out to the old man. "Mr. Kincaid, thank you for bringing my son home. Bannerman here will give you some refreshment and something for your trouble. One of the stable lads will drive you back to Thornhill."

He walked Shona to his study, where he poured her a large brandy to calm her nerves.

"Why, Conall? Why would they do this?" She sat on one of the chairs, the glass in her hand untouched.

His gut had told him something was amiss. Now, he knew that his instincts had been correct. But he wished he hadn't had to confirm it at the expense of Shona's tears.

He sat down in the adjoining chair. "I had my suspicions those men were after something."

Tears brimmed in her eyes. "But what would they want with Willow?"

Conall sighed deeply. He didn't want to speak his fears, because they would only cause more tears to fall down her cheeks.

"Ye don't think—" Shona stiffened. "Oh, no . . . do ye think they might try to rape her?" Horror twisted her features.

"Calm yourself, Shona. No, I don't believe they're planning to hurt her. But I do believe they plan to bend her to their will. Tell me—do you or Willow possess any wealth?"

Shona wiped her nose. "What do ye mean?"

"A dowry, perhaps, or some hidden treasure?"

"Of course not! If we had, do ye think we would ha' wound up as wards of the Poor Law?"

"What about land? You once said that your father had been a laird of a small estate. I forgot—what was the name of it?"

"Ravens Craig."

"That's right. What became of that when your parents were killed?"

"I dinna know. A *slaighteur* forfeits all holdings. I just assumed that Ravens Craig went to the clan chief, the Buchanan."

"Hmm. Assumptions can be wrong. Let's suppose for a moment that the land wasn't forfeited, that it never went to the Buchanan. That means it would still belong to your father's successors. Since your brothers were killed, that means that the land would be inherited by the next of kin."

Shona sniffed. "Which would be us."

"Yes. Or, more specifically, the elder of you two."

"Willow." Shona's damp eyes widened. "No wonder the McCullough wanted to know which of us was born first!"

Conall's mouth thinned. "If our surmises are correct, then the McCullough is trying to get Willow to marry into his family. If he succeeds, ownership of all of her property would then transfer to her husband. He is trying to make Brandubh the new owner of Ravens Craig."

"And I led them right to her. I told them where she was!" Shona squeezed her eyes, stemming a torrent of tears.

Conall pushed back a tendril of black hair that had adhered to Shona's wet cheek. "Hush, now. There's no point in self-recrimination. Let's think rationally . . . where could they have taken her? A church, perhaps, to solemnize the marriage?"

"This isn't England, Conall! Any person of worthless character can declare them legally married. A couple can marry without the benefit of banns, a kirk, or even a clergyman. All they would need is two witnesses . . . and Willow's consent."

"They shan't have it, then. Shall they?"

Shona shook her head. "Willow is fearful and easily dominated. They can tell her any tale and she'd believe it. I have to get to her, Conall. Before it's too late."

Bannerman came to the door. "Forgive me, sir. But Her Grace requests a word in private."

"Not now, Bannerman."

Bannerman stiffened in uncertainty. "What shall I tell Her Grace?"

"Tell her whatever you damn well please."

The valet hesitated. "Yes, sir," he muttered before closing the double doors.

By the time Conall returned his attentions to Shona, she'd already begun to unwind the bandages from her ankle.

"Don't do that. Your ankle still hasn't healed."

She puddled the linens on the chair. "It was never hurt to begin with. I just made believe it was." Her cheeks pinked. "To keep ye by my side."

Underneath Conall's baffled expression, she sprang up from the chair and marched to Conall's desk. She spun the ornate wooden box around and lifted the lid. And removed her dagger.

"What are you doing?"

"I'm going to get her back."

"No, Shona. I can't allow you to go off in pursuit of Willow. You'll get yourself hurt."

"Conall, this doesn't concern ye any longer. It's a matter of blood. They took my sister. My beautiful, perfect sister. I don't care why they did it. I'm going after her. And they will give her back or I will make them wish they had."

"What will you do? Try to poke them full of holes before they slice your throat? Give me the dagger."

Shona shoved it behind her. "No! I told ye, I can defend myself. Go on aboot yer wedding. I must find my sister."

He held out his hand. "Dammit, Shona, I said give me the weapon."

"Stay clear of me." This time, the dagger came out in front of her, its point aiming straight at him.

He raised a sardonic brow. "What are you going to do? Kill me?"

"I canna kill ye. I love ye."

The bemusement fled his face as his hand dropped to his side. "What?"

She bit her lip. "Ye heard me. Now get out of my way."

A smile inched across his face. "I've never known a woman to profess her love at the point of a dagger."

The emotion knotted up in her throat. "'Tis the love of a *slaighteur,* who must love from afar. And so great it is that I'll be content to withstand the separation from ye, Conall MacEwan, so long as ye're happy."

Conall took a step in her direction. Fresh tears brimmed in her moist eyes. He inclined his head and pressed his mouth to hers.

Her lips trembled slightly at first, but she kissed him earnestly and with abandon, knowing it to be their last. Her arms came around his neck, the blade still clutched in her hand. Conall wound his arms around her waist and pressed her forcefully against him. This is where he wanted her—in his arms, near his heart.

Languidly, he tasted her mouth. Her lips were salty from tears, but her tongue was sweet from the honeyed tea. She was a woman of such contrasts—caution and daring, knowledge and innocence, damage and completeness. Passion and revenge.

He twisted around and backed her against a chair. He sat her down, and knelt in front of her.

He held out his hand. "Let me have the knife."

She shook her head. "No. I'll need it to save Willow."

"Shona, do not disobey me in this."

"You dinna know these people as I do, Conall. Highlanders are violent, brutal men. They will stop at nothing to get their way."

He encircled his hand around the blade, and squeezed it closed. If she pulled it away, it would slice his palm wide open.

"Those who live by the sword will die by the sword. I won't let that happen to you. Let it go."

Shona's eyes searched his somber face. Slowly, her grip on the hilt loosened. Her fist opened, releasing her hold on the dagger.

"Do you trust me?"

She nodded.

"Good."

There was another knock at the door.

Conall grunted in frustration. "What is it?"

The door opened. The duchess herself stood in the doorway, surveying the scene before her eyes. The only movement was the winking of the jet beads that were sewn into the bodice of her burgundy silk dress.

"Your Grace, please allow us a few moments. Shona is much distressed at present."

A fine eyebrow flew into her alabaster forehead. "Another sprained ankle?"

Conall stood up. "That sort of remark is beneath you, madam."

"And that sort of girl is beneath you, sir. My God, you are about to be married to the heiress of one of the largest dukedoms in Great Britain. If you must take a mistress, kindly do me the dubious honor of selecting one that wouldn't be found amid the sweepings of a farmyard."

Conall took a step in front of Shona, as if to shield her from the duchess's diatribe. "You go too far, madam! How dare you insult her that way!"

"I am but illuminating you, sir. Anyone can see that the girl is fairly struck with you. And she is unquestionably trying to dissuade you from the honor of marrying my daughter."

"If Shona *is* struck with me, then that to me is the greatest honor by far."

"Really, sir! Have a care for your class. Have you so little appreciation for the nobility?"

His blue-fire gaze burned into the duchess's face. "The only nobility I recognize is the one inherent in a person's character. And it shines in Shona MacAslan. It is her kind of nobility that I should have sought from the beginning, and not the kind that you so begrudgingly offer." Conall took Shona by the hand. "I regret to inform you I will not be marrying Lady Violet. Find some other fool to foist that poor girl upon. Then go, exact your vengeance upon me. Do your worst. Because I will not inflict any more grief upon Shona. I desire *this woman*'s happiness above my own. And if marrying me will give her any measure of joy, then I am the luckier for it."

"Conall," Shona interrupted, rising behind him, "think what ye're saying. I know I've been selfish in wanting ye for myself. But I canna let any harm come upon Eric."

"Nor will I. Her Grace will simply have to see for herself which of us shall be the more vehement in protecting his child."

The duchess looked from Conall to Shona and then back again. "I am not willing to discuss this at present. I came to the study only to request your assistance in locating my daughter. It seems she went for a walk this morning and has not returned. Might I request that your footmen be instructed to search the grounds for her?"

The flame in Conall's eyes diminished to a slow burn. "No."

Her eyes flew open. "No?"

"I am organizing a search party for Willow, who has been abducted. The servants will be otherwise engaged. You may search the grounds yourself for your wayward daughter. Feel at liberty to ask Stewart to assist you."

The duchess's cheeks caved inward in affronted pride. She turned elegantly on her slippered heel and exited the study.

"Are ye sure ye know what ye're doing?"

He smiled. "Aye," he said, affecting his best Scottish accent. "'Tis ye I love, Shona MacAslan. And 'tis ye I want to marry." Tenderly, he kissed her mouth.

From the hall, a clock struck three. Mrs. Docherty knocked on the open door.

"Pardon me, sir. But yer brother asked me to deliver this letter to ye, and he commanded me not to do so before three o'clock precisely."

Puzzled, Conall tore open the folded sheet and read. A grin inched across his face. "The crafty devil. That's my brother for you. The only sweets he'll have are stolen ones. Mrs. Docherty, please inform Her Grace the Duchess of Basinghall that a search of the grounds for her daughter is no longer necessary. The Lady Violet has eloped with my brother."

Mrs. Docherty's face turned a paler shade. "Oh, sir. The duchess will be scandalized!"

"I know. I'm only sorry I won't be around to see it. But I'll have my own hands full trying to stop one marriage—" He took Shona by the hand. "And plan another."

TWENTY

Willow lived a thousand nightmares in that carriage.

Warring with the urge to become sick, Willow rocked inside the cramped walls of the conveyance over the bone-jarring roads. The scenery speeding by the window became ever less familiar, and the thickly overcast day had made her lose all sense of direction. Even if she could send word to someone for help, she wouldn't be able to tell them where she was.

In vain she looked for a directional sign that would indicate to which town they were headed. All that met her gaze were sparsely populated sheep pastures and solitary croft farms. Nowhere diminishing to nothing.

From her downcast face, her eyes flicked upward to regard the men who'd taken her. She knew only Horace Hartopp. He was an angry man, she remembered, always belittling Shona to puff himself up. Now, he refused to speak to her to explain why they had shoved her into a carriage or where they were taking her.

The other men also sat in stony silence. The older man, Duncan, had presented her a genial face at the linen draper's, but now his expression was forbidding. He was strong—far stronger than she—as evidenced by his heavy arms and barrel chest. The younger man, introduced to her as his son Brandubh, was someone she would have considered very handsome, with his full head of brown hair, intelligent navy eyes, and broad shoulders. But as he had her wrist imprisoned in an iron fist, and he only flicked her an occasional dispassionate glance, she thought him a fiend.

Eric. They had made her abandon the frightened wee boy in the shop like an unwanted parcel. She worried more for the child than for herself. It was still a mystery whether the shopkeeper was a decent enough man to have taken charge of getting the boy home. And whether his hearing was good enough to hear her shout the name of his father.

For the hundredth time, she berated herself for being so trusting of their attentions. Their expensively crafted kilts and coats, together with their fine linen cravats, never for a moment gave her the suspicion that they were anything but Scottish gentlemen. Now, she knew for certain . . . a well-dressed ruffian was still a ruffian.

She relived the moments so long ago when she was but a child of eight. Angry men with bloodied clothes had imprisoned her in their arms and burned her hand, all after murdering her family. All her kicking and screaming did nothing to stop these terrible things. But then, as now, retreat into herself gave her distance, offering her some measure of safety. Shona had always been frustrated by Willow's lack of boldness. But Willow knew that inside herself, all was quiet and peaceful, and evil could not touch her there.

But evil was all around her now, and Shona was not here to protect her from it. Willow wondered what had happened to her. The men told her she'd been abducted too, and threatened to kill her if Willow didn't do as they said. Poor Shona. If she had been taken, then she was probably already hurt, because Shona would surely not surrender easily.

"When may I see Shona?" she asked politely, trying to keep her voice from enraging her captors.

"As soon as we've concluded business," said the younger man.

"What business, my lord?"

"Ye will find out soon enough."

Their accents were distant and yet familiar. Highlanders they were, like her parents. Their tartan was also vaguely familiar, but certainly nothing she'd seen since they came to live in Dumfriesshire.

The carriage turned off onto a narrow road that was nearly swallowed by overgrown hedges. They rumbled between the reaching branches until they came upon a modest house that had been greatly neglected.

Once they came to a stop, Hartopp opened the door. "We're here, my lord McCullough. Welcome to my home."

The McCullough stepped out onto an overrun front garden that was more weed than flower. He gave a derisory sneer before poking his head back into the carriage. "Come on out, my dear. Stretch your legs. We've a great deal to accomplish."

He held out his hand for her, but the thought of touching this man made Willow feel ill. She got out on her own.

"Hmph. I hope ye quickly overcome yer aversion to us, Miss Willow. Ye're about to become one of the family."

"What?"

She didn't get an explanation. The younger man pushed her by her elbow through the front door.

After the light of day, the inside of Mr. Hartopp's home was nothing but blackness. It took a few moments for her eyes to adjust to the darkness. But a thick mustiness assaulted her nose, and she wondered what sort of a frog would feel at home in a place such as this.

Hartopp showed them into a sitting room that looked as if it hadn't been cleaned in months. He blew the dust off some glasses and poured them full from a decanter.

"Well, gentlemen," he said cheerfully, "it did not happen as planned, but success is ours nonetheless. What say ye to a victory toast?"

"The victor never counts the spoils until he's safely returned to his castle," Duncan replied. "Before ye start crowing again about a victory toast, ye'd be best off sending for someone to officiate the ceremony."

Hartopp set down his glass, and rushed out of the room.

Willow's voice began to shake with the threat of nervous tears. "My lords, please tell me why ye've brought me here."

Duncan adjusted himself in the chair. "How would ye like to leave yer life of service behind and become the lady of Ramh Droighionn Castle?"

"The lady?"

"Aye. My son Brandubh here is willing to marry ye. In a few years, I shall make him chief of Clan Mc-Cullough, and ye shall be his lady. What say ye to that?"

Willow looked nervously from Duncan to Brandubh. "No, thank ye, my lord. I am perfectly content to serve the laird of Ballencrieff."

Brandubh stood up in annoyance. "Well, ye don't

have to now. Ye'll have servants of yer own to look after ye."

"I don't want servants. I want to go home." Willow's eyes began to overflow.

Brandubh rolled his eyes heavenward in disgust as he downed his glass and served himself another. Duncan shifted forward in his chair.

"That's the beauty of it, lass. Ye *can* go home now—yer *real* home. Once ye become my son's wife, ye can return to Ravens Craig."

She wiped her eyes upon her sleeve. "What?"

"That's right. We're offering ye a chance to go back to Ravens Craig, the land of yer da and yer mum. Where ye grew from a bairn. Ye can see the old place once more, walk across its hills, whatever ye like—and know that it's yers."

"But how can this be? The land was forfeit to the Buchanan when my father failed to fight the McBrays alongside the clan."

"Not exactly." Duncan leaned back in his chair. "Oh, there was a fight, to be sure. In fact, that quarrel between the McBrays and the Buchanans has been going on so long, I daresay no one even remembers how it started. But yer father was a peaceable man, and even though the MacAslans owed their loyalty to the Buchanans, he thought 'twould be a step toward reconciliation if he married his eldest son to a McBray girl."

Willow had a distant memory of that girl. The McBray lass had had a soft smile and poetic eyes. She remembered her father talking enthusiastically about the marriage. And she certainly remembered the smile on Hamish's face whenever her name was mentioned.

"Yer father had requested permission of the Buchanan to abstain from the fighting. Naturally, he didn't want to fight the men that would soon become his own kinsmen. But the Buchanan said no, and insisted that John show his loyalty to his own chief on the battlefield." Duncan drew a large swallow from his glass. "John chose to follow his conscience instead of doing his duty. And it proved to be his undoing."

The harsh words spoken on the last day her father was alive had been seared into her memory. But they never truly made sense to her. "'Twas the Buchanan men that killed him, wasn't it? His own clansmen?"

"Aye. Perhaps if the McBrays had lost, John's failure to show on the battlefield would have been overlooked. He was a well-liked man, after all. But as it turned out, the Buchanans lost, and John's treason against his chief would not be forgiven."

"But why was my father never given a fair trial? 'Twas his right to state matters in his own defense. He should no' have been killed before he could give an account of himself."

"Ah, well, that is your saving grace, Willow. If he *had* been tried before the chief, he would have been executed just the same. And then all his land and possessions would have ended up in the coffers of the Buchanan. As it is, he was never termed a traitor. Except by *vox populi*."

Questions tripped over themselves in her head, each wanting to be answered foremost. "Then how is it that Ravens Craig is now yers to give me?"

Duncan glanced furtively at Brandubh. They exchanged silent arguments that only they seemed to understand.

It was Brandubh who answered. "It's not. It's yers to give me."

Willow's moist green eyes widened. "What?"

Brandubh sat down in front of her. "Ravens Craig sits waiting for the next in line to inherit it. *Ye* are the next in line."

"Ye mean to tell me that Shona and I could have gone home all this time?"

"In a manner of speaking," answered Duncan. "Children of eight are not fit to manage a large estate such as Ravens Craig. Least of all, female children. Fortunately for ye, yer father saw fit to leave ye in good hands. John MacAslan and I made a pact that one of his daughters would marry my eldest son."

Duncan opened his tartan coat and pulled out a parchment from the inside pocket. He unfolded it for her, and she took it from his hands.

"When we drew up that document, the lot of ye were still children. But when ye came of age to wed, John wanted one of ye to marry Brandubh."

Willow scrutinized the betrothal contract. She recognized her father's handwriting and his seal. It was a genuine agreement—her father had promised "one of his twin daughters" to Brandubh. Whichever one Brandubh chose.

"That was why when yer da was killed, I wanted my man Seldomridge to care for ye two until ye were twelve years of age, when Brandubh could legally marry ye."

At the mere mention of that name, Willow wanted to retreat into that place of safety inside once more. Mr. Seldomridge had been a cruel man, and he never displayed a kind gesture to the sisters. It was a miracle they managed to run away from the horrid man, and flee from the Highlands altogether.

The past terrors dissipated, leaving her squarely planted in the present one. "Ye're mistaken, my lord. Ravens Craig canna belong to me. The property must go to the next male child. Ravens Craig would belong to my little brother—"

"Camran?" said Duncan, miles ahead of her thoughts. "Camran MacAslan is dead."

The black script letters on the parchment in her lap began to blur as silent tears welled up in her eyes. *Camran,* she wanted to scream. He was all the family they had left. The hope of finding their brother had burned inside them like an unquenchable fire. And just like that, Duncan McCullough extinguished it with a puff of his breath. "How?"

"Torn apart by wild animals. I'm sad to say."

An image of blood, fangs, and teeth flashed across her mind. And just as quickly, it was gone.

Her eyes flew up to Duncan's face. There was no sorrow or consolation in them.

Willow gathered her courage as she refolded the parchment. "I'm sorry, my lord. But I've no wish to marry yer son."

A genial expression lifted Duncan's face as he threw his hands in the air. "Ye can marry me, if ye like! I'm a free man, now that my wife's passed on." He leaned in conspiratorially. "Truth be told, I'd prefer it if ye made *me* yer man. Ye were little more than skinned knees and tangled hair when John MacAslan and I made our pact. I had little expectation that ye'd become such a rare beauty, Willow MacAslan."

Willow pulled her shaking hand from his. "I've no wish to marry either of ye."

The smile never left his lips. "Then we'll kill ye and Brandubh will marry Shona." He ignored her horrified expression as he snatched the parchment from her hands. "Ye know as well as I do that a betrothal contract is just as binding as a marriage. The only difficulty in all this is that John MacAslan was so damnably unclear in his wording. If he had only given a name, this would be a concluded matter. Still, what matters to us is that Brandubh marry the eldest of ye. Whichever one of ye is to inherit Ravens Craig."

Willow felt her arms go weak with futility. She turned her face away, afraid to look at the dangers threatening her. How she wished Shona were there to tell her what to do.

It would be far simpler to just let them kill her. Then, at least, the nightmares would end. But these men would then embroil Shona in a forced marriage to a hateful family. And so the nightmares would begin for Shona. No matter how much it took out of her, Willow could never do that to her sister.

She couldn't imagine which would be worse . . . to marry the devil or be wed to his son. Bound to either for her natural life would feel like an eternity in hell. But which should she make her man?

My man. Something about that clanged in her head like a lead bell. It was something Duncan had said, something that finally began to materialize through the haze of fear.

My man Seldomridge, he'd said. Duncan had just said he'd instructed Mr. Seldomridge to raise Shona and Willow after their parents died until they were old enough to marry Brandubh. Why, then, was it that he was there on the Day?

"He was waiting for us."

Duncan's grizzled eyebrows wove together. "Pardon?"

"That day . . . at Ravens Craig . . . Mr. Seldomridge was there with the angry mob. You sent him there to collect us."

"Ye've a good memory, lass. What of it?"

"How did ye know that Shona and I would be orphaned that day?"

The corner of Duncan's mouth turned downward. His breathing accelerated almost imperceptibly.

Willow pressed on. "*Ye* sent that mob to kill my parents, didn't ye?"

Brandubh brushed past his father and seized Willow by the upper arms. "Keep a civil tongue in yer head, woman! Do ye know who ye're talking to?"

A boldness born of indignation coiled up inside her, and she met him glare for glare until he released her.

"I am speaking to Duncan, chief of Clan McCullough. A man who ought not to fear answering a simple woman's question."

"It's all right, son," Duncan said smugly. "I've nothing to hide."

The older man stood up from the chair and dropped his large frame in the seat beside her on the settee. He inched close enough to her that their knees touched. It took all of Willow's courage just to face him, for it was beginning to dawn on her just what this man was really capable of.

"John MacAslan made up his mind what his fate was going to be. He was doomed the moment he betrayed his clan. Had he been arrested and tried, he would have met the same end. Death at the hands of a clan executioner, or death at the hands of his clansmen . . . what does it really matter? This way, *ye* get to inherit all his worldly possessions, instead of them being seized by the Buchanan. All I did was help him find an end that benefited those he left behind. Ye really ought to be thanking me for arranging it."

Willow grew dizzy with the sickening discovery. "And what of Hamish? And Thomas and Malcolm? And my mother? Should they be thanking ye, too?"

Duncan shrugged. "They were . . . a necessary measure. Because ye, my dear, are now the owner of Ravens Craig. Think on it. Instead of all that land going to yer eldest brother and his McBray wife, it will now be inherited by ye."

Willow began to feel Shona's fire burning inside her. The McCullough had had designs upon her father's holdings for years. And when her father extended his hand in friendship to that man, little did John MacAslan know that a handshake with Duncan McCullough would seal his own death. The betrothal contract would ensure that Brandubh acquired legal possession of Willow. But Duncan had to remove all the sons who'd inherit Ravens Craig ahead of her. And he had to do it before any of them sired children. So he mounted a frenzied vengeance killing with the defeated Buchanans, slaughtering all the MacAslans who stood to inherit the land, and sparing only the daughters who would preserve his hold on Ravens Craig. And then to make sure no man would give them a second look, he branded them as *slaighteur* and sent them to be raised until they were old enough to marry the only man that *would* take them—

his son—who in a single day would acquire a bride and fertile Ross-shire lands. The McCullough was a man of unbridled craftiness, infinite patience—and unimaginable cruelty.

But his plan had failed. He hadn't counted on her and Shona running away. He hadn't expected the sisters to grow to the hardy age of twenty, old enough to know their own minds. And big enough to say no.

At first, it was only a gentle quiver of her shoulders and a shake of her head. But then, to everyone's surprise, Willow threw back her head and began to laugh.

"All this time," she said, chuckling into her hands, "I'd been thinking it was our fault. That we'd done something horrible to deserve such a fate. I tried to imagine what it was my da and my mumma had done wrong. Or what I had done that was so naughty. And all this time, it was nothing. It was all you . . . a common thief who coveted our happiness."

Willow rocked back and forth clutching her sides. The laughter rose up out of her in a way that made Duncan and Brandubh twist their faces in revulsion.

"She's mad," remarked Brandubh.

"Not yet she's not," snarled Duncan, and slapped her hard across the face.

But it was too late to subdue her. Willow had emerged from within herself. The safe place inside had suddenly grown too small to hold all she had become.

She cocked her fist back and slammed it into Duncan's nose.

His pinched face sprang back from the blow. Startled, he clambered from the settee, putting as much distance as he could between them.

Brandubh flew to his father's aid. Blood began to stream down from the hand he clutched to his nose.

A wicked grin curled her cheek, infuriating Brandubh even more. He gripped her by the front of her dress with one hand, hauled her up to a standing position, and pulled back his right fist.

"What in hell is going on?" Hartopp yelled.

Brandubh froze. His menacing stance did nothing to make Willow flinch. She lifted her face in open defiance, practically daring him to hit her.

"My lord McCullough," Hartopp continued after watching Brandubh release the girl, "ye're bleeding."

"Of course I'm bleeding, ye jackass! That girl broke my nose! Go get me something to soak up the blood."

"Aye, sir. Er, I've sent for someone to perform the marriage rite, just as ye asked. The local town clerk is not far, and he's done marriages before. I sent word offering an inducement, so he should be here soon."

"Fine, fine! Now hurry up and find me a cloth!" Hartopp raced out of the room to do as he was bid.

Brandubh stood shoulder to shoulder with Duncan. "Don't worry, Father. Once the ceremony's over, I'll make sure she pays for what she did to ye. What are ye laughing at, girl?"

Willow couldn't hide the chuckling. "There isna going to be any wedding."

Brandubh's nostrils flared as he pressed his lips together. "Is that so?"

"Aye. It doesna matter how many clerks or vicars ye bring. It isna going to happen."

"Ye're not giving yer consent, are ye?"

"No." She giggled softly.

Brandubh nodded. With lightning speed, he pulled his *sgian achlais* from inside his jacket, seized her by the knot of blond hair, and pressed the sharp edge of the shiny blade against her neck. "Then I'll just slash yer pretty throat."

"Ye canna marry a corpse. Go ahead and kill me. I won't marry ye. Ye can kill Shona too, because she won't marry ye, either. Ravens Craig will be lost to ye. Ye'll never get yer hands on it."

Brandubh removed the blade from her throat, leaving a thin red glistening line in its place. He moved the point of his dagger to her left eye.

"I'll give ye laurels for bravery, *slaighteur*. But dinna think for a moment ye can get yer own way in this matter. Will ye or nill ye, I'll have Ravens Craig. And whether or not—"

A sound outside pricked his ears. He twisted her around and put a hand over her mouth. He edged to the window and pulled back the drape with the edge of his blade.

"Is it the clerk?" asked Duncan.

"No. It's . . . Ballencrieff. With the other girl."

Willow groaned beneath Brandubh's palm. At once, she felt relief that Shona was not already a prisoner of Duncan McCullough's—and dread that she might soon become so.

Hartopp returned and handed Duncan a damp handkerchief. "Leave them to me, my lord," said Hartopp. "I'll send them away."

"No," grunted Duncan. "Lead them in here. I'll handle the rest."

Willow saw Duncan unsheathe his *sgian achlais,*

and watched as he flattened himself against the wall beside the door. He was mounting an ambush.

Willow listened as Conall and Shona came to the door. Words were exchanged with Hartopp. Then footsteps drew closer to the sitting room. Willow had to warn them, to let them know they were walking into a trap.

She screamed as loudly as she could, even though the scream was muffled in her throat. Then she heard Conall's voice.

"Shona, no!"

But Shona must have escaped his grasp. Shona burst through the door, and was jerked to one side by Duncan. He held her against his body, his blade dimpling the tender skin under her jaw.

Conall ran in but it was too late. Both women were being held at knifepoint, and Hartopp came up behind him with a pistol.

He raised his hands to the level of his shoulders. "What's going on here? McCullough, explain this!"

"'Tis my son's wedding day, Ballencrieff. Ye were not invited, but now that ye're here, ye can watch the festivities."

"I know what you're trying to do," he said, eyeing each woman nervously. "It won't work. You can't force a woman to marry you upon threat of death."

"I don't intend to," said Brandubh. "Willow is going to be very compliant now, aren't ye, sweeting? Otherwise, my father may decide to repay yer assault upon him with an assault upon yer twin. Isn't that right?"

Shona squealed as the blade went deeper into her skin. Her expression of pain brought out a reaction in Conall. He lunged at Duncan. But behind him, Hartopp raised his pistol and clobbered Conall on the back of his head with the stock of his firearm.

The blow drove Conall to his knees. Stunned and dizzied, he clenched his eyes as he tried to focus his vision. Shona cringed at his agony.

"Don't attempt anything foolish, Ballencrieff," Duncan said. "This matter doesna concern ye."

He drew a hand from the crown of his head, and found his fingers bloodied. "It does when you hold my fiancée at the point of a knife."

"Fiancée?" Bemusement crinkled the corners of his eyes. "Why on earth are ye marrying this surly wagtail? She owns nothing, ye know. Ye'd have been better off pursuing the other one. But now ye're too late. Willow's taken."

"Let them go, McCullough."

"We're just getting started. Let's make it a double wedding. Ye marry yer wagtail, and Brandubh will marry his. Happiness all round. What say ye to that, Willow?"

Dread filled her chest. Duncan was threatening to impale her sister on his dagger. She couldn't think clearly enough to predict what would happen if she said yes. But she knew precisely what would happen if she said no.

"If I marry Brandubh, will ye let Shona and Conall go free?"

"Aye. After the ceremony, of course."

"All right. I'll give my consent to marry Brandubh." Shona squirmed in his grasp. "No!"

"Dinna fash yerself, Shona," Willow said. "They'll be contented once Ravens Craig becomes theirs outright."

Shona twisted her head as high as she could to ease the pressure of the dagger's point. "Ye must no' marry that de'il! He'll only do away with ye once he's no more use for ye!"

A rivulet of blood trailed down Shona's neck. "Now, now," admonished Duncan, "ye must not interfere with yer sister's marital bliss."

Willow stared at Shona. She was impaled like a fish on a hook. All her squirming and wriggling was doing her no good. It was impossible to fight the evil that men do.

Shona's eyes met hers. In their silent language, Willow communicated a message of futility to her. *It's no use. Let them take me. Go and live your own life. The time for us to separate has come.*

"Wait!" Shona said as much to Willow as to the man who held her captive. "I know how we can settle this. Willow will give ye Ravens Craig. Here and now. It'll be yers, all of it."

"Just like that?" asked Duncan incredulously. "Free of charge?"

"Aye," she said, unable to keep the desperate tremors from her voice. "Do ye think either of us wants to live in the house where my parents were butchered? That place is no home to us now. Had I known Willow owned it still, I would have burned the place to cinders long ago. In fact, ye'd be doing us a blessing if ye'd take it from us."

The knife lowered slightly, allowing Shona to descend from her tiptoes.

Shona did not relent. "Hartopp . . . he can draw up a paper for Willow to sign. She'll transfer Ravens Craig to ye. And yer son can still be free to marry whomever he likes."

"What makes ye think he doesna want Willow for himself?"

"Look at him," she responded. "He's young and virile. Why would he want a cold, meek woman in his bed, one who wakes up screaming from nightmares? Let him find a wife who will warm his bed and inflame his passions."

Duncan squeezed her. "Like ye?"

Conall growled. "McCullough!"

Shona continued. "Brandubh can have Ravens Craig *and* his choice of wife. All we ask in return is that you let us all go free. Now."

Duncan leered at her. "Ye must think me the biggest fool on two legs. I let ye go and then ye organize a battle against me."

"Don't be daft," she replied. "A battle with what? We have no people. Who's going to ally themselves to a *slaighteur*'s cause? No one joins a knave's revolt. Even if we could gather anyone to fight with us, how many armies of men do ye have at yer disposal? We want no quarrel. Look at us . . . we came here unarmed. More's the pity," she muttered for Conall's benefit.

They heard a carriage drive up. Brandubh looked out the window. "The clerk's here. What do ye ken, Father? I'd rather no' marry this woman. I canna make up my mind if she's simple or barmy."

"Neither. She's crafty." He pushed the knife in a little deeper, making Shona wince. "They both are."

"McCullough!" yelled Conall from the floor. He clambered to his feet. Though Hartopp pushed the barrel of the gun into his back, he continued. "That's enough. Let Shona go."

"What are *ye* going to promise me, then? A castle in Wales? A palace in Australia?"

"Nothing. Ravens Craig belongs to the ladies, and they

can do with it whatever they like. I promise you nothing—except unending misery if you make an enemy of me."

"Dinna make idle threats to Highlanders, Ballencrieff. We dinna take them lightly."

Conall snorted. "Highlanders. No matter how important you think you are, McCullough, the Highlands are but an annoying speck to the rest of Great Britain. If it weren't for the occasional uprising, London would never even know it existed." He chuckled. "It's the appendix of the United Kingdom."

Brandubh harrumphed. "Arrogant. Just like a fucking Sassenach. Try saying that in Inverness, and they'd have yer balls for their haggis."

"And just like a Highlander, Brandubh, you're a coward. You crow when you're amid your clansmen, but alone, you're not man enough to take on an opponent of your own size. You resort to bullying unarmed women. Even after they've surrendered to you."

Brandubh pointed his dagger at Conall. "If it's a fight ye want, Englishman, it's a fight we'll give ye."

Conall sniffed. "Three against one? That's hardly sporting, old boy."

"Just the two of us, Ballencrieff. Yer choice of weapons."

"Brandubh, enough!" yelled Duncan. "He's goading ye, boy. Ye must learn to control yer temper. Still, he's right about one thing." With a brusque shove, Duncan propelled Shona at Conall. "Never let it be said that Highlanders are brutes where women are concerned."

Conall couldn't hide his look of relief. "Are you all right?"

"Aye," she responded. Conall tugged at his cravat,

and unwound it from around his neck. He applied the cloth to the bleeding wound below her jawline.

"Hartopp," continued Duncan, "give me the gun. Now, fetch something to write on. Ye'll write to my dictation. Willow will sign it, and then we'll get that town clerk out there to witness it."

While Brandubh pushed Willow to the settee, Shona let Conall tend to her wound. With her head tilted back, allowing Conall to pat away the blood, she surreptitiously pulled her dagger from her bodice.

Conall gave her a surprised glance. The dagger had no crossguard, and the sheathed weapon concealed easily between her generous breasts. She pushed it into his hands, and he quickly slipped it inside his coat.

"Sit down," ordered Duncan, and motioned to the chairs with the pistol.

Hartopp returned with a sheet of vellum and ink. He sat on the edge of a chair and leaned over the table with the quill at the ready.

Duncan rattled off language effectively deeding Ravens Craig to Brandubh McCullough in perpetuity. Hartopp dutifully scratched the words onto the vellum, and then blotted the still-pooling lines.

Brandubh went out into the hall to bring the clerk into the sitting room.

"Good afternoon, all," said the affable man. He had a face full of ginger whiskers and a fly plaid with a brooch that had the seal of the magistrate court. "My name's Sean Ferguson. I hear there's going to be a wedding. Which of ye is the happy couple?"

Duncan, who'd hidden the pistol behind his back, wrapped an arm around the clerk. "Ye heard wrong, Mr. Ferguson. We're drawing up a bill of sale, and we'd like ye to witness the document for us, if ye'd be so kind. Of course, we'll make sure that ye're rewarded for yer trouble."

"A pity," he said. "I was rather looking forward to hearing the 'I dos.' I do love weddings. I've performed forty-nine ceremonies so far, and I was hoping to finally bring that number to fifty. Still, I'll be happy to help in any way I can."

"Glad to hear it. Mr. Ferguson, this is Miss Willow MacAslan. She's here to transfer ownership of her property to my son. Here's the document. Please take yer time and look it over."

The clerk stroked the ginger whiskers on the side of his face. "Hmm. Just a moment . . . is this correct? Miss MacAslan, are ye handing over these lands *gratis*?"

Willow cleared her throat. "Well, ye see—"

"It's a decrepit property," interrupted Duncan. "Hardly worth more than the cost of this vellum. We're accepting it in trade."

"In trade for what?"

"An old debt," he answered.

"I see. Well, Miss MacAslan, if ye have any other properties ye want to get rid of, make sure to let me know. It's a price I can afford to pay."

He chuckled at his own joke, but no one else joined him. He handed back the paper to Willow, who signed her name at the bottom. Brandubh signed next, then Mr. Ferguson, and finally Hartopp.

"Right," said Mr. Ferguson. "Now all ye need is the proper stamp on this at the registry office. Shouldn't cost ye more than a couple of shillings. Then it'll be official."

"Thank ye, Mr. Ferguson. Hartopp here will give ye something for yer trouble and see ye out."

After Mr. Ferguson left, a heavy quiet descended upon the gathering.

"Now may I take these ladies home?" Conall asked Duncan impatiently.

"Aye," he answered. "Our business with them is finished."

Conall took Shona and Willow by the hand and escorted them out the front door.

But before they reached his carriage, a voice drew up behind him. "But my business with ye is just beginning."

Conall turned around, and Brandubh swung. Hard.

The force of the blow to Conall's cheek rocked him backward, and he fell against one of the horses.

"Call me a coward, will ye?" Brandubh growled, as he brought his fists up. "Let's see what ye call me once I send ye down to the ground in yer own blood and teeth."

Conall righted himself, and straightened his coat. "I might have expected you'd fight like a brigand."

"Come on with ye, then!"

Shona grew worried. "Conall, please. He's a bully. Let's just go."

"The bully lives only as long as the cowardly let him. Get in the carriage, you two. I'll join you presently."

"Conall—"

"Now, Shona. Do as I ask."

Begrudgingly, Shona ascended the carriage after Willow.

Conall slipped off his coat and threw it onto a hedge. Within the conveyance, Shona gasped. The dagger was hidden in the coat's inside pocket. Conall was now defenseless.

She gazed upon the spectacle in horror. Brandubh stood four inches above Conall and outweighed him by at least three stone. And when he removed his own jacket, Brandubh revealed a physique that seemed accustomed to physical brutality. Wide shoulders, long arms, and a heavy stance spreading the folds of his kilt.

Conall looked so English in his white linen shirt, silk waistcoat, and fawn breeches. A discoloring red blotch began to spread on Conall's cheek where Brandubh had hit him. It was sure to be his first lesson that Highlanders fight dirty. Highlanders didn't observe rules; they fought to win.

Conall approached him with a light step. Brandubh took another swing at his head, but Conall ducked. He took another swing, and again, Conall weaved beneath it. This time, Brandubh stomped toward him and landed two punches on Conall's head in quick succession.

Conall reeled backward from the force of the stronger man, and landed on his arse. Shona gasped, fearing for Conall. It must have hurt terribly. She silently wished he would accept defeat before he was injured further. Brandubh McCullough seemed intent on hurting everyone she loved.

But even if Conall could hear her mute pleas, he ignored them. He clambered back to his feet and assumed a defensive stance.

A razor-blade smile cut across Brandubh's face as he advanced upon Conall. He had struck Conall on the jaw and gashed him on the right side of the forehead. "Come on, hit me, ye flowery Sassenach! Ye probably bleed rose water. Have at me! Fight like a man! What are ye waiting for?"

"Four," he answered cryptically.

"Eh?"

"Four punches. That's all I'll need to take you down."

Brandubh tossed his head back and laughed.

In the doorway, his father and Hartopp echoed the amusement. Duncan cupped a hand to the side of his mouth. "Let's see ye land just one first."

"Very well," Conall said. And then he dropped his hands down at his sides. "Come for me."

From inside the carriage, Shona held her breath. *What is he doing?*

Brandubh narrowed his eyes, and with a snarl, accepted the invitation. He cocked his fist back and swung with all his might.

Time seemed to slow as the clenched fist arced toward Conall's face. He just stood there, defenseless, waiting for the deathly blow like a lamb before the slaughterer's knife.

But just as Brandubh's fist almost connected with his face, Conall dodged beneath it. Then he brought his fist up beneath the taller man's outstretched arm, and projected a punch straight into Brandubh's armpit.

Brandubh roared, curling over his injured side.

Conall jumped backward. "An injury to the axilla will traumatize the nerve bundle distal to the brachial plexus. I daresay you will be in incredible pain for several days."

Enraged, Brandubh came at him again, but this time, he held his elbow down to protect the injury, neutralizing the reach from his dominant arm. With his left arm, he swung at Conall, but Conall parried it. Conall then sidestepped him, and slapped him in the ear with a cupped hand.

Dazed and unbalanced, the taller man staggered and clutched his ear in pain.

"The tympanic membrane in your ear has just been

perforated. The disorientation, the high-pitched ringing, and the loss of hearing may not be permanent. My medical advice would be to concede defeat, and then sit down. Before you fall down."

Brandubh shook his head, but could not dislocate the pain or dizziness. He took a few steps at Conall, but it seemed like he was waiting for Conall to get back into focus.

"You're a very difficult patient. Perhaps this will help you to follow my advice."

Conall drove a fist into the side of Brandubh's thigh. The man screamed in pain, his knee buckling.

"A contusion of the quadriceps will cause temporary paralysis of that muscle and excruciating pain. If you cannot stand, you cannot fight. Accept your incapacitation, and concede defeat like a gentleman."

But Brandubh seemed only to be listening to the goading from his father and Hartopp. Sweat broke on his forehead as he stood back up. One unsteady leg was bent beneath him, and one elbow was pinned to his side, covering an injury that seemed to be sending lightning bolts of pain throughout his body.

"No fuckin' Sassenach is going to get the better of me," he said as he grabbed hold of Conall's waistcoat and jerked it toward him. Having imprisoned Conall inches from his own body, he thrust his meaty fist into the center of Conall's stomach over and over again.

He stopped only when Conall was so winded that he hung in the man's grasp. Brandubh let him go, and Conall crumpled to the ground, gasping for breath.

Brandubh then delivered a rib-cracking kick to the fallen man, and Conall twisted in pain. Leaves and dirt clung to his sleeves as he writhed on the ground.

Amid the cheers of the Scotsmen in the doorway, Brandubh drew back his foot again.

But this time, Conall was ready for him. He caught the man's foot in his hands, and twisted it. Brandubh's entire body was forced to turn in the same direction, and he too fell to the ground facedown.

Furious, Conall rose to his knees. "You asked for this," he said, and delivered punch number four. Right into the man's kidney.

Brandubh cried out, yelling something inarticulate. But he was not getting back up. He pounded his fists into the ground in vain, almost like a child throwing a tantrum, battling with the invisible pain coursing throughout his body. Dry heaves racked his body.

Conall clambered to his feet. He plucked his coat from the hedge and threw it back on.

"Now our business is concluded," he said to Brandubh, who had managed to draw himself up on all fours like a dog. "Don't let others call you flowery when you start to pee rose water."

"Ballencrieff!"

Conall turned around to see Duncan raise his pistol.

"You've shamed us, Ballencrieff. And the McCulloughs don't live with dishonor long."

Conall narrowed his eyes upon the face of the man who would not lose at any cost. In one swift movement, he reached down and grabbed hold of Brandubh's disheveled hair while simultaneously removing the dagger from his coat pocket.

"Very well," Conall replied. "I shall end the dishonor here and now. I will slice your son's carotid artery, and he will exsanguinate in just a few minutes. Or," he said, moving the knife to Brandubh's groin, "I could cut him in the femoral artery, ending his suffering even faster. Or would you prefer that I just castrate him and thereby end your miserable bloodline once and for all?"

Brandubh made no resistance. He was in too much pain to be afraid for his life . . . or his manhood. The blows Conall gave him probably made him wish he was already dead.

Hartopp put a hand on Duncan's arm. "Don't do this, McCullough. Ballencrieff won fair and square. Let him go. Ye have what ye came for."

Duncan cast a momentary glance at Hartopp before lowering his weapon.

Conall dropped Brandubh, who collapsed in agony onto the ground. "Don't ever let me catch either of you south of Glasgow again."

He turned on his heel and headed back toward the carriage. A line of blood oozed from the cut above his eye. Shona sharpened her gaze upon Duncan, terrified he might shoot her beloved in the back.

Conall snapped the reins, and the horses jolted into movement. She watched as the house disappeared behind the green overgrowth, and then they made breakneck speed for home.

TWENTY-ONE

Shona leaped out of the carriage when it finally came to a stop outside Ballencrieff House.

"Conall! Are ye all right?" She climbed up to the perch.

In the driver's seat, Conall was clutching his side, grimacing in pain. Fresh blood still rolled past the dried blood above his left eye, and a purpling blotch discolored his cheek.

"Willow, go get help from inside. He's too hurt to climb doon himself."

Bannerman ran out of the house toward the driveway, together with two footmen recently returned from the search party. They lifted him from the perch and carried him up to his bedroom. Shona followed them up the stairs, her worried thoughts flapping about like a bat in her hair.

Conall was lowered onto his bed, and the valet began to remove Conall's boots. "Miss, you really ought not to be here," said Bannerman.

"Then try and make me go," she replied, her eyes never leaving Conall's pained face.

"Miss, I really must protest. I'm about to disrobe the master. He will be indecent—"

"It's all right, Bannerman," Conall managed. "I'm

going to need some help, and Shona isn't squeamish or prudish about matters of the body." He shifted on the bed. "Besides, I know what the sight of blood does to you. The last thing I need right now is for you to faint dead away on top of me."

"Very well, sir," he conceded, but his relief was evident in the grateful look he tossed at Shona.

"You can serve me best by getting me my medical valise in the study. And bring me the tray of brandy."

"Right away, sir." Bannerman withdrew.

Shona stood next to him. "Should we send for a doctor?"

"I am a doctor," he growled.

She pursed her lips. "Another one, I mean."

"No. I can take care of myself."

"Hmph. We'll see aboot that. Let's have a keek at what that jackanape did to ye." She knelt on the bed behind him. Gingerly, she pulled off Conall's swallow-tail coat, and tossed it aside. Instantly, she was awash in admiration. The broad shoulders beneath the oversized shirtsleeves, the tight abdomen hugged by the green and silver waistcoat—it had been a mistake to think his fine clothes made him the weaker opponent. He had clearly emerged the victor against that Highlander. And even though physically Brandubh looked more menacing, the greatest weapon in that battle had rested between Conall's ears.

Her fingers reached around him to undo the buttons of his waistcoat. The warm silk on her fingertips wreaked havoc on her senses. Her face came down to his neck, and breathing in his scent—heated sandalwood—made her fingers fumble in their simple task. She wanted so to steal a kiss, but she feared that the pressure of her lips on his bruised face would do more harm than good.

Somehow, she was able to accomplish her task, even though she was more focused in absorbing the feel of the rock-hard abdomen rather than in unbuttoning his waistcoat. Open it fell, and he groaned in pain as he bent his arms backward to allow the fabric through.

"Sorry. Only one more bit of clothing to go."

As she began pulling the white shirt out from the waist of his breeches, Conall unfastened two of the topmost buttons to help ease the fabric out.

"Raise yer arms for me."

She couldn't see his face, but she heard him groan. Only one arm made it above his head.

Once she succeeded in pulling his shirt off, he immediately fell backward upon his pillow. He shut his eyes tightly as the pain washed over him.

Shona's eyes raked down his naked chest. Between the wide pads of muscle of his chest, a deep valley furrowed from the *V* at the base of his throat down to his navel. On either side of it, delicious rows of muscle bricked his abdomen. The half-open breeches revealed a triangular pad of muscle that aimed at the very thing she had been thinking about for weeks.

But poor Conall's skin was discolored horribly. A deep red bruise had spread along the top of his abdomen, and his side where Brandubh kicked him had purpled darkly.

"You can leave if you want to."

Her eyes met his. "Eh?"

"It was unfair of me to urge you to stay. Ladies shouldn't have to behold such gruesome sights."

Shona realized her face reflected the pain he must feel. "I am made of sterner stuff than that."

A gentle smile touched his mouth. "Yes. I believe you are."

"Besides, ye once promised to teach me how to treat people with injuries. Now would be a good time to start, don't ye think?"

Conall sighed. "So it would."

Bannerman returned with the medical valise and the tray. A brief look at the master's injuries, and sweat broke out on his upper lip. He poured some brandy into a glass and then made a hasty withdrawal.

"Right," Conall said, forcing himself to a sitting position against his pillow. "First things first. Go get me a mirror. And a moistened towel."

Shona returned with the items he requested. She watched as he daubed the blood from the gash above his eye.

Irritation colored his face. "Damn. It's longer than I thought. Open my case and pull out a jar marked 'Blue Vitriol.'" He told her how to mix it—one part powder to four parts water.

"It's a pretty color," she said. "As blue as yer eyes. What is it?"

"It's a styptic. It'll burn the wound so that it bleeds no more."

Shona's heart turned to water. Burning his wound? Hadn't he been through enough pain already?

She moistened a gauze with the blue liquid. "Take a deep breath." She applied the gauze to the gash. Conall winced, inhaling through his teeth.

"Damn and blast! I hope to God my head broke the man's knuckle."

Shona grinned as she wiped the excess vitriol off his forehead. "In my experience, 'tis a very hard head, indeed. Mayhap your jaw broke another knuckle."

He harrumphed, shifting his jaw. "I doubt it. And it still hurts like hell."

"It's getting fair black, it is. I think I can help ye with that. Ye know, the best thing for bruises is cow dung."

"Cow dung?" Conall chuckled, and then winced from the pain.

"Dinna laugh! Mayhap ye dinna use it in London, but up here 'tis good medicine."

He tried to bite down his laughter, but it escaped his clenched teeth.

"Keep laughing like that and I'll pinch ye in the ribs."

"No. I'm sorry. I didn't mean to make sport of it."

"Ye could do worse than to try it. I can go get some fresh cow pats if ye like."

He battled to keep the laughter in. "No. But thank you all the same."

She shrugged. "Please yerself."

"All right. There's one more thing I need you to do for me. Place the flat of your hand here, right on my ribs."

She did as he asked. Shona had wanted to touch his body for some time, but this was not as she had imagined it would be. The skin was hot, and he winced with the slightest touch.

"Right. Now I'm going to cough. I want you to tell me if you feel crepitation under your fingers—that is, any rattling of the bones. Can you do that?"

"Aye, I think so."

Conall took a deep breath and coughed. The exertion made him grimace in agony.

"I felt nothing, Conall. No—rattling."

"Good. That means the bones aren't broken." He swallowed down the brandy before lying back down, exhausted.

Watching him suffer, Shona's heart broke for him. "I'd give anything to trade places with ye."

He stretched out his hand and stroked a thumb across the small puncture wound made by Duncan's knife on Shona's jaw. "You've been through so much already, your whole life. If I could, I'd take all your hurt onto myself if it meant that you'd feel it no longer."

Emotions knotted up in her throat. He fisted his hand in her hair and brought her face down to his lips. In that kiss, Shona did the one thing she never thought she'd do. She surrendered.

Her hand undulated over his shoulders and along the ridges of his muscled chest. How strong he was, in body and mind, and she wanted to be joined to all that strength.

"Ye were so incredibly brave in that fight with Brandubh McCullough. I was so proud of ye, knowing just how to put a man doon. Would ye teach me all that ye know?"

"Only if you promise not to use any of it on me."

She bit her lower teeth. "So what else can I do to give a man excruciating pain for a very long time?"

He harrumphed. "Introduce him to a Scotswoman."

Her mouth fell open in mock affront. "So that's how ye feel, is it?"

He chuckled at her reaction, but immediately winced. "I withdraw that comment. I'm in no condition to wage war with you."

She gave him a sidewise look. "Very well. Apology accepted."

"And speaking of apologies," he announced loudly,

"you and I must have a reckoning on that lie you told me yesterday."

"What lie?"

"That fiction you made up about the sprained ankle, attended by that superb bit of acting that continued all the way to this morning."

"Oh. That."

"When I get out of this bed, I shall put you over my knee."

A wicked grin slid across her face. "What makes ye think I'm going to let ye out of bed?"

An expression of inaccessible lust came over him. "By Jove, you're a cruel woman to provoke an injured man like that."

She shrugged. "I am as ye find."

"Perhaps. But there is one thing I intend to change about you at the very first opportunity." Conall spread his fingers behind her head and brought her lips closer.

"What's that?" she asked, her words smoky against his nearness.

"Your last name."

Six weeks later, Shona and Conall found themselves again in his bedroom. Except now, they were man and wife.

Below, they could still hear the revelry of all the tenants, friends, and former clients who had turned out to celebrate their wedding. Stewart and his bride, Violet, had toasted the happy couple, having organized a wedding breakfast for more than three hundred people. Hume and Iona were among those crowded into the ballroom or spilling out into the garden, joining in the spirited Scottish dancing.

Conall went to the window. Squares of light fell over his tall form, melting across his wide chest, over his belted waist, and down his kilted hips.

Shona grinned appreciatively at the profile of her husband. *Now* he looked like a born-and-bred Scotsman, every inch of him. The height of a warrior, the wide shoulders of a caber-tosser, the firm butt lifting the blue and green tartan of the MacEwan kilt. He closed the last of the drapes, blotting out the light and muffling the noise from downstairs.

He turned to face her, his massive silhouette darkened by the muted light behind him. Shona's sexual anticipation hit her full force then. She had anxiously waited for this day for weeks, and now their wedding night was upon them.

She stood, the folds of her gown swishing down to her legs. It was a sky-blue silk, its bodice and hem decorated with tiny flowers and leaves in royal blue and emerald green, echoing the colors of her new husband's tartan.

Husband. Never in her wildest dreams did she think she'd become someone's wife. As if her feral character were not enough to scare suitors away, the scar of the *slaighteur* upon her hand advertised a warning to any man who might fancy her.

But here was a man who not only accepted her, but also protected her and wanted her.

And she wanted him, too.

Now.

She advanced upon him with steely determination. She wanted to feel the pressure of his body against hers. Touch his face. Smell his hair.

She slid her arms up around his neck. Oh, she could

hang on these massive shoulders and he would hardly feel the weight of her. She slanted her mouth against his, demanding a real kiss—not the tender I-love-you kiss when he proposed, not the gentle peck permitted after they spoke their vows, but the wedding-night, private-bedchamber, take-me-like-a-pub-wench kiss.

His mouth was perfect—warm, full lips that could make her want to kiss him forever. But there was another organ that was demanding attention, and she wanted him to finally make her his woman. Her breasts were flattened against his chest, and every subtle movement he made rubbed her growing nipples, heightening her desire.

He pulled away, breathing heavily. "Slow down, Shona. I want to make you keen for me."

"I'm already keen," she whispered. "Come on, let's have the belt," she said, reaching for the buckle.

He gripped her hands. "No. Not just keen . . . keen *for me*. Now sit down for a moment. There's something I want to give you."

He cast her a bemused glance while she plopped herself on the bed. He reached into a drawer and pulled out a slip of paper.

"This is your first gift. Happy birthday, wife."

She smiled. It was her twenty-first birthday. At midnight, she was liberated from her apprenticeship, and by noon, she'd been married. Twelve hours of freedom, then once again belonging to Conall MacEwan—this time, for the rest of her life.

Iona had said that marriage was another form of indentured servitude, but she was wrong. Shona could leave Ballencrieff this minute if she wanted to, and never come back. Love—that was the enslaving force.

And Shona knew that she had already been bound to the man beyond all redemption.

She unfolded the paper. It was a letter.

To the Much Honored the Laird of Ballencrieff

Sir—

In reply to your request, I can offer the following information. The boy Camran Slayter was smuggled into this parish by an unnamed woman of Clan McCullough, who claimed with all desperation that the child would be killed by her kinsmen if left in her care.

After a stay in our parish orphanage under an assumed name, the boy was sent to be taught seamanship with the Royal Navy, where he has served these many years. At last inquiry, upon the age of seventeen, he was aboard the HMS Lionheart, *ordered to engage Napoleon's fleet in the Mediterranean.*

I have left word at the offices of the Admiralty to notify Mr. Slayter of your interest in reuniting the young man with his remaining family members. I have no doubt that once his ship puts to port, he will be permitted to communicate with you.

I extend hearty congratulations on your upcoming nuptials, and I wish you and your bride every happiness.

Yours sincerely,
Ian Newton, Churchwarden

Joy leaped inside her. "Camran's alive!" Shona's eyes glistened with happiness.

"Yes, my sweet. It took three solicitors working round the clock to find out what had happened to him. It appears that McCullough had ordered Camran to be killed along with the rest of your family. But it takes a man with no heart to kill a five-year-old child, and apparently the one ordered to do so took pity on him. How it happened, no one knows, but Camran wound up in Glasgow in a parish orphanage, and since then, he's been serving with honor in His Majesty's service."

Shona jumped off the bed and threw her arms around Conall's neck. "Thank ye! Thank ye for finding my brother!"

He hugged her in return. "I'm delighted it pleases you."

The mere knowledge that her brother was alive, and not torn apart by animals as the McCullough had said, was reason enough to rejoice. But soon her young man of a brother would learn that his sisters were seeking him, and he would know precisely where to find them. For the first time in her life, her hope turned into something solid and tangible, a hairsbreadth away from becoming reality.

"Thank ye for gifting me with my brother. Camran was one of the two things I most desired in the world."

"And the other?"

"I'm holding him right now."

The corners of Conall's eyes crinkled as he placed a soft kiss on her lips.

Shona caressed his hair. "Do ye think that once Camran comes home, he'll be able to claim Ravens Craig as his own?"

"He'll have to fight Brandubh McCullough to wrest it from him. And speaking from experience, that will not be an easy matter. But Ravens Craig is his by rights, and he's entitled to it." He pulled back from her grasp. "Would you now like your second gift?"

Her eyes shone. "It couldn't possibly be better than the first."

The long dimple in his cheek deepened. "I have a feeling you'll like it all the same."

His head descended and pressed a passionate kiss upon her mouth. The sensation was pure heaven. Here, now, Shona felt safe. The world was no longer something she had to fight to overcome. The man in whose arms she hung had overcome it for her.

Her hand cupped the chiseled cheek, the sandy sideburns tickling her fingertips, as she returned the kiss with ardor.

Soon, her body began to respond in its own language. The pure maleness of him awakened all that was feminine in her, and her desire began to thread itself throughout her body. His chest was a wall of impenetrable muscle, imprisoning her in his embrace. His hands gripped her bottom possessively, rushing heat down to her nether parts. And now, his tongue speared into her mouth, demanding her surrender. Once the safe cocoon of his protection, now she felt as if his body were attacking her from all sides.

A vine of pleasure grew inside her and snaked itself through to her limbs, which reached for him. Of its own volition, her knee lifted, sliding itself up his kilted thigh. But her gown stopped all progress.

"Take me, Conall. Now."

He smiled lazily. "No."

"Why no'?" she moaned.

"It's my second gift to you," he said, guiding her to the brown leather Chesterfield sofa. "You're going to learn precisely how much pleasure your body is capable of."

Now, her face was at a level with the object of her desire—his cock. Impulsively, she reached for the sporran, which, though beautiful with its stamped black leather and silver cantle, stood between her and the feel of Conall's manhood.

He slapped her hands away. "No touching yet. You mustn't get ahead of me."

She pouted up at him. "But . . ."

"It would give me great pleasure to just mate with you, Shona. But I want you to have much more than that." He lifted the hairpins out of her hair, letting the black locks tumble down. "Open your senses and feel what I'm about to do to you." His voice became chest deep. "I want you to notice everything."

His nearness alone was making her breath quicken, but admittedly, the sensation of his fingertips in her hair made pleasure slide down her body. The hair tickled her cheeks and shoulders as he fanned it around her.

He knelt in front of her. Her predatory gaze burned trails all down his body, devouring him hungrily. She reached out her arms and drew him close.

He pulled away. "You are a stubborn creature."

"I want to feel you," she demanded. "You belong to me, and I've a right to what's mine."

"Right," he said, yanking the cravat from around his neck. "You asked for this." He began to entwine the fabric around her wrists. "If you think I'm going to let you dominate me in the bedchamber, you've got a harsh lesson coming your way."

The silk fabric whispered across her hands as he tied a knot, awakening feelings of confusion . . . and a secret thrill.

His mouth was set in grim determination as he enforced his will. He took her bound wrists and raised them above her head. His mouth fell upon her throat, pressing hot kisses there. She felt it not just on her skin, but deeper, right into her flesh. His tongue flicked at a spot just below her ear, and it immediately weakened any resistance. Lower his mouth descended, planting small kisses along the exposed part of her chest. And when he reached a spot below her shoulder, just above her breast, his tongue darted out and danced upon the skin, sapping all the strength out of her.

Too late she realized that he was doing to her as he had done to McCullough. He was using his superior knowledge of the body to overpower her. Except now, he was going to overpower her with exquisite pleasure.

And torment. Liquid heat pooled inside her, and she ached for him. His mouth traveled down to her breasts, still cinched by the bodice of her wedding gown.

"The buttons are in the back, Conall. Reach behind me to—"

"The dress stays on."

What torture was this? She wanted to rip off every stitch of her clothing and his. She didn't know if the English made love with their clothes on, but if they did, she would have to teach him the way Highlanders do it.

Conall caressed the underside of her breast with a thumb. She cursed all the fabric that stood between her and that delicious hand. He watched her face as his fingers danced upon her breast, searching for a spot. When the back of his nails stroked her sensitive nipple, intense pleasure made her womb contract and she moaned. Conall smiled triumphantly, and clamped his mouth upon the spot.

She felt the heat of his mouth even through the silk and the boned chemise she wore, and the heat flooded her belly. But when Conall grazed his teeth over her imprisoned nipple, she could stand it no longer.

"Conall, please," she mewed, arching into him.

He grinned. He reached down and removed her heeled slippers. Air bathed her sex as he lifted her exquisite blue dress to her waist. His mouth breathed hot kisses up one stockinged leg and down the other, driving her mad with desire. If he wanted her to be attentive to the sensations, it was working. Nothing else existed but the things he was doing to her.

Finally, he rewarded her patience by bringing his tongue to her womanhood. She grew light-headed as all her awareness focused on that area, which was weeping with need. His expertly trained fingers stroked and thrust, prodded and penetrated, until Shona was no longer sensible to her surroundings. Conall seemed to know her body better than she knew it herself. He was awakening sensations she never dreamed were possible.

Her breathing descended into panting as Conall's tongue flicked a rhythm on her nub. White-hot pleasure spread from her V to her breasts, and across her arms to her bound wrists. She was keen for nobody but him.

And then, instead of hot breath, she felt cool air. Conall pulled back and sat down upon his haunches. Her half-closed eyes began to widen.

"Don't stop," she managed. "I'm ready for ye, Conall. It's ye I want. Only ye." She glanced down at his kilt. His sporran was lifted at an odd angle, his cock pushing the damned thing up. Clearly, he wanted her, too.

"There's a lot more I want to show you. Come to the bed with me."

She seized him by the shirtfront and brought his face to hers. "Conall, if ye don't mate with me now, I swear to heaven I'll kick ye in the pink parts. And that'll make neither of us happy."

Conall narrowed his eyes upon her. "I can't believe I'm married to a wildcat. Right. If it's mating you want, it's mating you'll get."

He stood and lifted her up with him. With an unceremonious push, he tossed her forward over the tufted leather back of the Chesterfield. Brusquely, he yanked up her skirt over her waist. Cool air connected with her bottom.

She tried to raise herself up, but the bound wrists limited her movement. Behind her, she heard the chain of his sporran snap, and he threw it across the room. He kicked her legs open and wedged himself between them. Her womanhood thrummed in expectation as he raised his kilt.

She felt the slick plum-tip of his penis push between her well-licked folds. She had asked him to mate with her—no, ordered him—but now she was concerned that there might be pain.

Above her head, she heard his sharp intake of breath as he fought to control himself. There was a remarkable strength to him . . . and restraint . . . for which she was grateful. He pushed in an inch at a time, and she winced. There was no sharp pain, only pressure and stretching. But more of him came, and then more and more, and she never thought she'd feel the end of him.

Finally he was buried up to the hilt in her, and both of them were panting. He thrust in and out, slowly at first but with increasing speed. She was full of him, with not an inch to spare. Her womanhood became alive again, singing pleasure into her body. Over and over he hammered himself in her, and she was highly attuned to the delicious feeling that it gave her. His hands on her hips, his thighs between hers, his sex inside hers. It was glorious.

She had wanted him so badly that she had run out of patience for him. All that desire had come rushing upon her all at once. But instead of quenching her appetite for him, his thrusting only made it keener. Soon, the single note in her womanhood turned into full-blown harmony, and she climaxed. Her sex clamped down upon his, squeezing every last bit of pleasure from him. And when he too could stand no more pleasure, he buried himself inside her and came.

Shona absorbed every sensation of the incredible experience. She'd just been joined to the man of her dreams. And she couldn't wait to do it all over again.

He pulled out of her and lifted her. Her legs were still weakened from pleasure, and she leaned in his arms for support.

He raised her bound wrists, and pulled apart the knot he'd made. Gently, he turned her hand over and placed a lingering kiss upon the *S* of her scar. He raised his eyes suggestively, sending her an unspoken invitation. He was so handsome, so dangerously intelligent. And he was hers.

"Know what I like better than a man in a kilt?" she asked.

"What's that?"

A hungry grin edged across her face. "A man oot of one."

The comment made him smile. "There isn't a shred of modesty to you, is there? What on earth did I do to deserve you?"

"I dinna know. Let's go over yer sins one by one."

She kissed him, all the while pulling the white shirt from within the belted kilt. She exposed his back to her eyes before he ducked out of the shirt. Standing straight, naked to the waist, Conall looked every bit a fearsome Scot, his shoulders towering over his narrow waist. The only thing missing was a weapon. Except, of course, the one between his legs. And that one was all hers.

She unfastened his belt, and undid the buckle holding the kilt in place. How she loved seeing the awed fascination on his face.

He let her unravel the kilt from his waist, and the fabric slid down his narrow hips. Leisurely, she stared at the sculpted form of his body, and it stirred her desire once more.

"Ye're a beauteous man, Conall MacEwan. And I want ye every night of my life."

Conall kissed her. "I can't tell you what good it does me to hear a wife of mine say that," he whispered.

Pity crept into her chest for him. His first wife had abandoned their bed long before she died, and he hadn't deserved her betrayal. She vowed that morning before God and witnesses never to do that to him, and she meant every word.

He unbuttoned her beautiful silk dress, and it slid down over her shoulders to the floor. He unlaced her boned chemise, and it puddled around her feet. As he undressed her, warmth began to suffuse through her womanly parts once more. She reached out and kissed his mouth, and she could taste herself on his lips.

"In the tollhouse, ye promised to teach me something. Something that ye were going to take yer time doing. Do ye remember?"

He brushed a thumb across her full lips, and she could swear that his cock began to stir once more. "I assure you I have not forgotten."

"Well, we have the rest of our lives together. How long do ye think it will it take?"

"Not long," he said, as his pupils went dark with lust. "But I have not had my fill of your moans just yet." He lifted her hair and brought his lips to her ear. "I know a spot on your body that will make your body scream with pleasure."

A smile slid across her face. "Really? Show me."

Fortunately, the revelry below drowned out the noise.